Look Alive

Black Curtain Press
PO Box 632
Floyd VA 24091

ISBN 13: 978-1515425434

First Edition
10 9 8 7 6 5 4 3 2 1

Look Alive

Miles Burton

I

The car, a rakish-looking two-seater of uncertain age, drew up outside the house in Surbiton. The driver, David Wiston, was about to get out and ring the bell, when the door was opened and Annabel Dorset appeared. "I'm ready, for once," she remarked. "It was sweet of you to ring up and offer to take me for a run. Where are we going?"

"I'd take you to the sea, somewhere, if I could spare the petrol," David replied. "But I'm afraid that's out of the question. What about Fembrake Forest?"

"Fembrake Forest!" Annabel exclaimed. "You're not suggesting that we should pay a call on my great-aunt, surely?"

"Good heavens, no," David replied. "The old lady would hardly welcome us with open arms, I fancy. The Forest is big enough for us to wander about in it without troubling her. And then we could look in at my father's place. He'll give us a cup of tea."

Annabel took her seat in the car, and they drove off. They were both young, Annabel in her early twenties, a tall, graceful girl, generally described as attractive. Pretty was not the epithet to be applied to her. She had too much of the Lavant blood in her for that, and the Lavants were a notoriously ugly family. But she had merry grey eyes, an unfailingly cheerful expression, and an irresistible smile. She was quite as much sought after as many far prettier girls of her own age.

Of this she was fully conscious. But, having thoroughly learnt her way about the world—she had served in the W.R.N.S. during the latter part of the war—she did not attribute this entirely to her personal charm. She was very well aware that, as far as any one could be these days, she was an heiress. And this knowledge caused her to regard advances on the part of the opposite sex with a half-amused suspicion. David, for instance. They had known one another for years, and David knew what her prospects were as well as she did herself. She had been expecting him to come to the point for some little time now.

Perhaps this was the opportunity he had contrived. A stroll through the secluded glades of Fembrake Forest, culminating in a romantic declaration?

Romantic, yes, but none the less tiresome. Annabel had by no means made up her mind about David. All she would admit, even to herself, was that she liked him the best of any man she had met so far. But that was quite a long way from feeling an ardent desire to marry him. Why couldn't he be content to let things go on as they were? They had always been content in one another's companionship. Why seek anything further?

The answer came with shattering realism. Because it was not herself, but her money, he was after. David was a quiet, rather reserved young man, with the keen appreciation of his own interests derived from his Welsh ancestry. The son of a doctor, he had himself recently qualified in that profession, and was now a house-surgeon at St. Lucy's. He was not at all the sort of person to encumber himself so early in his career with a wife for purely sentimental reasons. The fact of the matter was that he dare not wait, lest he should see the golden apple snatched from the tree before his very eyes.

Annabel had plenty of time for these meditations, for the attention of her companion was concentrated upon the control of the car. David was not a very experienced driver, and had only lately acquired this restive discard from some sportsman's garage. Fortunately Annabel was not of a nervous disposition, and regarded their antics as they negotiated the traffic with more amusement than alarm. Anyway, she was spared the necessity of conversation.

David's intentions were becoming clear to her. Fembrake Forest, followed by a call at Dr. Wiston's house at Ridhurst for a cup of tea! What a delightfully natural setting! But Annabel saw, or thought she saw, the romantic drama which was to be played against it. Saw it with complete detachment, as though she were sitting in a cinema, watching the scenes as they flashed across the screen. The lovers wandering side by side beneath the overshadowing trees. The sudden passionate avowal, the bashful response, as she subsided gracefully into David's embrace. Then the pilgrimage of the affianced couple to David's father, to seek his parental blessing. Annabel wriggled in her seat at the contemplation of such hideous banalities.

She blamed herself for not realising all this before. She should never have accepted David's invitation, for her intuition told her that the expedition was bound to end in a quarrel. If he thought that things were going to be as easy as all that, he would find that he was vastly mistaken. Ridicule, rather than indignation, would be her line. Amazement at the aspirations of a presumptions child. Did he really suppose that she was going to fling herself away upon a man who had hardly set his foot upon the first rung of the ladder of his career? If he did, he had better think again. Meanwhile—oh, for mercy's sake let's talk about something else.

They left the main highway at last, turning off along a less-frequented thoroughfare which, as the signpost indicated, led to Ridhurst. But David did not follow this very far, turning off again into a by-road as soon as they reached the outskirts of the Forest. "I know just the place," he explained. "I used to ride all round here on my bicycle in the old days, when I was at home for the holidays. I don't suppose there's been much change since then. Let's go and see."

Annabel raised no objection. If the situation had to be faced, the scene hardly mattered. They followed the by-road for a couple of miles or so, passing only a few isolated houses on the way. The Forest was by no means continuous woodland, rather wide groves of trees interspersed with stretches of open ground covered with gorse and bracken. Suddenly David applied the brakes and the car drew up jerkily at the side of the road. "This is the place!" he exclaimed.

He had pulled up at a low stile, beyond which a footpath wound through the trees. They got out of the car, climbed the stile, and set off along the footpath. It was obviously to some extent a public right of way, as for some distance it was littered with orange-peel and empty cigarette cartons. However, after a while these evidences of a refined civilisation were left behind, and they found themselves in what might have been almost virgin country. The path had led them to the edge of a sheet of water, long but not very wide, with trees and undergrowth stretching down to the water's edge. Through a narrow gap in these they caught a glimpse of a large house on the farther side of the lake. It was a hideous castellated structure, without a single redeeming feature. The tall beech-trees surrounding it seemed to express by their grace the clumsiness of man's handiwork. Beyond the house, in the distance, could be seen between the trunks of the beech-trees the outline of a high wall, capped with fragments of broken glass, glittering evilly where they caught the sun.

Annabel, who was not without artistic appreciation, frowned at this spectacle. "Whoever desecrated such a lovely spot by building a house like that!" she exclaimed. "And that cruel wall! What is it, David? An asylum for criminal lunatics? Or does somebody really live there?"

David shrugged his shoulders. "I couldn't say," he replied off-handedly. "I suppose I must have seen the house before, but I never noticed it particularly. I dare say some trees have been cut down since I was last here. What about a bathe in the lake?"

"My dear man!"Annabel protested. "What a preposterous suggestion! Your lake looks to me more mud than water, and it's probably full of slimy weeds. I hate bathing in fresh water. Besides, I haven't brought a bathing-dress with me, and I don't fancy myself as a nudist. But if you feel you must take the plunge, don't let me stop you."

"I'm more than tempted," David replied. "Just a few minutes' swim, and then dry off in the sun. Sure you'll be all right?"

"Of course I shall," said Annabel. "What do you think is likely to happen to me? What I'm wondering is whether you'll be all right. Never mind, if you get caught in the weeds, just sing out, and I'll come and rescue you."

David went off among the bushes, she supposed to find a secluded spot in which to undress. It was what the town-dweller describes as a perfect summer's afternoon, with a cloudless sky and the temperature somewhere in the seventies. Under the trees nearby Annabel found a bed of withered leaves, and, having satisfied herself that the spot was comparatively free from insects, curled herself up upon it. She felt half-relieved and, for some reason she could hardly explain, half-resentful. Things hadn't turned out at all as she had expected. Unless the invitation to bathe in this unfrequented environment had been the first step towards seduction. David being the sort of person he was, that was quite unthinkable.

Where she lay, it was extraordinarily silent. At the height of the summer afternoon not a bird twittered. No sound came from that appalling house, now mercifully hidden from her eyes. She imagined herself as Ariadne, abandoned—rather to her relief—by Theseus on Naxos, but with very little chance of Bacchus appearing to her from among the trees. The fancy pleased her, and she played with it for a while, until it became merged in other nonsensical visions.

She woke up, to find David standing beside her. "Hallo, Theseus!" she murmured dreamily. "So you've come back? That's all wrong, you know. You ought to have gone on to Ridhurst. Your father, watching for the approach of your two-seater, and seeing its black hood raised, would have flung himself out of the window for grief."

David stared at her. His strictly practical education had included no smattering of Greek mythology. "What are you talking about? You've been to sleep, that's what's the matter with you. You'd much better have had a bathe."

Annabel shook her head as she got up. "Don't feel like it," she replied tersely. "Where do we go from here?"

David shrugged his shoulders. "It's up to you. Personally, I feel like a bit of exploring. Let's go on and see where this track leads to."

It was all one to Annabel, and she followed him as he moved off. Only single file was possible, for the track was narrow, and so little frequented that in several places they had to push away the undergrowth to make their way through. The track twisted about among trees and brushwood, through which at intervals they caught a glimpse of the lake. At its head was a ruinous structure which they took to be a boat-house. But the track did not approach it closely enough to allow of investigation. Having negotiated a final bend, they found themselves confronted by another low stile. Beyond this was a narrow road, hardly more than a lane, running roughly parallel to the one on which they had left the car.

They climbed the stile, and Annabel looked about her. "Have you the remotest idea where we are?" she asked.

"Well, not exactly," David replied. "I don't remember having come this way before. But now we're here, let's see if we can't find another way back, round the other side of the lake."

They turned to the right, and followed the road for some little distance, to find that it meandered rather purposely through the forest. Finding no sign of a path leading in the direction they desired, they were about to turn back. Then, without warning, they came to a gateway on the right, beyond which stretched a sandy drive. And by the side of the gateway there was a post surmounted by a board, bearing the words, "To The Brake."

Annabel stared at this, then rounded upon David. "You old humbug!" she exclaimed. "You knew all the time!"

"What's come to you now?"David replied with an air of injured innocence. "What am I supposed to have known all the time?"

"You know perfectly well," she exclaimed petulantly, pointing at the board. "The Brake I That's where my great-aunt lives."

David shook his head. "My dear girl, I know nothing of your great-aunt beyond what you've told me yourself, that her name was Mrs. Lavant, and that she had a house somewhere in Fembrake Forest. That we should have stumbled on the estimable lady's abode is quite accidental. Now that we have done so, would you like to pay a dutiful call?"

"Not I!" Annabel replied. "I've never set eyes on her in my life. She must be eighty if she's a day, and I don't suppose she has the dimmest interest in her great-niece. Do you suppose The Brake is that hideous house we saw just now?"

David hesitated. "Might be. But I think we must have come farther than that. I expect we're on the farther side of that high wall with the broken glass on top of it. There's nothing to prevent us going down the drive and seeing for ourselves. It's not marked private."

"Only a little way, then," said Annabel. "I should hate my great-aunt to think that I was butting in." With the furtive air of a pair of conspirators they passed through the gateway and started up the drive. Before they had gone very far, it turned out that David had been right. They had rounded the end of the wall, which now appeared to their right, running parallel to the drive. Beyond it they could make out the roof of the house they had already seen. And, as they progressed, they discovered on their left a second lake, very similar in size and shape to the first. And, facing this lake, with a lawn sloping gently down to it, was another house, smaller and of more pleasing architecture. "That'll be The Brake," David remarked. "Not at all a bad-looking place. Care to have a closer view of it?"

"I feel horribly guilty," Annabel replied. "But there seems to be nobody about. Let's go on just a wee bit farther." The front entrance to The Brake was on the side of the house farthest from the lawn, and towards this the drive wound through the trees, never diverging far from the wall. But this was not the side they wanted to see, for the lake frontage appeared far more enticing. They came at last to a ragged shrubbery, through which a path led off from the drive in the direction of the lawn. "Let's go along there and have a peep," David whispered.

But Annabel shook her head. "I'm not going a step farther. You can go if you like. But if you're caught, I shall disown you."

David nodded, and crept off on tiptoe. Annabel entered the shrubbery and took up a position where she wasn't very likely to be noticed. Left alone, she felt a strong inclination to panic. How on earth could she explain her presence if her great-aunt, or any one else for that matter, bore down upon her? It was with difficulty that she restrained herself from taking to her heels and bolting back down the drive by the way she had come. She was still struggling with the impulse when David returned, grinning broadly. "There's only one person about, and she's fast asleep," he whispered quietly. "It must be your great-aunt, I think. Come and look for yourself. It's quite safe."

For a moment Annabel held back. But her curiosity got the better of her, and she allowed David to lead her along the path. They reached the farther edge of the shrubbery, and peeped out between the bushes.

The lawn lay spread before them, with the lake beyond. In the centre of the lawn was an elaborate hammock, fringed and tasselled, swung from a complicated framework, with a brightly-coloured canopy above. In the hammock lay a woman, dressed in white, and wearing an almost barbaric profusion of jewellery. Her attitude was one of complete repose, and her face was hidden by the newspaper she had allowed to fall upon it.

Annabel giggled faintly. "Yes, that's Great-aunt Claire," she whispered. "There's a photograph of her at home, which shows her all got up with trinkets like that. She was an actress, you know, before she was married. Well, I shall be able to tell my astonished parents that I've seen her, anyhow. Now let's get away quickly before any one comes."

They retraced their steps through the shrubbery to the drive, which, as they found, led on past the front entrance to the house. "There's another gate, I expect," said David. "If there is, it must be on the road where we left the car. We may as well go on and get off the premises that way."

Once again his sense of direction proved correct. They followed the drive for some little distance, with the forbidding wall never far away on the right. Then ahead of them appeared the expected gate, and beside it, hidden among the trees, a gloomy building, not unlike a medieval castle in miniature, and evidently the lodge. As they hurried towards the gate, the door of the lodge opened, and a man emerged to intercept their passage.

He was a rough-looking type, but there was something about his appearance that fascinated Annabel. A ridiculous flash of her daydream returned to her. This was Bacchus, then, though he seemed very much alone, and was certainly unaccompanied by any jovial convoy of Bacchanals. Nor did he display any trace of the exuberance of the wine-god. He was young, perhaps a few years older than David, with a shock of dark curly hair and a pair of sardonic deep-blue eyes. He stood there, with his hands on his hips and elbows outspread, frowning menacingly. There was no avoiding him, and David and Annabel came to an awkward halt.

The man eyed them contemptuously. "Thought you'd slip out without being seen, did you?" he growled in a deep and curiously resonant voice. "Who might you be, and what have you been a-doing of?"

Annabel looked at him with increasing interest. He was wearing a faded blue shirt, open at the neck and revealing a hairy chest, a pair of dirty slacks, and gum-boots. His appearance and articulation were rough, but for some indefinable reason it seemed to Annabel that this roughness was deliberately assumed. But to David the encounter seemed highly disconcerting. He flushed and hesitated, and when he spoke his voice was high-pitched and querulous. "You've no right to talk like that. We're doing no harm. Let us pass, please."

But the man made no move, and his tone became even more offensive. "Gam! Don't you try to play the high and mighty with me. You and your young woman are trespassing, as you know well enough. And I'm Mrs. Lavant's keeper, I am, and my orders is that I'm to give folks like you in charge."

"Nonsense!" David exclaimed hotly. "If you're Mrs. Lavant's keeper, you ought to have learnt to speak civilly to your betters."

"Betters?" the man sneered. "I'm not so sure of that. You and your girl may be dressed-up folk, but it's my belief you're up to no good. Looking around to see what you can pick up, I dare say. But I'm not standing for any nonsense like that. You'll come into my lodge and stop there while I call for the police."

"We shall do nothing of the kind!"David exclaimed, with an angry glearn in his eyes as he took a step forward. But the keeper merely glanced at him contemptuously. "I'd keep quiet, if I was you," he said. "Why, I could pick you up with one hand and break your neck like a rabbit. Just you do as I say and come along with me."

It was obvious to Annabel that David was quite incapable of dealing with the situation. He was, in fact, making a perfect fool of himself. Now, if further unpleasantness was to be avoided, there was only one thing to be done: to make herself known to the keeper's mistress, and to secure her intervention with her surly servant.

Annabel turned and ran lightly up the drive, half-expecting to be pursued by the keeper, whom her mind still envisaged as Bacchus. But no footsteps followed her, and she reached the house without seeing any one on her way. She ran on past it, and turned along the path through the shrubbery, queer problems racing through her brain. How did one address a great-aunt whom one had never met? One could hardly awake a sleeping stranger with the words, "Oh, Auntie Claire, I'm your great-niece Annabel." But perhaps she had woken up by now.

She hadn't. The white-clad and bejewelled form still lay motionless in the hammock, with the newspaper lying undisturbed upon the face. Annabel cheeked her speed, and walked decorously towards the hammock. She had made up her mind to address her great-aunt respectfully in the first place as Mrs. Lavant. She reached the hammock and hesitated, awed by the complete inertness of the recumbent figure. The long chain of beads which lay on her ample bosom were undisturbed by any rise and fall due to respiration. Tentatively she stretched out her hand and removed the newspaper.

To her eager gaze was revealed the face of an old woman, so

elaborately made up that all evidence of extreme age was obliterated. That it was the face of the photograph, taken many years earlier, there could be no doubt. But the immobility of those features struck Annabel with a cold rush of fear. She realised that her great-aunt must have lapsed into unconsciousness. More disconcertingly still, she might even be dead.

II

Annabel was not the sort of person to dither in the face of
emergency. Her thoughts came rapidly, the first thing was to
summon a doctor. David? David was apparently still in
altercation with the keeper. No good going back there and
recounting her discovery. The keeper, in his insufferable
obstinacy, probably wouldn't believe her. There must be help
nearer at hand. A companion, or a maid, somebody. She turned
from the hammock towards the house. A french window stood
open, and towards this she ran, calling as she went. No answer
came. She reached the window and entered the house, to find
herself in a wide and lofty hall. "Is any one here?" she called at
the top of her voice. Faint echoes resounded from the walls, but
no answering sound or movement. She caught sight of a brass
dinner-gong and snatching the stick that hung beside it, beat
upon it desperately. The resultant clamour filled the house with
a pulsating ocean of noise. As it died away she waited tensely.
But even this deafening summons evoked no reply, and the
house reverted to its uncanny stillness.

As she looked helplessly around her she perceived a table,
half-hidden by a curtain, and on it a telephone. Dr. Wiston,
David's father! Her great-aunt was probably his patient. Annabel
didn't know his number, but the exchange would, of course. She
snatched up the instrument, vaguely noticing as she did so that
it seemed a very old-fashioned affair. "Hallo, exchange, hallo!"
she called. "This is an urgent call. Put me through to Dr. Wiston
at Ridhurst, please."

She heard a clicking noise, but no acknowledging voice. She
repeated her message, but the silence persisted, broken only by
a renewed clicking. At last she decided that the line must be out
of order. The Fates were conspiring against her attempt to seek
aid. She flung the instrument down, and turned despairingly
towards the window by which she had entered.

Then, with a gasp of relief, she ran out. David had
unaccountably materialised, and was standing by the hammock.
Swiftly she joined him, to find him holding her great-aunt's wrist

and frowning at the inanimate features. He looked up as she came. "Oh, here you are!" he muttered incoherently. "I say, this is pretty grim. The woman's dead."

"There's nobody in the house," Annabel replied wildly. "I tried to telephone, but the line's out of order. The only person about the place seems to be that awful keeper. We shall have to get him. Where is he?"

David shook his head in complete bewilderment. "In his lodge, I think. The fellow's behaviour is most extraordinary. I never met such a truculent brute in my life. But when you ran off he didn't say any more. Just turned away and strode into the lodge. He'll have telephoned for the police by now, I suppose. I don't like it a bit."

It seemed to 'Annabel that David was proving a broken reed. The keeper, however offensive he might be, would probably be more capable of dealing with the situation. "I'm not exactly enjoying myself either," she replied sharply. "But we must do something. The keeper may know where the domestic staff are to be found. Anyhow, if there's a telephone in the lodge, it surely can't be out of order too. My idea was to get your father to come."

David nodded with an air of relief. "You've got it. He'll know what to do. All right, then. Come along." They hastened down the drive, seeing no sign of human activity. They reached the lodge, to find the door shut and all quiet within. David hammered on the wooden panel, but no reply came. He tried the door, to find it locked. "We can't get in," he said helplessly. "And that brute of a keeper doesn't seem to be about. I say, wait a minute!"He looked up at the frowning walls of the building and pointed. "There's no telephone line running to the place," he continued excitedly. "And there aren't any poles beside the road either. The fellow was bluffing when he said he was going to ring up the police."

"I feel as if we'd blundered into a mad-house," Annabel replied wearily. "There's only one thing for it. We shall have to drive to Ridhurst in the car. That is, if it's still there and hasn't vanished by this time."

They passed through the gateway, and set off along the road towards the spot where they had left the car. Before they had gone many yards, they passed the end of the wall, and a short distance farther on came to a second gate, secured with a chain and padlock. Attached to the gate was a board with the inscription, "The Retreat. Strictly Private."

"The Retreat?"David remarked. "That must be the other house we saw across the lake, the ugly one. I don't think it's much good trying there, for that glass-topped wall rather suggests a barrier to intercourse between the two houses. We'd better keep going until we get to the car."

Rather to Annabel's surprise, the car was still standing as they had left it. Her adventures had been so topsy-turvy that any normal happening was becoming unexpected. They got into the car, which rather unusually responded to the starter, and drove off at speed towards Ridhurst.

They covered the three miles or thereabouts in a few minutes, and drew up at Dr. Wiston's door. Avoiding the ceremony of ringing the bell, David led the way through the garden entrance, and into the house by a side door. Dr. Matthew Wiston was in his study, writing at a desk. He was a middle-aged man, slight and of athletic build, with a capable expression and twinkling eyes. As the door opened and his unannounced visitors burst in, he looked up sharply. "Why, bless my soul!" he exclaimed. "Make yourselves comfortable, and I'll ring for tea."

David shook his head impatiently. "Can't do that. Father. We want you to come with us at once. We've just stumbled on Annabel's great-aunt, Mrs. Lavant, at The Brake, and found her dead. She's a patient of yours?"

This sounded incomprehensible, but Matthew Wiston had more experience than his son of emergencies. "Mrs. Lavant has never been a patient of mine," he replied as he rose from his chair. "I know her, for I have met her at Sir Julius Blackrock's. But if you say that the good lady is dead, it would seem that there is not very much I can do for her."

"Oh, you must come. Dr. Wiston!" Annabel pleaded. "There's nobody there, only a rough sort of keeper, and he seems to have vanished. We can't leave her alone like that, in a hammock on the lawn."

Matthew Wiston was greatly puzzled. Not so much by the news of Mrs. Lavant's death, for she was a very old woman. But these two young people had evidently been through some experience which had given them a considerable shock. It was incredible that there should be nobody there. He knew little of Mrs. Lavant, but enough to be aware that she did not live alone at The Brake. It would be as well for him to go and find out how things really stood. No doubt one of the other doctors in the town had attended Mrs. Lavant. He could learn which of them it was, and turn the job over to him. "All right, I'll come," he said shortly. "I'll get my car out. It's more reliable than David's rattletrap. Come along."

They set out, and reached the entrance to The Brake. The gate was shut, the position into which it swung naturally unless hooked back. Since there was no sign of the keeper, and the lodge appeared to be shut up and deserved, David got out to open it. As he did so, he saw on the sandy surface of the drive the track of tyres, which had certainly not been there when he and Annabel had come away. "Someone has got here before us," he remarked, as he resumed his seat in the car.

"Eh?" his father replied. "Then there's no need for us to butt in. Still, as we've got as far as this, we may as well go on, I suppose."

He drove along the drive, and pulled up at the front door, where another car already stood. The three of them got out and David rang the bell. They waited, but there was no reply. "I told you there was no one in the house!" Annabel exclaimed fretfully. "Let's go round, through the shrubbery, and you'll see."

She and David led the way, and Matthew Wiston followed them, expecting to find one of his fellow-practitioners on the spot. They reached the farther edge of the shrubbery, and Annabel uttered a half-stifled cry of amazement, "Oh!"

The sight which greeted them was certainly strange enough. Mrs. Lavant was sitting up in the hammock, her legs dangling over the edge. She was dressed completely in white, down to her shoes and stockings, and the jewellery with which she was generously adorned flashed in the sun. She was talking vivaciously to a young man who held a note-book and pencil in his hands, while another young man, equipped with a camera, was moving round taking photographs of her from various angles. A third man, middle-aged and tall, stood in the background, surveying the proceedings with a somewhat sardonic expression.

At the sound of Annabel's cry, Mrs. Lavant looked round and

frowned at the three standing on the edge of the lawn. "Go away!" she exclaimed in a deep contralto, waving an arm upon which the many bangles tinkled musically. "I only see people by appointment. Write and tell me what it is you want. I can't attend to you now." And without troubling any more about them, she reassumed her ingratiating smile and continued her conversation with the reporter.

Clearly there was nothing for it but undignified retreat. Crestfallen and in silence the intruders retraced their steps to Matthew Wiston's car and drove off. Not until the gate had again opened and they were on the road outside, did any of them speak. "Have you young people been pulling my leg?"Matthew Wiston asked severely.

It was Annabel who replied, half-hysterically, "Oh, no, Dr. Wiston! She was dead, I'm sure she was. And David said so too. Didn't you, David? We can't both have been dreaming."

"Mrs. Lavant now displays every symptom of exuberant vitality," Matthew Wiston remarked with some acidity. "I'm very much relieved that she didn't seem to recognise me. I should have found explanation more than difficult. We'll go home and have tea, and between you, you can tell the whole story as coherently as you can."

As they sat in the doctor's study, they recounted the afternoon's adventures. Annabel did most of the talking, for David seemed rather ashamed of the part he had played, and was in consequence inclined to be sulky. Matthew Wiston listened with kindly sympathy. He had wondered, before now, whether David had thoughts of marrying this girl. It seemed to his acute perception that the afternoon had done nothing to increase any mutual affection. Rather the reverse, for Annabel seemed to blame David for their experiences. "It was David who suggested we should go and have a peep at The Brake," she complained. "If he hadn't been so inquisitive, all this wouldn't have happened. I believe he knew all the time who lived there."

"I didn't I "David replied. And then, somewhat inconsequentially, he added: "After all, the woman is your great-aunt, not mine."

"That's got nothing to do with it," said Annabel firmly. "I should never have gone inside the place if it hadn't been for you. And then, when we met that keeper, you were so silly. If you'd been more tactful, and apologised to him for trespassing, he'd have let us out. I'm sure he's not really so disagreeable as he pretended to be. And when you saw her you said definitely that she was dead, you know you did."

Matthew Wiston hastened to interpose. "Elderly people, when they are asleep, often look alarmingly death-like. And David hasn't enough experience yet to recognise death at first sight, without detailed examination. I'm not surprised that you both got rather a nasty shock. However, you'll soon get over it."

The two young people drove back from Ridhurst, neither of them inclined to conversation, and David left Annabel at her house in Surbiton. Annabel did not ask him in, nor did she speak of her adventures until after dinner, when she was alone with her parents in the lounge. Her father. Henry Dorset, was a man of fifty, well set-up and good-looking. He was a director of a firm of merchants in the City, and though he took no very active part in the business, attended at the office two or three days a week. His hobby was yachting on a modest scale, and during the war he had served in the R.N.V.R., spending most of his period of service in a minor post at the Admiralty.

Annabel's mother, Irene Dorset, was a couple of years younger than her husband. She was a cheerful, pleasant-faced woman, her appearance somewhat marred by her inheritance of the Lavant features, always a shade distressing in the female members of that family. She was a woman of wide interests, allowing nothing, however, to intervene between herself and her husband and daughter. It had already struck her that Annabel had been strangely reticent about her afternoon excursion. But she was far too wise to ask questions. If, as she half-expected, David had brought himself to the pitch of a proposal, she would hear about it in her daughter's own good time.

It was Annabel who broached the subject. "I met Great-aunt Claire this afternoon," she remarked in an elaborately casual tone.

Her father was glancing sleepily at an evening paper as he smoked a pipe. But at this amazing announcement, he started bolt upright, his pipe dropping from his mouth as he did so. "Confound it!" he exclaimed, groping on the floor. "Your great-aunt? What are you talking about? Where on earth did you come across the old lady?"

"David says it was an accident," Annabel replied. "I'm furious with him, for he led us both to make fools of ourselves. I've had such a ridiculous adventure that I'm beginning to believe I must have dreamt the whole thing. I met Great-aunt Claire at her own house, and I'll tell you what happened there."

Her parents listened to her story with unconcealed amazement. "I never heard of such a thing in my life!"Henry Dorset exclaimed when she had finished. "Whatever possessed the pair of you to butt in like that? It's my belief the old girl's a witch, and that she enchanted you. Serve you right, too. And you dragged Matthew Wiston there to certify her death. I wonder he didn't certify you both as lunatics."

"It was David who said she was dead," Annabel replied. "And, having just qualified, I thought he ought to know."

"Whereas she was merely enjoying an afternoon nap," said her father scornfully. "My own personal sentiment is that it's a pity he wasn't right. Well, she didn't know who you were, that's a comfort."

"She didn't even recognise Dr. Wiston, whom she knows," Annabel replied. "She was far too busy showing off to her visitors to take any notice of us. I'm going to bed to try to sleep it all off."

Irene Dorset very shortly followed her example, leaving her husband puffing thoughtfully at his pipe. Annabel's adventure had disturbed him more deeply than he cared to reveal. That young fellow David. Had he beguiled the girl to The Brake for some mysterious purpose of his own? According to Annabel, he seemed to have behaved rather wildly throughout. Anyhow, inexperienced though he might be, he ought to have known the difference between sleep and death.

It was many years since Henry Dorset had met Mrs. Lavant, once so well known as Claire Gabriel, the actress. She and the Dorsets had nothing in common, and they had kept out of one another's way. Although Mrs. Lavant was Irene's aunt, they never corresponded, and neither of the Dorsets had visited her at The Brake. They had heard little of Mrs. Lavant, except on that occasion three years ago when The Brake had acquired a momentary publicity. That had been a rather unsavoury story, revealing if not actual cruelty, at least a callous lack of consideration on Mrs. Lavant's part. But, even before that, it had been notorious that she was apt to behave with the reverse of kindliness towards those dependent upon her.

She was a remarkably selfish old woman, of that there could be no possible doubt. And vain too, as her adornment and her behaviour before the camera showed clearly enough. The universe and its inhabitants revolved about herself. And it seemed, from the vitality she displayed, that she might live for ever.

Henry Dorset allowed his thoughts to dwell on that subject. He didn't really grudge Mrs. Lavant her continued existence. But always at the back of his mind was the knowledge that on her death the income she enjoyed would revert to Irene. She and her family could put it to good use. There was Annabel to be thought of. Both her parents believed that she was rather aimlessly drifting towards an engagement to David. Mainly, perhaps, because comparatively few eligible young men had come her way. David was a decent young fellow, but, with pardonable pride, her father felt that Annabel was worthy of someone more distinguished than the son of a provincial doctor. Given more money to spend, her parents could take her about-give her the opportunity of meeting people beyond the suburban environment of Surbiton.

But, while Mrs. Lavant lived, that must remain a castle in the air. Back then to Annabel's unaccountable adventure. She was far too sensible a girl to suffer from hallucination. Incredible though the suggestion seemed, was it possible that she and David had not been mistaken? That the unfortunate affair of three years ago had been repeated. That a woman, some member of Mrs. Lavant's household, had lain dead in the hammock? Mrs. Lavant wouldn't have allowed a trifle like that to interfere with her afternoon's enjoyment. Annabel had never seen her great-aunt, and it was to be supposed that David hadn't either. They had probably both been too flustered to look very closely. That the woman they had seen then was Mrs. Lavant was no more than an assumption on their part. It might well have been a companion, or merely a visitor.

Of course, all this was sheer nonsense. If any one had died at The Brake, even Mrs. Lavant would be constrained to do something about it. But once again a faint shadow of mystery had fallen across the place. Obviously it was not a matter to be reported to the police, who would demand to be shown a non-existent body. Nor for that matter, as Henry Dorset realised, was it any affair of his. But he felt a natural curiosity, and an overwhelming desire to discuss the situation with some sympathetic but disinterested friend.

He knew the very man in whom to confide. While serving at the Admiralty, he had come into contact with a certain Desmond Merrion, who had occupied an important post in the Intelligence branch. Merrion's almost uncanny aptitude for solving the knottiest problems had become proverbial. Henry Dorset had kept in touch with him since then, and knew that he was frequently in London, where he rented rooms in the St. James's district. He determined to find out in the morning if Merrion was at hand.

In fulfilment of this resolve, he rang up the number from his office. The call was answered by Newport, Merrion's faithful retainer, who to Dorset's relief told him that his master was at home. Merrion came to the telephone, and uttered a hearty greeting. "Hallo, Dorset! Only the other day I was thinking that it was quite a while since I'd heard from you. How are things with you and the family?"

"We're all flourishing, thanks," Dorset replied. "I'm very glad to have found you in London. If you can spare the time, want your opinion on what seems a rather queer story. Can we meet somewhere?"

"Of course we can," said Merrion unhesitatingly. "You know my voracious appetite for queer stories. Come along here as soon as you like, and stay to lunch with me. That will give us plenty of time to talk."

III

When Dorset reached Merrion's most comfortable rooms, he found his host alone and waiting for him. "I'm delighted to see you again," he said. "We'll have a glass of sherry before lunch while you spin your yarn. You can talk here in perfect confidence, and without the slightest fear of interruption."

"That's most awfully good of you, Merrion," Dorset replied. "Now that it comes to it, I hardly know where to begin. I'm afraid I shall have to inflict on you a certain amount of family history, if it won't bore you to extinction."

Merrion laughed. "Family history is often most entertaining. Go ahead in your own way."

Dorset took a sip from the glass which his host had poured out for him. "We needn't go further back than the last century," he began. "In Yorkshire, somewhere about 1830, a boy, Oliver Lavant, was born. We don't know definitely who his people were, but tradition has it that his father was a prosperous farmer. Anyway, the boy did not follow the plough, but turned his attention to industry, in which he proved highly successful. He became a manufacturer on a fairly extensive scale, and prospered exceedingly. Before his death he sold his business for what in those days was a very considerable sum.

"Oliver Lavant died in 1894. Perhaps because in his earlier years he was too busy making money to have any time to spare for romance, he gave no thought to marriage until he was forty. By that marriage he had two sons, a second Oliver, born in 1871, and William, born in 1876. There were no other children. It may have been because neither of his sons displayed any natural aptitude for business that their father sold out.

"The dispositions of the two sons were entirely different, and one imagines that they were mutually antagonistic. Oliver junior was a charming person, universally popular and his father's favourite. Unfortunately, as I have said, he displayed no enthusiasm for the factory. Agriculture being in his blood, he took to farming, mainly, I fancy, as a means of enjoying a comfortable and rather ineffective life. He was one of those people who are always on the verge of doing great things which somehow never come off. His principal achievement was marrying a wife as charming as himself, by whom he had an only child, a daughter, Irene. Both her parents died not very long after I married her. We, too, have an only child, a daughter, Annabel. You may remember having met her in the last year of the war, when she was in the Wrens."

"I remember very well meeting your daughter," Merrion replied. "And a very jolly girl I thought she was."

"We're proud of her," said Dorset. "She's twenty-four this year and naturally we're beginning to wonder whom she'll marry. However, that's by the way. We come now to old Oliver's second son, William. He was the typical hero, or villain, of the romantic novel of his period. His father died when he was eighteen. Three years later, a few days after his twenty-first birthday, when he became his own master, he astonished his acquaintances by marrying a village maiden, Mary Stoke. It is alleged that he had previously seduced her, but whether that is true or not I can't say. This young woman did not survive very long, for in 1898 she died in giving birth to a daughter, Althea.

"William was thus left a widower, with an infant girl on his hands. However, this responsibility did not weigh very heavily upon him. He was living in London, and engaged a series of females, from wet-nurse to governess, to look after the child as she grew up. He had other interests which claimed his attention, for he had fallen under the spell of the stage. Not as an actor himself, but as a dilettante playwright and critic. Although this became his passion, it was never a very profitable means of livelihood. But he had his own income, as I'll explain in a few minutes, so that didn't matter very much. The point I want to make is that all his friends were people of the stage and of the minor literary and journalistic circles. He had no interest in his brother or his family, and they very rarely met. I believe that Oliver junior and his wife suggested that their niece, Althea, should spend some part of her time with them. But, for some reason or other, William refused to countenance the arrangement. Disliked the idea of any sort of family tie, I dare say.

"Then, when Althea was sixteen, and already fairly headstrong, the first World War broke out. It was her father's intention to have her trained for the stage, but the war put an end to that. Two years later she hurled herself into some form of war work, I don't know what. She took to bringing various men in uniform to the house. And one fine morning in 1917 William found on his desk a note from her, announcing that she had eloped with a boy-friend whom William particularly disliked, a thorough waster of the name of Jack Rayner.

"It was too late to do anything about it, for by the time William got on the track of the couple they were already married, Althea having stated a false age. William took a firm line, insisting that having made their own bed, they must lie on it. He made it clear that under no circumstances would that piece of furniture be accommodated in his own house. What became of Althea and her husband for the next year or so, I don't know. But Jack Rayner contrived to get himself killed in the last days of the war, and in 1919 Althea gave birth to a posthumous boy, who was christened Roy. One supposes that she subsisted on a pension, possibly eked out by an allowance from William. At all events the disconsolate widow did not return to her father's roof.

"Meanwhile, not very long before Roy's entry into the world, William Lavant had once more embarked upon the troubled waters of matrimony. This time he had chosen as his consort a woman older than himself, nearly ten years older, I believe, a then well-known actress, Claire Gabriel. On her marriage she retired from the stage, and she and her husband continued to live in London, keeping company with what must have been a raffish lot. Again I must emphasise that my wife's side of the family saw very little of them. William gave them no encouragement, and his new wife even less. She was, and is, a domineering woman, and I imagine it didn't take her very long to get her husband completely under her thumb. It was quite certain that she had no use for her stepdaughter.

"Then, in the early thirties, Althea was killed in a motorcar smash, and the problem of the orphaned Roy arose. Someone had to become responsible for his maintenance, and the obvious person was his grandfather. One might have supposed that he would have boarded him out somewhere, but things didn't turn out that way. As soon as Claire Lavant set eyes on him, with the sudden and unaccountable impulse to which women of that type are subject, she took an instant fancy for him. He seems to have been quite a prepossessing child, with good looks and ingratiating manners. Claire Lavant insisted that she and William should take charge of him.

"As might have been expected, her infatuation soon wore off. I don't know any details of the life the three of them led for the next few years, but there is reason to believe that his step-grandmother's treatment of Roy oscillated between bullying him and ignoring his existence. What is quite certain is that he was allowed to drift into foolish ways. A case of evil communications corrupting good manners, I take it. His grandparents' associates were hardly of the type to exert a steadying influence on a growing lad. Anyhow, there was a particularly unpleasant scandal, which found its way into the newspapers. Something about a valuable fur coat which disappeared from a night club, and was subsequently offered for sale by Roy. He narrowly escaped gaol, as a first offender.

"This was in 1938. At the beginning of the following year William died and, incidentally, the last time I saw Claire Lavant was at his funeral. Her behaviour on that occasion was in the best theatrical tradition. She played the part of the bereaved widow to perfection. Actually, her husband's death can't have affected her greatly, for she carried on much as usual. But, on the outbreak of war, she closed the London establishment, and went to live in a house called The Brake, in Fembrake Forest. I believe the place was put at her disposal by a friend of hers in some way connected with the stage. She sent me a curt notification of her change of address, but I have never been to The Brake to see her. Nor has she invited me to do so.

"Roy Rayner did not accompany her. What became of him immediately after the incident I have mentioned I don't know. He was not in evidence at his grandfather's funeral. But it seems that either before or after war broke out he drifted into the Army. I imagine that by that time all communication between him and Claire Lavant had been completely severed. And she only saw him once again.

"There is no doubt that there was a criminal taint in Roy's blood, possibly inherited from his father. At all events, his next and final adventure reads like a scene from a picaresque novel. After his demobilisation he joined, or for all I know organised, a gang of smugglers. There was a rather amateur attempt to land a cargo from a fishing-boat somewhere on the south coast. The police got wind of the affair beforehand, and boarded the boat as soon as she dropped anchor one dark night. I dare say you may have seen the sensational story that appeared in some of the papers. There was a wild sort of struggle; the smugglers were armed, and one of the police was seriously wounded. In the confusion the smugglers jumped overboard, and it was thought they had got away.

"But next morning a body was found in the water, considerably battered. I imagine the police had used their truncheons to some effect. From the information they had been given, they had reason to suspect the identity of the dead man. They brought Claire Lavant to the spot, very much against her will, one supposes. A glance was sufficient to enable her to identify the body as that of her step-grandson."

Merrion nodded. "Yes, I remember reading that story at the time. Mrs. Lavant is still alive, I gather? '

"Very much alive," Dorset replied with a faint grimace. "I'll tell you about that in a minute. But first I must hark back to something else. I said just now that William Lavant had an income of his own. This he inherited from his father, old Oliver, the provisions of whose will I'll explain as clearly as I can.

"I'm no lawyer, and I can't hope to set out the proper terms. What it amounts to is this. Old Oliver left all his estate in trust. The income from this trust was to be divided equally between his two sons. On the death of either of them, his share passed to his wife if she outlived him. On the death of both parents, the share passed to the children, if any, and so on. If the succession in either branch of the family failed, that share would pass to the other branch. The trust was to be wound up, and the capital distributed, on the death of the last of old Oliver's great-grandchildren. Have I made the position sufficiently clear?"

"I think so," said Merrion, as he poured out a second glass of sherry for his guest. "Let me see if I can work out for myself how things stand at the moment. Oliver Lavant junior's share of the income is now enjoyed by his daughter, Mrs. Dorset. It will pass from her to your daughter, Annabel, upon whose death the trust will be wound up. William Lavant's share is now enjoyed by his widow, Mrs. Lavant. Had Roy Rayner survived, this share would have passed to him on her death. But, as matters stand, the succession of that branch is at an end, and upon Mrs. Lavant's death her income will fall to Mrs. Dorset, and, after her, to Annabel. Is that right?"

"Perfectly," Dorset replied. "And I don't mind confessing that Irene and I are profoundly conscious of the situation. Rightly or wrongly, we feel that we could put the money to at least as good use as Claire Lavant. She's eighty and more, and she can't live for ever. In fact, as recently as yesterday afternoon, Annabel had reason to believe that she was dead. And now at last I've come to what I really want to talk to you about."

Merrion glanced at the dock. "Newport will be telling us that lunch is ready, any moment now," he said. "Finish your sherry, and you can tell me all about it while we're having our meal."

So it was over the dining-table that Dorset repeated the story of his daughter's adventures. Merrion listened with close attention, putting in a question now and then to elucidate a point that was not quite clear. "Well, there you are," Dorset concluded at last. "It's perfectly safe to assume that those two young people didn't invent the story. What do you make of it?"

"I hardly know," Merrion replied thoughtfully. "There are many points about it which strike me as very queer. The accident which brought your daughter to The Brake at all, for one thing. She had never been there before?"

"Never!"Dorset exclaimed. "We knew that Claire Lavant's address was The Brake, and that it was somewhere in Fembrake Forest, which is a description covering a very considerable area, a great part of which is no longer forest. Beyond this, we had no idea where the house was, or how to get there."

"And you didn't know in what circumstances Mrs. Lavant lived, or what sort of an establishment she kept?"

Dorset shook his head. "We knew nothing at all about her. It was a pretty safe guess that at her age she was not likely to be living alone. But we had, or have, no knowledge of the constitution of her household."

"Chance plays strange pranks," Merrion remarked. "As for the central episode, one is inevitably driven to the conclusion that your daughter and David Wiston were both mistaken in thinking that Mrs. Lavant was dead."

"Of course," Dorset replied, a trifle impatiently. "That's the only reasonable solution. But there's just the faintest shadow of doubt at the back of my mind. You see, it's not the first time that a woman's dead body had been found at The Brake."

Merrion eyed him shrewdly. "Is that so? Would you care to tell me?"

"I'll tell you what I can," Dorset replied. "But, to start with, you must understand that I only had the story at second or third hand. From David Wiston, who got it from his father. It happened some three years ago, not long before Roy Rayner's spectacular demise; Claire Lavant was acquiring a familiarity with dead bodies about that time.

"It seems that very shortly after she took up her residence at The Brake, she acquired a companion. I'm very vague about who this woman was. A foreigner of some kind from one of the Baltic States, driven from her home by the Russian occupation. Needless to say, I never met her. Well, one fine morning her body was found in the lake which I am told lies in front of The Brake. She had left the usual heart-broken letter behind her. She found herself unable to endure life in exile, and had decided to end it. She hoped that her action would not unduly inconvenience Mrs. Lavant.

"The dramatic value of the event must have appealed to Mrs. Lavant, and she made the most of it. She appeared at the inquest in flowing black robes, and bedewed her evidence with the most convincing tears. Her pose was that she had lost her dearest friend, and she certainly gave her a sumptuous funeral. But, according to Wiston, there was a good deal of whispering locally. From what I know of Claire Lavant, I shouldn't be a bit surprised if there was some truth in it. It was rumoured that from being a companion, the woman had become a drudge. That her mistress had heaped all the housework upon her, and grumbled at her incessantly. Led her a dog's life, in fact. And that the true reason for the suicide had been that the wretched woman simply couldn't put up with Claire Lavant's behaviour any longer. It was established that she had no friend in this country, and nowhere she could go to."

"You don't paint a very engaging portrait of Mrs. Lavant," Merrion remarked. "You spoke of the faintest shadow of a doubt. Do you connect this incident with the strange adventure of your daughter yesterday?"

Dorset hesitated. "It seems the most utter nonsense when one tries to put it into words. But history has a way of repeating itself. Another of Claire Lavant's associates may have found her companionship intolerable."

Merrion smiled. "If there really was a body, we shall no doubt hear more of it. It will hardly escape the notice of Dr. Wiston, who lives nearby. Tell me more about him and his son David."

"I've known Matthew Wiston nearly all my life," Dorset replied. "We are much of an age, and we were at school together. We kept in close touch after that, and I was in fact best man at his wedding. At that time he was the partner of a doctor in the suburbs, and we saw a lot of one another. I married a couple of years after he did, and our respective wives became very good friends. In a sense his boy and my girl grew up together. Then, about twelve years ago, Matthew dissolved his partnership and bought a practice at Ridhurst. His wife, poor soul, was killed by enemy action in 1940. She had come up to London to see some friends, and was killed in an air-raid.

"Naturally, after he went to Ridhurst, Matthew and I didn't see one another so often. And then the war intervened. David served in the latter part of it, and then resumed his interrupted studies. When he went to St. Lucy's as a student, he often came to see us at Surbiton, and he has continued to do so ever since."

"Being always a welcome guest?" Merrion suggested.

"Perfectly," Dorset replied. "If only for his father's sake. But latterly Irene and I have had pretty shrewd ideas that the friendship of their childhood was developing into something stronger between him and Annabel. We shouldn't dream of standing in her way, of course. The girl is perfectly free to marry the man of her choice. But—"

Merrion nodded understandingly. "You'd like to offer her a wider choice, I dare say. David Wiston was already aware that Mrs. Lavant was your daughter's great-aunt. How much more did he know about her?"

"Quite a lot, I imagine," Dorset replied. "He insisted to Annabel that he didn't know where The Brake was until they came by chance upon the notice-board. But he had heard about her from his father, for, as I said, it was he who told us about the suicide of the companion. And he must have heard us talking about her. We have come to regard Claire Lavant and her ways as something of a family joke. Against ourselves, that is."

Merrion did not put the direct question. But it seemed to him pretty certain that David must know to whom Mrs. Lavant's income would revert on her death. "Look here, Dorset!" he said. "You've told me a most intriguing story. You have, in fact, excited my curiosity to the extent of inspiring me with a desire to learn more about The Brake and its surroundings. To that end, I should very much like to make the acquaintance of Dr. Wiston."

"I'll ask him to come up to my place in Surbiton and you can meet him there," said Dorset.

"No need to drag him away from his practice," Merrion replied. "Sit down now and write a letter of introduction, describing me quite simply as an old friend of yours. Armed with that, I'll run down to Ridhurst and see him."

"It's awfully good of you to take so much interest," Dorset replied. "Better still, I'll run down with you myself."

But Merrion shook his head. "Indulge my whims. One of them is that I like to make the first acquaintance of anybody at an interview with no one else present. You write me that letter, and I'll try to get to Ridhurst to-morrow."

Dorset complied with this request and departed, apologising for having taken up so much of Merrion's time. It was arranged between them that so soon as Merrion found himself at leisure he should dine with the Dorsets at Surbiton.

After his guest's departure, Merrion sat down with a cigarette. He was inclined to discount a good deal of what Dorset had told him of Mrs. Lavant's character. Dorset was evidently prejudiced against his wife's aunt, on account of her obstinate longevity. He had hardly made a secret of the fact that her decease would be very welcome. As for the story he had told, it was certainly remarkable. There might be nothing in it beyond the heated imagination of two panic-stricken young people. On the other hand, there were several points in it, the significance of which seemed to have escaped Dorset himself. And Merrion could never resist the urge to crack the hard shell of circumstance in the endeavour to disclose the kernel within.

IV

On the following afternoon Merrion drove himself to Ridhurst. He had no difficulty in finding Dr. Wiston's house, for it stood in one of the main streets and exhibited a brass plate. He rang the bell, and when the maid appeared handed her the letter which Dorset had written. "Will you take that to Dr. Wiston, and ask if I may see him?" he said.

The maid showed him into the doctor's waiting-room, and very soon returned with the message that Dr. Wiston would be delighted to see him. She led him to the study, where Matthew Wiston was seated very much as he had been when so rudely disturbed by David and Annabel two days earlier. He rose as his visitor came in, and advanced with outstretched hand. "I am more than pleased to make your acquaintance, Mr. Merrion," he said heartily. "You are hardly a stranger to me, for Henry Dorset has spoken to me of you more than once. Sit down and tell me to what I owe the pleasure. This is not a professional visit, I take it?"

Merrion laughed. "It is a visit of pure and undisguised curiosity, I'm afraid. Dorset lunched with me yesterday and told me the oddest story of an adventure which befell his daughter and your son in this neighbourhood. I hope you won't think it a piece of confounded impertinence on my part part if I ask you for your version of what happened?"

"Not at all," Wiston replied readily. "I know that Henry has a very special interest in Mrs. Lavant's welfare. I'll willingly tell you what I saw at The Brake the day before yesterday. And, as it happens, I am able to confirm it."

He stretched out his arm towards a newspaper rack, and drew from it a paper which he laid open for Merrion's inspection. It was a copy of the Pembroke Forest Standard and Ridhurst Post, bearing the date of the previous day. In it was a photograph of Mrs. Lavant, seated in her hammock, with a winning smile and a graceful gesture. Accompanying this was an account of her theatrical career, as related by herself.

"They're doing a series of personalities living in the district,"

Wiston explained. "One every week. Needless to say, I had not the slightest idea that they had chosen Mrs. Lavant for this week's issue. You can guess my amazement when I saw her sitting there posturing. She really is the most astounding old woman."

"You are acquainted with her, I believe?" Merrion suggested.

"Acquainted, no more," Wiston replied. "Fortunately, she didn't recognise me on this occasion. I'll tell you how I came to know her. When I bought this practice some few years before the war, I found among my other patients Sir Julius Blackrock, who lives at The Retreat, in Fembrake Forest. Sir Julius is an old man, not very much younger than Mrs. Lavant. He was at one time a leading theatrical manager, and I gather that he and Mrs. Lavant have known one another for half a century or more. She appeared in plays that he put on.

"Sir Julius is in many ways a queer old chap, but I have always got on very well with him. His chief eccentricity, if it can be described as such, is a passion for privacy. He lives alone at The Retreat, attended by an aged housekeeper, Mrs. Moffatt. There is also a gardener, nearly stone deaf, who is in some way related to Mrs. Moffatt. Both of them, I understand, were in some way connected with the stage. It will give you some idea of the rigidity with which privacy is guarded when I tell you that the entrance gate of The Retreat is normally kept locked. It is only unlocked for a couple of hours every morning to admit the postman and the various tradesmen, who have to call during that period or not at all.

"I call on Sir Julius periodically. There is nothing very seriously the matter with him, but he likes to consult me upon his minor ailments. More than that, his sight is failing, and he can't read for very long at a time. He likes someone to talk to now and then, but only in small and infrequent doses. I am careful not to intrude too often, or to stay too long. The procedure is strictly laid down. The Retreat is not on the telephone. I write a note to Sir Julius, telling him that I propose to visit him on a given afternoon at a given time. When I get there in my car I find the gate unlocked to admit me, and the gardener standing by. When I come out again, the gardener is still there, waiting to lock it behind me."

"When you first knew Sir Julius, Mrs. Lavant was not living

at The Brake?" Merrion suggested.

"No, the house was empty," Wiston replied. "Some years ago, twenty-five or thereabouts. Sir Julius bought the property on which the two houses. The Retreat and The Brake, stand. It is a fairly extensive strip of land lying between two lakes, East and West Moon. The Retreat looks out upon West Moon, and The Brake upon East Moon. And the first thing Sir Julius did was to build a wall between the two houses, running the whole length of the strip of land. A high wall, topped with broken glass, to deter any one from attempting to climb it. He told me long ago, with some pride, that there is only a single narrow gate in the wall, of which he jealously keeps the key."

"Sir Julius seems to have immured himself pretty effectively," Merrion remarked. "Does he ever use that key?"

"Presumably he does when Mrs. Lavant visits him," Wiston replied. "I say when she visits him, for I'm fairly certain he never visits her. He doesn't care about venturing out of his own domain. The truth is that he is becoming too blind to venture far afield by himself, and he wouldn't dream of allowing any one to lead him.

"About the time that war broke out he told me that he had consented to let The Brake, to a very old friend of his, the widow of a man he had known very well in his more active days. Even so, I gathered that he would have preferred to remain without a neighbour. He said that his consent had been influenced by a fear that The Brake might be requisitioned as a hostel for evacuees, or something horrible like that. It was not until some time later that I met Mrs. Lavant for the first time. I called one afternoon and Mrs. Moffatt showed me as usual into the room Sir Julius calls his library. There sitting with him was an obviously old woman, though her face was miraculously camouflaged. She was dressed like a girl in her teens, and was almost smothered in gaudy jewellery.

"Sir Julius introduced us, and when she heard that I was a doctor she froze up. She said she would go and talk to Mrs. Moffatt while I interviewed my patient. She has told me quite frankly since that she doesn't like doctors, though she was prepared to make an exception in my favour so long as I refrained from offering her professional advice. Her contention is that doctors had never done her any good, and had conspicuously failed to save her husband's life. Once she got that off her chest, she has seemed to regard me without aversion."

"You meet her fairly often, I suppose?" Merrion suggested. Wiston shook his head. "I don't suppose I've met her more than half a dozen times in all. I go to see Sir Julius once every three weeks, on the average, but I very rarely find Mrs. Lavant at The Retreat. Perhaps he warns her when I am coming, and she keeps away. I have never met her anywhere else. But when I am there he often talks about her, and that is how I know the little about her concerns that I do."

"When you first met her, did you know that Mrs. Lavant was Mrs. Dorset's aunt?" Merrion asked.

"I guessed she might be," Wiston replied. "I knew that Irene Dorset had an aunt whose name was Mrs. Lavant. And after my first encounter at The Retreat I wrote to Henry, asking if this was the lady in question. He wrote back that she must be, for they had heard from her that her address in future would be The Brake, Fernbrake Forest."

Merrion nodded. "Dorset doesn't seem to have taken any steps to establish contact with his wife's aunt. Perhaps he suspected that any advances on his part would be repulsed. Do you know what sort of establishment Mrs. Lavant keeps up at The Brake? She must have a domestic staff of some kind, one supposes?"

"She has," Wiston replied. "That's the part of those young people's story that I can't understand. They say that there was no one about but the keeper, and that they couldn't attract any one else's attention. But, according to Sir Julius, she had a couple living with her for some years. A Mr. and Mrs. Lingfield, theatrical folk, of course. At one time they appeared together as a music-hall turn, as Lance and Linette. I think I remember those names on the bills in the old days. But I can't say now what particular form of talent they displayed."

"Do the Lingfields comprise the whole of the staff at The Brake?" Merrion asked.

"The whole of the resident staff, so far as I know," Wiston replied. "Mrs. Lavant employs a jobbing gardener, who lives in a cottage about a mile away, and his wife does a few hours' housework at The Brake, but neither of them are there every day. Then there's that keeper who behaved so oddly the day before yesterday. I had never heard of his existence before then. I fancy he must be a comparatively recent acquisition."

"At one time Mrs. Lavant had a companion, a foreigner, hadn't she?" Merrion asked.

Wiston smiled. "So Dorset told you that story, did he? Yes, a Madame Tallinn, or some such name. A highly-educated woman, with a perfect mastery of the English language. Or so at least Sir Julius told me. It seems that Mrs. Lavant took her to The Retreat and introduced her, and Sir Julius took a great fancy to her. She used to go and read to him fairly often. I never met her, at least until after her death, the cause of which the coroner asked me to ascertain."

"She drowned herself in one of the lakes, didn't she?" Merrion asked.

"Yes, in East Moon," Wiston replied. "She seems to have thrown herself into it one night, for Lingfield found her body there next morning. There's no doubt that her mind was deranged. The evidence at the inquest brought that out clearly enough."

"Dorset's theory is that she found life with Mrs. Lavant impossible," Merrion remarked.

"Yes, I know," Wiston replied, a trifle impatiently. "It's true that at the time there were rumours of persecution, as there always are in such cases. But nothing of the kind was suggested at the inquest. Between ourselves, Mr. Merrion, I'm inclined to believe that Mrs. Lavant is not quite so black as Dorset is apt to paint her. She may have acted unkindly towards that unfortunate young fellow, Roy Rayner. But she seems to show every consideration for people she likes, the Lingfields, for instance. They appear to be devoted to her."

"I gather from what you say that the Lingfields were already living at The Brake at the time of the tragedy?" Merrion remarked.

Wiston nodded. "They had been there for some time, a couple of years, perhaps. After they came, another woman, Lingfield's stepsister, or something of the kind, joined them. I've only heard her referred to as Loretta. So that there were five people living at The Brake. Mrs. Lavant, Madame Tallinn, Lingfield, his wife, and his stepsister. And by all accounts until shortly before the tragedy, they were a perfectly happy family."

"Do I infer that shortly before the tragedy there was some disagreement?" Merrion asked.

"Well, yes," Wiston replied. "That came out at the inquest, in the evidence as to the state of mind of the deceased. It seems that for no reason whatever, she had taken to being very rude to Loretta, to such an extent that she, Loretta, had left The Brake to take up a theatrical engagement somewhere, in Australia, I believe. That rather suggests that Mrs. Lavant must have taken Madame Tallinn's part. The fact that the pair of them were very fond of one another does not depend upon Mrs. Lavant's evidence alone. Both the Lingfields testified to it.

"That was by no means the only evidence that Madame Tallinn's mind had become deranged. The witnesses described how she had taken to wandering up and down by the brink of East Moon, wringing her hands and muttering to herself. And when her room was entered after her death, it was found that she had destroyed what little she possessed. All that remained was a letter declaring her intention of committing suicide."

"Yes, Dorset told me of that," said Merrion. "How did Mrs. Lavant react to the tragedy?"

Wiston pointed to the newspaper still lying open on his desk. "Mrs. Lavant has a taste for publicity, as you observe. She organised a wonderful funeral procession from The Brake to the church, in which she herself played the principal part. But, when that display was over, her reaction seems to have been one of genuine grief. Sir Julius told me that she didn't go to see him for at least a fortnight, and that when she did she appeared considerably subdued."

"You have seen Mrs. Lavant yourself since then, I take it?" Merrion suggested.

"Three or four times, I dare say," Wiston replied. "The last time I saw her, if we except that unfortunate contretemps the day before yesterday, was a couple of months ago. She was at The Retreat when I called to see Sir Julius, and was her usual spectacular and vivacious self. She really is a marvellous old lady, there's no getting away from that. The malicious might say that her physical fitness is due to the fact that she has kept herself out of the hands of the medical profession. It sometimes seems to me that she has discovered the trick of growing younger instead of older. Henry Dorset will have to curb his impatience as best he can, for I see no reason why she shouldn't live to be a hundred."

"Bar accidents, of course," said Merrion lightly. "Look here. Doctor. This is a perfectly ridiculous question, as I am well aware. There was never the faintest suspicion of foul play in the case of Madame Tallinn?"

"Foul play!" Wiston exclaimed. "You mean that someone might have pushed her into the lake? There was certainly never the slightest suspicion of that. The evidence was perfectly straight-forward, and was confirmed by the letter she left. Besides, there was a complete lack of motive. What earthly reason could any one have had for murdering a penniless, homeless, and slightly demented refugee? You may say if you like that Loretta had a grievance against her. But Loretta had left The Brake some days before it happened. No, it was a case of suicide, you may set your mind at rest about that."

Merrion laughed. "I will. You must forgive my suspicious nature. But I must ask you to bear with it for a few minutes longer. You're perfectly satisfied that nobody died at The Brake the day before yesterday?"

"I am," Wiston replied firmly. "And I'll tell you why. But I insist upon you having tea with me. I'll ring the bell, and they'll bring it in here. We can go on talking while we refresh ourselves."

After the maid had brought in the tea-tray, Wiston went on: "I quite appreciate your last question, Mr. Merrion. The possibility of such a thing presented itself to me. Only because I imagined that my lad had learnt his job sufficiently to be able to recognise a dead woman when he saw one. So I have been making discreet inquiries.

"To begin with, no death at The Brake has been reported. And, when you come to think about it, if there had been a stray body on the premises, even Mrs. Lavant could hardly have behaved as I with my own eyes saw her behaving half an hour later."

"Half an hour?" Merrion interposed. "Were you on the scene as soon as that?"

Wiston stroked his chin thoughtfully. "Half an hour is perhaps an under-estimate. Let's work it out. From the lawn to the place on the roadside where David left his car must be all of a mile. Give them a quarter of an hour to walk that distance. Eight minutes for them to reach here. Ten minutes for them to tell me what was wrong, and for me to get my car out. Finally, ten minutes for us to reach the house."

"Forty-three minutes," Merrion remarked. "Say three-quarters of an hour. Sorry I'm so meticulous."

"I don't mind in the least," Wiston replied. "Accuracy is always a virtue. But the point is that there never was a body, for all those to whom it might have belonged are accounted for. I mentioned the jobbing gardener, and his wife who goes to The Brake as a charwoman. Their name is Edgefield, and they are on my panel. Joe Edgefield, the gardener, attended my surgery yesterday evening. He'd got a thorn into his hand, and it was beginning to fester.

"While I was dealing with his trouble, I took the opportunity of chatting to him about The Brake. I needn't trouble you with all he said, for most of it was quite irrelevant. But the salient points are these. The day before yesterday was Wednesday. That morning, both Joe Edgefield and his wife were working at The Brake. The only occupants of the house then were Mrs. Lavant and the two Lingfields. Joe went to work again there yesterday morning. While he was in the kitchen garden, Mr. and Mrs. Lingfield came and had a few words with him.

"You see what that means. Since David's unpardonable mistake, the only three people at The Brake have been seen alive. I myself saw Mrs. Lavant, making a spectacle of herself for the benefit of the local paper. Edgefield saw Mrs. Lingfield and her husband. And I utterly refuse to believe in the apparition of some casual visitor, lying dead in the hammock, arrayed and bejewelled in exact imitation of Mrs. Lavant."

"That sounds convincing enough," Merrion agreed. "Your son and Miss Dorset must have been mistaken?"

Wiston nodded. "There's no other explanation. I offer no excuses for David, who, as I say, ought to have known better. But there's just this in extenuation. Both he and Annabel were in a disturbed state. They were conscious of intrusion, and had just come from a most unpleasant altercation with the keeper. Add to that the fact that, oddly enough, the place seemed to be completely deserted, increasing the sinister aspect of the situation. According to Annabel, she kicked up enough din to rouse the Seven Sleepers. When you take all that into consideration, it becomes less difficult to understand how they came to jump to a false conclusion."

"It's rather odd that the telephone should have been out of order on that particular afternoon," Merrion remarked.

"Telephones have a way of going out of order, and always at the most inconvenient moments," Wiston replied. "Until Annabel told me of her attempt to get through to me, I didn't know that The Brake was on the telephone. As I've told you, The Retreat isn't." He reached for the directory and consulted it. "Mrs. Lavant's name isn't here," he went on. "Perhaps she's one of those people who like to keep their numbers to themselves. It's curious, though, for as a rule she likes to display her name as prominently as possible."

Not long afterwards, Merrion took his leave and drove back to London. Some days before, he had invited a very old friend of his, Inspector Arnold of Scotland Yard, to dine with him that evening. During the meal, he entertained his guest with an account of the odd adventure at The Brake on the previous Wednesday. "This Mrs. Lavant appears to be a bit of a character," he remarked. "And she has had some rather strange experiences. Her husband's grandson by his first wife, Roy Rayner by name, tried his hand at smuggling, and got killed in a scuffle with the police, some three years ago. Do you remember anything about that?"

Arnold frowned. "Remember it? Of course I do, and it makes me swear whenever I think about it. That affair was properly bungled. If they'd gone about things the right way, they'd have rounded up the whole gang. I had nothing to do with it, for I wasn't on the job. But it was I who got the information in the first place."

"Let's hear the yarn," said Merrion encouragingly.

"Am I to confess to a failure on the part of the police?" Arnold growled. "Well, since it's only you, I don't mind. We'd known for some time that there was smuggling going on. And we had reason to believe in the existence of a gang of demobilised, or deserted, ex-servicemen, though we didn't know who they were. And then, almost by chance, I arrested a deserter. He put up a pretty poor show, and squealed to save his own skin. Among other things he told me was that he had been approached by a man named Rayner. This man told him that he was the leader of a gang which had got hold of a fishing-boat and meant to run a cargo to a certain spot on the south coast on a given date. Rayner had invited him to bear a hand, but for some reason or other my man declined.

"It occurred to me that Rayner was probably a professional crook, and I looked up our records to see if we had any facts about him. We had, but they didn't amount to much. A year or so before the war he had been arrested on a charge of theft. He had got off under the First Offender's Act, and for that reason we had no record of his fingerprints.

"That's all I know at first-hand. As I say, I wasn't put on the job, which was given to an inexperienced officer because he had served in the Navy and might be expected to know how to handle a nautical job. But he made a mess of it. He and his whole party boarded the boat as soon as it came in, without leaving any one on shore to stop the bolt-holes. It was as dark as pitch, and they had a proper battle by the light of their torches. One man, obviously the ring-leader, had a revolver, and didn't hesitate to use it. He got knocked on the head for his pains, and fell, or jumped overboard. The rest of them followed his example. You'd hardly believe it, but they got into the dinghy the police had come aboard from, and got clean away, leaving the police marooned upon the fishing-boat.

"Remember, it was pitch dark, and they were hampered by the fact that the only one among them who had any knowledge of nautical matters was badly wounded, with a bullet through his chest. It took them some time to lower the fishing-boat's dinghy and set out in pursuit. By that time, of course, it was far too late. They found their own dinghy abandoned on the shore, but the members of the gang had got clear away. It wasn't until daylight came that they found the body of one of them washed up on the beach.

"There was never any doubt who the dead man was, though there was nothing in his pockets to identify him. But he had a revolver hung round his neck by a lanyard. Only one of the gang, the ring-leader, had been seen to use firearms. My man had told me that the leader was Rayner, but for a definite identification a more reliable witness was necessary. Our records showed that at the time when Rayner was convicted of theft he had been living with his grandparents at a London address. Their name, Lavant, came back to me just now when you mentioned it.

"Our inquiries revealed that though Mr. Lavant was dead, Mrs. Lavant was alive; and in the country. We dug her out, but of course we were anxious not to give the old lady too violent a shock. We told her that her grandson had met with a serious accident, and offered to take her to see him. She wasn't very keen, and said that she had long ago severed all connection with her husband's grandson. She was at pains to make it clear that Rayner was no blood relation of hers. However, we persuaded her to view the body, which she identified as that of Roy Rayner, aged twenty-seven, and, so far as she was aware, single. I dare say she wasn't over-grieved to know that the young scamp was dead."

"There are others who can't have been over-grieved, either," Merrion remarked. "But that wouldn't interest you. Tell me about the crimes you've been investigating since I saw you last."

V

It would be no exaggeration to say that Annabel's adventure preyed upon her mind. In the first place, she was profoundly irritated by David's behaviour. He must surely have deliberately led her to The Brake, for some obscure purpose of his own. And having got her there, the part he had played had been contemptible. He had come off very badly in his encounter with that curiously enigmatic keeper. Then, to crown everything, he had declared Mrs. Lavant was dead, a piece of folly on his part which had led to that ridiculous fiasco.

But there was more to it than mere annoyance with David. Her unexpected visit to The Brake had filled Annabel with an insatiable curiosity. Hitherto, her only knowledge of her great-aunt had been derived from hearing her parents talk about her. Her mother, good-natured and tolerant, never introduced the subject. But her father, especially when anything had happened to annoy him, was always bringing it up. Mrs. Lavant seemed almost to be an obsession with him, and the picture his imagination drew of her was not favourable. A cross-grained, selfish old woman, who spent her not inconsiderable income entirely on herself, without giving a thought to her relations. She must be well over eighty, probably bed-ridden, certainly decrepit, physically and mentally.

Now, Annabel had seen for herself. Far from being decrepit, Mrs. Lavant had exhibited a vigorous vitality. And what about the charge of selfishness and neglect of her relations? That cut both ways, for Annabel's parents had made no advances. Never even inquired after the old lady's health or comfort. Mrs. Lavant might retort with justice that it was she who had been neglected. As for the old stories of her unkind treatment of others, Annabel had only heard one side. There might be quite a lot to be said on Mrs. Lavant's behalf.

Annabel fully realised that after all these years, it would be hopeless to expect her parents to take any steps. But she had the imagination, and perhaps the impetuousness of youth. Gradually an idea took shape in her mind. Why shouldn't she, of a younger generation, attempt a rapprochement? Descend out of the blue upon Mrs. Lavant, and present herself to her as her great-niece? True, she had already been shooed away with the intimation that Mrs. Lavant saw nobody except by appointment. But that had only been because Mrs. Lavant had supposed the intruders on her lawn to be strangers. She would surely consent to receive her great-niece, if only out of curiosity.

By Friday, the day of Merrion's call on Matthew Wiston, Annabel's mind was made up. She announced casually at lunch that she proposed to spend the afternoon with a friend of hers, a statement which she hoped would turn out to be true. She went by train to Ridhurst, and set out from the station there on foot, being careful to avoid the street in which Dr. Wiston's house stood. She was a swift walker, and as she traversed the country road towards The Brake, she allowed herself to indulge in rosy anticipations. Her great-aunt would be surprised, but her astonishment would turn to affection. She would grasp the olive-branch held out to her in her old age, and all misunderstandings would be forgotten. Annabel would return home with at least a cordial message of good wishes for her parents.

Another thought passed through her mind. Cerberus, guarding the gate. Would he appear and forbid her entrance? She rather hoped he would, for she felt perfectly competent to deal with him. It had only been David's silly blustering that had made him so offensive. She felt sure that he wasn't really so rough as he had pretended to be. It was his job to keep trespassers away, and in the exercise of his duties a certain amount of rudeness and bluff was justifiable. He would turn out to be civil enough when she told him who she was.

She reached the entrance to The Brake, and it seemed to her that no one was about. But, as she laid her hand on the gate, the door of the lodge swung open, and the keeper appeared, dressed as she had seen him on the previous occasion. He strode on to the drive, and stood before her, frowning menacingly. "I've seen you before," he growled. "You were hanging around here the other day, with a young chap. Lucky for you both I was called away when I was. Now, what is it?"

Annabel smiled at him disarmingly. "I don't want to trespass," she replied. "I'm on my way to call on Mrs. Lavant.

She's my great-aunt, you see."

The keeper's air of ferocity changed to one of complete bewilderment. He stood motionless, staring at Annabel as though she was a visitor from another world. And when at last he spoke, his voice had lost all its roughness. "It may be as you say, miss. Did you see Mrs. Lavant when you were here the day before yesterday?"

Annabel did not feel inclined to enter upon the details of her previous visit. "Oh, yes, I saw her," she replied. "But I couldn't speak to her then, for she was busy giving an interview to some reporters."

This answer seemed to satisfy the keeper, for he stood aside, and his features relaxed into a positively friendly grin. "Very well, miss," he said. "If you'd told me who you were the other day, I shouldn't have spoken as I did. You won't say anything to Mrs. Lavant when you see her? You're sure to find her at home."

"Oh, no, I won't say anything," Annabel replied brightly. She went on her way, triumphant in the thought that she had completely tamed the man. He was quite nice, really, and an interesting if rather puzzling character. She wondered what his origins had been. It was quite obvious that his roughness of speech and manner were assumed. His natural voice was deep and cultured, and there was something engaging in the way he had asked her not to report his previous insolence. And he was certainly good-looking, when he wasn't pretending to be so fierce. By the time she came within sight of the house, Annabel had reached the conclusion that she quite liked him.

There was nobody in sight, but this time she did not propose to indulge in any game of hide and seek. She had come to pay a formal call, and the regular procedure must be observed. She rang the front-door bell, and stood there waiting. Some time elapsed before it was answered, and in the silence Annabel's confidence began to fail her. Suppose she received a resounding snub? Suppose her great-aunt told her that she wished to have nothing to do with her or her parents? She had no wish to expose herself to anything like that. Wouldn't it be better to turn back by the way she had come?

She was still standing irresolute when the door opened, to reveal a man whom she recognised instantly. The scene on the lawn recurred to her vividly. This was the man who had been standing apart, watching the proceedings with a cynical air. Annabel wondered who he might be. Certainly not the butler, for he was not dressed in the least like a servant. He was middle-aged, tall and of spare and athletic build. Clearly he did not recognise the visitor, but eyed her with a puzzled and, Annabel fancied, a rather worried expression. "Er—good afternoon," he said vaguely.

"Good afternoon," she replied. An awkward pause followed, while she tried to frame a suitable form of words. She mustn't appear to treat him as a servant. "I've come to call on Mrs. Lavant. Perhaps you can tell me if she is at home?"

"Mrs. Lavant is at home," the man said slowly. "But it is not her habit to see strangers, except by previous appointment."

Annabel was getting rather tired of this formula. "But I'm not a stranger," she replied briskly. "I was. passing this way, and I thought it only right to call. My name is Annabel Dorset, and my mother is Mrs. Lavant's niece."

The man appeared utterly astounded. He stared at Annabel with eyes so wide open that she was irresistibly reminded of the Frog Footman. And so of the Duchess, probably no more formidable than her great-aunt might prove to be. But she couldn't push past him as Alice had. And at last his expression relaxed. "Forgive me, Miss Dorset," he said. "It is so long since we have heard anything of your parents that you took me completely by surprise. Let me in turn introduce myself. My name is Lance Lingfield, and my wife and I have lived with Mrs. Lavant for many years. Do come in. I'm quite sure that Mrs. Lavant will be delighted to see you. Dear me, what a pleasant surprise for her!"

He led Annabel through the hall which she remembered so well, into the drawing-room which opened off it. "Do you mind waiting here for a minute or two?" he went on. "Mrs. Lavant is upstairs with my wife. I will tell her you are here."

He went away, leaving Annabel sitting by the open window. Through it she could see the hammock standing on the lawn, but now unoccupied. The room was richly furnished, though in rather blatant style. All the tables were covered with large photographs in silver frames. Most of these depicted Claire Gabriel in various roles. The rest were of men and women in costume, signed with names now nearly forgotten.

Annabel had not long to wait before two women entered the room. The first was Mrs. Lavant herself, a trifle bent, but walking with surprising agility for her age. She was not quite so elaborately dressed as when Annabel had last seen her, wearing a gaily-coloured frock and not quite so much jewellery. Her cunning make-up could not entirely conceal the wrinkles, but her hair was a profusion of platinum blonde. Annabel strongly suspected that it must be a wig.

The second woman was less spectacular in appearance. She was middle-aged, tall, slim, and handsome, plainly dressed without any adornment. Her expression was submissive, and she watched Mrs. Lavant as though ready at any moment to take her cue from her. Just how the companion of a domineering woman might be expected to look, Annabel thought. This of course must be Mrs. Lingfield.

As Annabel rose, Mrs. Lavant came towards her with outstretched arms. "So you are Annabel!" she exclaimed in her rich contralto voice. "How nice to meet you at last! Sit down, dear, and tell me all about yourself and your mother."

Mrs. Lingfield had remained in the background. "Shall I leave you alone for a little?" she asked.

"Yes, do, dear," Mrs. Lavant replied curtly. She said no more till Mrs. Lingfield had left the room, then continued in a far less effusive tone. "What does this mean? Who sent you here to see me?"

Annabel felt as though a pail of cold water had been flung over her. "Nobody sent me," she replied. "I came to pay my respects to you, because it seemed absurd that I should never have met my mother's aunt."

"Nonsense!"Mrs. Lavant exclaimed sharply. "You may as well tell me the truth. Your parents sent you here out of curiosity."

"I assure you that they didn't," Annabel replied. "It was entirely my own idea. I didn't even tell them I was coming."

Mrs. Lavant seemed slightly mollified. "Well, I'll believe you," she said grudgingly. "I'm glad in a way that you came, for I don't want to lose touch entirely with the other branch of the Lavant family. Your mother and father are quite well?"

"Quite well, thank you," Annabel replied. "They often speak of you."

"I dare say they do," Mrs. Lavant said grimly. "You may tell them that you have seen me in the best of health and looking forward to many years of life yet. I'm afraid the news won't be very welcome. And you may tell them that I wouldn't for the world put either of them to the trouble of coming to see me. I have my own friends, and I find their attentions quite sufficient. I shall be glad to see you from time to time, and you can give me news of them. But don't burst in upon me like this, write and tell me when you are coming. Now you shall stop and have tea with me. Will you press that bell by the fireplace?"

Annabel got up and pressed the bell-push. In a very short while the Lingfields appeared, bringing in the tea between them. Mrs. Lavant presided over the meal, talking volubly. But she seemed to have forgotten all about the Dorset family, and made no further inquiries concerning them. The conversation was virtually a monologue, Mrs. Lavant's reminiscences of her successes on the stage, interspersed with admiring comments from her listeners. "Dear Julius always tells me I ought to write a book," she babbled. "He says my memory is so wonderful. Well, perhaps I shall, some day. And then, Annabel dear, I'll send you an autographed copy for your very own."

Annabel took her leave as soon as she felt she decently could. Before she went, Mrs. Lavant presented her with a copy of one of the photographs taken on Wednesday for the Pembroke Forest Standard, inscribed with the flowing signature "Claire Gabriel." "I'm sure your parents will like to have that," Mrs. Lavant remarked maliciously.

As Annabel walked down the drive she felt a trifle disappointed. Her welcome had certainly not been so cordial as she had hoped. But she comforted herself with the thought that she had at least made a beginning. At least she hadn't been turned away, and her great-aunt had given her gracious permission to call again. Perhaps in time she would relent so far as to suggest that her mother, if not her father, should accompany her.

She had forgotten about the keeper, but it was evident that he had not forgotten about her. As she approached the gate he emerged from his lodge and came towards her, most respectfully this time. Annabel was flattered by the thought that he had been looking out for her, and welcomed him with a smile. "I beg your pardon, miss," he said. "But did you see Mrs. Lavant?"

"Oh, yes," Annabel replied. "I saw her and she gave me her photograph!"

"You found Mrs. Lavant quite well, miss?" the keeper asked deferentially. "You'll forgive my asking, but I haven't seen her lately. I haven't been to the house this week, and it isn't often Mrs. Lavant comes here."

"Perfectly well," Annabel replied. "I've just been having tea with her and Mr. and Mrs. Lingfield."

This remark seemed to cause the keeper some astonishment. "Mr. and Mrs. Lingfield?" he repeated. "Were they both there? I thought Mrs. Lingfield had gone up to London to stay."

Annabel shook her head. "If she did, she's come back again. Now, I've told you who I am. Will you tell me your name? It's so awkward talking to people without knowing what to call them."

The keeper grinned. "I don't know that my name can mean anything to you, miss. But it's Tom Hopton, at your service."

"Thank you, Mr. Hopton," Annabel replied. "Good afternoon. I hope I shall see you again when I come here next time."

Hopton opened the gate for her, and she started off on her walk to Ridhurst. It amused her to think that though she might not have been a striking success with her great-aunt, she had been with the keeper. The man had revealed himself in his true light, friendly and at the same time respectful. His solicitude for his employer's health showed that beneath the assumed roughness of his exterior he had a warm heart. She thoroughly approved of him.

As it turned out, the trains were inconvenient, and Annabel had to wait some little time at Ridhurst station. The result was that she got home later than she intended, and entered the house as her parents were sitting down to dinner. "Hallo, child!" Henry Dorset exclaimed. "We were beginning to wonder what had become of you. Where have you been all this time?"

"Oh, only having tea with Great-Aunt Claire," Annabel replied with elaborate carelessness.

"What!" her father exclaimed. "You mean to tell us that you've been to The Brake again? I should have thought that your adventures there on Wednesday would have cured you of any wish to see the place again."

"You are an extraordinary girl!" said Irene Dorset. "Why did you find it necessary to tell me you were going to spend the afternoon with a friend of yours?"

"Because I wanted to be able to tell her that neither of you knew I was coming," Annabel replied. "And it was quite true. Great-auntie was friendly in her own way. She gave me a photograph of herself she said you'd like to have."

"A photograph!" her father exclaimed disgustedly. "Well, sit down and let's hear all about it."

Annabel recounted her adventures, making no mention of the keeper, who was of no importance to her present story. "I'm going to call her Auntie in future, for short," she went on. "She was really as nice to me as I deserved. She's a thoroughly vain old woman, and utterly self-centred. There's no getting away from that. But I don't think there's any real harm in her."

Henry Dorset grunted. "There are at least two people, now dead, who would hardly have agreed with you. Your mother and I know better than that. What about those other two folk you met there?"

"The Lingfields?" Annabel replied. "They seemed all right, though a trifle subdued. Mr. Lingfield told me that he and his wife had been living with Auntie for years. So far as I can make out, their position is something between companions and domestic helps. And Auntie mentioned someone whom she called dear Julius, whoever he may be."

"The Lingfields have plenty to put up with, I dare say," her father remarked. "So the old woman sent us her photograph, did she? I'm bound to say I'd rather you'd brought home an invitation to her funeral."

After dinner Annabel produced the photograph, and they laid it beside the one they already possessed, taken many years earlier.

"She hasn't changed much in recent years," said Irene Dorset. "She hardly looks a day older in this last photograph than she does in the other. Her face seems to have changed a little, that's all."

Annabel laughed. "Her face is what she makes it. Having been an actress, she's up to all the dodges. She was so heavily made up this afternoon that she was practically disguised, and I'm pretty sure that her hair can't be her own. But still, if you look closely enough, you can see the wrinkles. They don't show in the photograph."

"I can understand her making up to have a photograph taken," said her father. "But why should she take all that trouble when she wasn't expecting anybody? Hardly for the benefit of the Lingfields, I should think."

"Because she likes to pretend that she's still on the stage," Annabel replied. "This afternoon I felt that I was acting in a drawing-room comedy, with Auntie as the leading lady. The setting was perfect, with all the theatrical properties. The Lingfields were the deferential attendants, and I was the long-lost grandchild. It was rather fun in a way, especially as all I had to do was to make an appropriate comment whenever Auntie paused in her soliloquy."

"I'm glad you found it fun," her father remarked. "Whatever possessed you to pay a formal call like that?"

Annabel shrugged her shoulders. "Curiosity, mainly. I wanted to make quite sure that I hadn't been dreaming on Wednesday. And I hadn't, for everything was just as I remembered it. As I went through the hall I saw the telephone that wouldn't work and the gong I had pounded. Even the hammock was still in the same place on the lawn."

"With a dead woman lying in it?" her father suggested.

"Don't be so silly!" Annabel exclaimed. "Of course there wasn't. There never was a dead woman. It was David who made such fools of us. It was Auntie I saw, so fast asleep that she looked as if she was dead. Of course, being fast asleep, she looked a little different then. But there's no doubt it was her, for she was dressed exactly as she was when the photograph was taken later. And this afternoon I recognised some of the jewellery she was wearing."

"It's a thousand pities she ever woke up," Henry Dorset muttered. "Well, you can please yourself about going to see her again. It might be a good thing if you did, now and then, to make sure she doesn't pop off without our hearing about it." He paused, then added darkly: "And without the trustees hearing about it either."

VI

Perhaps, if Merrion had been busy during the week-end, he would have devoted little further thought to The Brake and its occupants. But, having kept a business appointment on Saturday morning, he found himself free from further engagements for the next forty-eight hours. He had further business to transact in London during the following week. It was hardly worth while going back to High Eldersham, his permanent home, especially as his wife Mavis was away visiting friends. So he resolved to amuse himself as best he could.

The solution of a problem of any kind was the form of amusement which appealed to him most. It was natural, therefore, that his mind should dwell upon his conversations with Dorset and Matthew Wiston. But did The Brake present a problem? On the face of it, it did not. From all that he had been told, it seemed to be definitely established that no death could have occurred there on Wednesday. But Merrion was never content to survey merely the face of things. He felt instinctively that some mystery was involved in the story he had been told.

Of the truth of that story he had no doubt. His very slight acquaintance with Annabel Dorset was sufficient to assure him that she was not the sort of person to invent a yarn like that. He was also prepared to accept, with slight reservations, the background which Dorset and Wiston had supplied. Reservations, because Dorset was obviously prejudiced against his wife's aunt, and Wiston's knowledge of events at The Brake was derived almost entirely from hearsay. But, on the whole, the sketches that had been drawn were probably correct enough, from their own points of view.

The situation was by no means unprecedented. The central figure was an old woman, whose death would be advantageous to a certain group of people. But, in this case, the Dorsets and their circle were to all intents and purposes complete strangers to Mrs. Lavant. According to Dorset, they did not correspond, nor had he or any member of his family visited The Brake until Wednesday. On the other hand, Mrs. Lavant was surrounded by her own friends, who, in the case of the Lingfields, might be assumed to be dependants as well. They could have no expectations from Mrs. Lavant, since she was not free to bequeath any part of her income to them. It was therefore in their interest that she should live as long as possible.

Much as Henry Dorset might look forward to Mrs. Lavant's death, Merrion was not inclined to suspect him of having taken any steps to hasten that event. On the other hand, there was that extraordinary illusion of Wednesday afternoon. It might be that Mrs. Lavant had fallen into so deep a sleep that she had passed into a coma resembling death. But in that case was the sleep entirely natural? Might it not have been induced by some soporific drug?

Merrion's fertile imagination began to work upon this. Was it possible that an unsuccessful attempt had been made on Mrs. Lavant's life that afternoon? That she had been given some drug, in quantity incorrectly calculated to be fatal? And that she had recovered from the effects sufficiently to play her part before the camera? This theory, if correct, would throw light upon many points which had hitherto seemed obscure.

Correct or not, it seemed to Merrion a theory well worth following to its logical conclusion. The question was, who could have made such an attempt? Not the Lingfields, for they had everything to lose by Mrs. Lavant's death. The only people who had anything to gain were the Dorsets and those closely associated with them. Though Henry Dorset had not said so in so many words, he clearly expected that his daughter would eventually marry David Wiston. If things turned out that way, since Annabel was the eventual heiress, David must be included among those to whom Mrs. Lavant's death would be an advantage. And, from his point of view, if he contemplated hastening her death, he would best escape suspicion by doing so before he married, or even proposed to, Annabel.

So much for motive. It seemed to Merrion that opportunity was even clearer. It had been David's suggestion that he and Annabel should spend the afternoon in Fembrake Forest. He had professed ignorance of where The Brake was, but even Annabel had her doubts about that. It was certainly odd that he should have led her almost straight there. Almost, but not quite, for a period had intervened during which they were separated.

How long that period had been was uncertain. According to Annabel, David had gone for a swim in West Moon, leaving her beneath the trees nearby. She had gone to sleep, and could not tell how long she had slept. It might have been half an hour at least. David had not gone for a swim. He had made his way round the head of the lake and the wall to The Brake, taking the route by which he had subsequently led Annabel. He had found Mrs. Lavant asleep in her hammock, he had administered the drug, probably hypodermically. Being on the staff of St. Lucy's, he had access to drugs and syringes. Having done this, he had returned to Annabel by the way he had come.

Merrion's critical brain proceeded to seek flaws in this. How had David foreseen his opportunity? How could he have known in advance that he would find Mrs. Lavant asleep on the lawn? The answer was that for some time past he had kept The Brake under observation, and discovered that this was her invariable habit at that particular time and season. How did he know that the Lingfields would not be present? Again by observation. He had learnt that they always took advantage of Mrs. Lavant's siesta to absent themselves from the premises.

To continue the story. David had then cajoled Annabel to the lawn. He had administered a dose which he believed would be fatal. But, in his anxiety not to overdo it, and so run the risk of post-mortem detection of the drug, he had under-estimated the dose. It would do no harm to afford Annabel a glimpse of her great-aunt asleep in the hammock. When Annabel heard later that Mrs. Lavant had died in her sleep, she would not question the fact.

There would have been nothing more for David to do after that, if their departure had not been intercepted by the keeper. In order to rescue them from the predicament, Annabel had run back to awaken her great-aunt. David's only course had been to follow her. He had not been deceived into believing that Mrs. Lavant was dead when she wasn't. But, imagining that she must certainly be dead by the time they could return with Dr. Wiston, he had said that she was already. He had therefore agreed with Annabel that the best course would be to fetch his father.

Merrion fully realised that all this guesswork was no sort of evidence against David Wiston. Further, that even had there been an attempt to murder Mrs. Lavant, it was no business of his. But Henry Dorset had come to him for advice. Was it Merrion's duty to impart to him his suspicions, in the strictest confidence? Merrion decided that it was not. At all events, not until a reconnaissance had proved, or disproved, the possibility of his theory.

His first step was a careful study of the one-inch Ordnance Survey of Fembrake Forest. On this he had no difficulty in tracing the route described by Annabel. The two Moon ponds were marked, and on the isthmus between them two houses were indicated. Both lakes were long and narrow, and they were approximately the same size, with their longer axis running north and south. To the southward of the lakes ran a lane, on which the entrances to both houses were situated. About a mile to the north of this was a second, and roughly parallel lane. From this was access to the more easterly of the two houses, which must be The Brake, though the names of the houses were not given on the map. There appeared to be no access to the more westerly house. The Retreat. A footpath was shown, running from one lane to the other, to the west of West Moon. It must have been at the southern end of this footpath that Annabel and David had left the car. Approaching from the London road, they would have reached the spot from the west. They would not, therefore, have passed the entrance to either house. A measurement of distances on the map suggested that the estimate of three-quarters of an hour as the period which had elapsed between their leaving the lawn and their return with Dr. Wiston, should be about right.

What had happened at The Brake during that period? The return to consciousness of Mrs. Lavant. If she had been doped, she must have felt a bit muzzy when she woke up. But she must have been expecting the visit of the representatives of the local paper, and she had sufficient strength of will to pull herself together. The Lingfields had returned from wherever they had been. The car with the newspaper men in it had driven up to the front door.

Merrion considered when it would be best to carry out his reconnaissance in secret. It might be expected that, during a fine week-end, people would be strolling at large through the Forest. But from Monday onwards his time would be too fully occupied to allow him the opportunity. In the end he decided to visit the spot during Sunday night. The moon, being at her full, would afford him sufficient light for his purpose.

So some time before ten o'clock he took out his car and set out. He was wearing an old grey flannel suit, and was equipped with a powerful torch and a short tyre lever—this last a very useful tool should he find it necessary to force open anything. He followed the main road southward, turning off towards the outskirts of the Forest. Once he had left the main highway, he had the lanes to himself. His map had shown him a sandpit within a mile of his destination. He found this without difficulty, and drove the car into it, leaving it where it was hidden from the road. Then he started on foot for the southern end of the footpath to the westward of West Moon.

The moon was shining brightly, and the night was very still and sultry, presaging thunder. As he walked swiftly and noiselessly in his rubber-soled shoes, the sound of a distant bell striking eleven o'clock came to his ears. He was not likely to meet any one in this sparsely-populated district at such a time of night. The only person for whom he need be on the alert was that confounded keeper, who might be given to nocturnal prowling in search of poachers.

He reached the stile at the southern end of the footpath without meeting anybody. Climbing this, he started along the path. Litter was more than ever in evidence, showing this to be a favourite week-end resort. But as the path narrowed and became more difficult to follow, the litter was left behind. It became obvious that after a couple of hundred yards or so the path had fallen into disuse.

Merrion was not greatly concerned to follow the path. His first object was to find some point of vantage from which he could gain a view to the eastward. Some little distance ahead of him the ground rose in a slight fold, and towards this he pushed his way. He reached the shoulder of the slight ridge and forced his way upward through the tangled brushwood. Then he turned towards the lake, and in a few yards reached the edge of a miniature cliff, falling steeply to the surface of West Moon, a few feet beneath him.

He could not have found a better place for his purpose, for the whole panorama was spread out before him. In the immediate foreground was West Moon, shining like silver in the bright moonlight. On the farther side of it was the tree-clad isthmus, with the unsightly frontage of The Retreat clearly visible. Through several gaps in the trees he could see stretches of the wall, looking even more formidable than it had been described. Beyond the wall rose the roof of The Brake, the house hiding the lawn on the farther side of it. But here and there, through the trees on either side of it, gleams of more distant silver showed the position of East Moon.

Merrion stood for some minutes taking in these details. One thing was quite obvious. From no point on this side of West Moon could observation be kept on the lawn of The Brake. In order to do that from a secure distance it would be necessary to secure a post on the farther side of East Moon.

He turned and pushed his way through the undergrowth until he regained the abandoned footpath. He walked along this as rapidly as the encroaching branches would allow him, then stopped abruptly as a sound reached his ears. A movement of some sort near at hand. The sound was repeated, a furtive scurrying, then a squeak. Merrion smiled and went on his way. Only rats.

He had not much farther to go before he reached the northern end of the path, and found himself up the upper lane. He turned eastward along this, keeping a sharp look-out for any means of access to The Retreat, but his map had not misled him, and he found none. In a short time the extremity of the wall became clearly visible, for it ended only at the high thick hedge bordering the lane. Not far beyond this was the gateway with its notice-board. But Merrion had no intention of trespassing in that direction. The risk of a possible meeting with the keeper was too great. He went on for some little distance until the lane became unfenced and bordered only by the trees and brushwood of the Forest.

Choosing what seemed to be a comparatively open space, he left the lane and steered a course southwards. After half a mile of difficult going, he saw on his right the glint of water in the moonlight. He made his way cautiously towards this, until he was within a few yards of the east bank of East Moon. Invisible among the trees, he looked out over the trees. He was right opposite the front of The Brake, with only a stretch of water and the lawn between himself and the house. Every detail was visible, to the hammock and its canopy standing on the lawn. As he surveyed the prospect, once more the sound of the distant bell came to his ears, striking midnight.

Well, that was that. From where Merrion stood, the closest possible observation could be kept upon The Brake and the doings of its occupants. And in reaching that spot the observer himself would be hidden. It seemed unlikely that the land on this side of East Moon formed part of The Brake property, so it would not be patrolled by the keeper. Merrion had seen all he wanted, and the next question was how he should return to the sandpit where he had left the car. The shortest route would be to go on till he reached the southern lane, and then to follow that. But that would lead past the entrance where the lodge was. Merrion decided that he would return by the way he had come.

As he made his way back through the undergrowth, it seemed to him that the air had become more sultry. And a few minutes after he had reached the northern lane he heard a distinct rumble of thunder. He quickened his pace, for if the storm approached it would obscure the moon, to say nothing of bringing drenching rain with it. Already there was a dark cloud in the western sky, and a few seconds later a faint glimmer of lightning. The peal which followed was louder and closer at hand. Merrion hurried along the lane towards the stile at the upper end of the footpath.

But when he had surmounted it, his progress was greatly slowed down. The branches of the shrubs seemed to have entered into a conspiracy to delay him. They twined themselves around him, and as often as he pushed them aside, whipped back into his face. Under the trees the moon cast little light, and he was compelled to employ one hand in holding the torch. He plunged through the sultry stillness, perspiring freely and swearing softly to himself.

Then again he heard that queer scuffling, apparently on the same spot where he had heard it before-close at hand, to his left, where a legion of rats seemed to be holding high festival. He wondered what on earth this wilderness could hold to attract the brutes. He stopped and flashed his torch into the undergrowth. Bright eyes instantly reflected the light. And he became aware that the thunder-laden air was tainted with a faint and nauseous smell.

That explained the presence of the rats. A dead animal of some kind. But it was odd, just the same. As he swung his torch slowly round, he saw a track through the undergrowth, where branches had been broken short, as though a passage had been forced. By the animal on whose carcase the rats were feasting, no doubt. It must have been a big animal, Merrion thought. And then, with an unwitting gasp of horror, the idea came. What if it had not been an animal?

Fighting back his disgust for rats, Merrion followed the track of broken branches. The scuffling was all about his feet now, punctuated by angry squeaks. And that nauseous smell grew more powerful with every step he advanced, making his gorge rise. Within a few yards the undergrowth came to an end and he halted abruptly as one foot sank into yielding mud. A flash of lightning turned the surface of West Moon to fire.

He was standing in the open, and the moon, still unclouded, revealed his surroundings. Beside him was a wooden shed, evidently a boat-house, for one end of it abutted upon the water. The doors at that end were closed and secured with a rusty chain and padlock. At the landward end was a single door, also secured in some way, though no lock was visible. The woodwork of the boat-house was in a state of disrepair, and showed a multitude of holes, especially at ground level. Merrion took the tyre-lever from his pocket, and with it beat upon the outer wall.

Immediately, through the holes at his feet, poured a colony of rats. Dozens of them, monstrous in the moonlight. Merrion sprang back in horror, but the brutes were too gorged to attack him. They scampered heavily away into the brushwood, their squealing drowned in a deep peal of thunder. And at that instant the storm cloud swept over the moon, plunging the world in darkness. Merrion felt the first big warm drops of rain upon his face.

His first impulse was to get away as quickly as he could from this horrible place. He sensed the rats all about him in the darkness, waiting to resume their grisly feast. But he steeled himself to withstand the ordeal. The emergence of the rats showed that whatever had attracted them was within the boat-house. His torch revealed an insecure plank, hanging loosely from its fastenings. With his tyre-lever he wrenched this away, to fall back overcome by the stench which poured out upon him.

He recovered himself and, holding his breath, extended the hand holding the torch through the opening.

Merrion was used to horrors, but what the torch revealed was more ghastly than anything he had ever known. One glance was more than enough. He recoiled, bent double, and was violently sick. He craved for a cigarette, but by now the rain was pouring down steadily, and it would be impossible to light one. Obviously there was nothing he could do, for this was a matter for other hands than his. Meanwhile, it would be wise to conceal the traces of his visit. With the tyre-lever he knocked the dislodged plank back into its place. Then he turned away and regained the footpath, the unseen scurrying ghouls all about him.

The storm was now reaching its height. Incessant flashes of lightning, followed almost instantaneously by deafening peals of thunder. As he struggled on through the entangling branches the rain, penetrating the leaves of the trees, drove down upon him. Somewhere, too near to be pleasant, a resounding crash and a momentary flashing glare told him that one of the trees in the Forest had been struck. With a shudder he thought it was a pity it had not been the boat-house, to destroy all vestige of its awful contents. His imagination pictured the rats following him stealthily, ready to spring upon him from behind. It seemed a century before he reached the more frequented stretch of the footpath and was able to quicken his pace. By the time he reached the car, he was drenched to the skin.

As he drove back to London, the storm abated. He put the car away and let himself into his rooms, where he lost no time in lighting a cigarette and pouring himself out a strong drink. It was two o'clock in the morning, but he knew very well that sleep was impossible. Even if it came, it would bring intolerable nightmare in its train. He gulped down his drink, then had a bath, hoping that the physical ablution would conduce to the mental. Then, wrapped in a dressing-gown, he sat down to consider the steps that must be taken.

Obviously, the proper course would be to inform the local police, but Merrion shrank from that. His midnight prowling in the vicinity of the boat-house would be far too difficult to explain. It would be immediately suspected that he knew more than he was prepared to reveal. But, fortunately, he knew how to provide himself with an intermediary. Arnold, he was aware, was not on night duty that week. Merrion rang up Scotland Yard, with a message to be given to Inspector Arnold as soon as he arrived. Would he come to Mr. Merrion's rooms immediately, on a matter of the utmost urgency?

VII

Arnold appeared when Merrion had breakfasted and had consequently regained his poise. "Well!" Arnold exclaimed, as Newport showed him into the room. "What's all this about, with your utmost urgency?"

"I've something to show you," Merrion replied. "It's urgent because very soon there won't be anything of it left. I've cancelled my engagements for the day, and you'll have to do the same. We won't waste time talking here. Newport has brought the car round and put a bottle of disinfectant in it. We'll get along, straight away."

As he drove, Merrion described his nocturnal reconnaissance. "Never mind what I was after," he said. "We can put that on one side for the present. On my way back I had the curiosity to look into an abandoned boat-house. There I got a shock from which I haven't entirely recovered even yet, although I'm not particularly squeamish. My excuse must be that, in a thunderstorm at midnight, to come upon a human body being eaten by rats is enough to give any one a shock."

"A human body?" Arnold exclaimed. "So that was what you were looking for, then?"

"It most certainly was not," Merrion replied heartily. "If it hadn't been for the rats, I should never have suspected its existence. And I may as well say at once that I haven't reported it. That'll be your job. All the credit of the discovery will be yours. Acting upon information received will come much better from you than it would from me."

He said no more, and when they reached the outskirts of the Forest, he diverged along a route which brought them to the northern lane. He pulled up at the stile at the upper end of the footpath. By daylight the track was easier to follow. The storm had passed, leaving behind it a fine bright morning. Merrion led the way, brushing aside the intruding branches. Before they had gone very far, a rat scurried across the path in front of them. "There's one of the beasts!"Merrion exclaimed with an involuntary shudder. "But they aren't likely to be so bold now as they were last night."

A few yards farther on a glimpse of the boat-house showed through the bushes. It could plainly be seen that a passage had been forced through them, and Merrion pointed this out. "It was like that at midnight. I may have broken off a few more branches, but someone had been through before me. There, look!"

As they approached, a dozen rats scuttled out through the holes in the wall of the boat-house. Arnold went up and examined the door on the landward side. He found a keyhole silted up with dirt and fragments of dead leaves, but the door was locked and no key was visible. "It's pretty flimsy," Merrion remarked. "Here, take this."

He handed the tyre-lever to Arnold, who inserted it in the jamb. After a couple of wrenches the door flew open. Arnold retreated, overpowered by the stench, but Merrion took from his pocket the bottle of disinfectant and flung it through the doorway against the opposite wall. "That'll do the trick," he said as the bottle broke. "Give it a minute or two to work, then we'll go in."

After a suitable interval they entered the boat-house. At the farther end, cut off from the lake by folding doors, was a dock, in which was a derelict skiff, stove in and waterlogged. Between the dock and the door by which they had entered was a strip of dry ground. One of the wooden shingles of the roof was missing, and through this aperture dead leaves and twigs had drifted in from the overhanging trees, forming a thick carpet. On this lay a body, which the dress indicated to be that of a woman, though the features were unrecognisable. Even Arnold, to whom a dead body was a commonplace, turned shudderingly away from this ghastly spectacle. "We'll have to get her out of this," he muttered.

"Exactly," Merrion replied. "But that, I take it, is a job for the local police. You've made the discovery for yourself now. Shall I drive you into Ridhurst to report?"

Arnold agreed, and they drove to the local police station, which Arnold entered, leaving Merrion in the car. In a few minutes he came out again. "I saw the sergeant," he said. "Fortunately when I told him I was from the Yard he was too impressed to ask awkward questions. He's coming along with a van and a man to help him."

"Then we'd best go back and wait for him," Merrion replied. Not very long after they had returned to the stile a van drove up and the sergeant and a constable descended from it. Arnold led the way to the boat-house and helped to raise the body. Between the three of them they carried it to the van. The two local policemen got into the front seat and drove off in the direction of Ridhurst. "We won't follow them yet," said Arnold. "I want to look round first. There may be something in the boat-house to throw a light on all this."

They returned to the place and set to work to examine it thoroughly. It was quite evident that the folding doors opening on to the lake had not been opened for some time, probably years. But, turning their attention to the other door, they found the key in place on the inner side of the lock. Merrion tried it and found that it turned quite easily. "That's curious," he remarked. "It rather suggests that unhappy woman had locked herself in. Which, in turn, suggests suicide. Hallo, what the devil's this?"

In turning from the door he had tripped over something buried in the carpet of dead leaves. Bending down to see what it was, he scraped away the leaves to reveal a bone, dry and with no flesh adhering to it. "Here, come and lend a hand," he said to Arnold. In increasing amazement the pair of them shovelled away the debris with their bare hands. Their efforts disclosed a complete human skeleton.

"This place is a regular charnel-house!" Merrion exclaimed. "We shall have to dig over it and see if there are any other human remains. I don't know enough about anatomy to tell whether these are male or female. It won't do to move them, or the bones will fall apart. What can this mean?"

"I'm blest if I know," Arnold replied. "You seem to have blundered into things a bit. Who does this boat-house belong to?"

"Being on this lake, it belongs to The Retreat, I suppose," said Merrion. "I've been told that Sir Julius Blackrock lives there, but I've never met him. Come outside, and I'll show you the house." From the edge of the open space outside the boat-house the whole length of West Moon was visible, and to the left of it The Retreat. "My information is that Sir Julius is a recluse, old and nearly blind," Merrion went on. "It isn't very likely that he's a Bluebeard, who disposes of his victims here. All the same, let's see if there's any sort of way to the house." He set off to explore, but very soon returned. "The bushes have grown up all round the boat-house," he reported. "There are traces of a path running down the east side of the lake, but it has grown over with brambles and stuff long ago. I'm ready to swear that no one has been along it for a year or more. Leaving the skeleton out of consideration, the other body didn't come that way. It may have come by water, landing where we're standing now. But, from the broken branches, it seems most probable that it came along the track from the stile."

"Alive or dead?" Arnold inquired significantly.

Merrion shook his head. "We can't hope to answer that question yet. All we've got to guide us at present is the locked door, with the key on the inside. But that's not final, of course. Someone may have prised open one of the weatherboards, as I did last night. If so, we ought to be able to see where."

But a minute scrutiny of the structure of the boat-house disposed of that theory. With the exception of the loose board Merrion had found, all the rest were secure and had obviously not been tampered with. The removal of this single board would not leave a gap wide enough to admit a human being. And nothing much larger than a rat could have entered by any of the existing holes in the woodwork.

"The door, I think," Merrion remarked. "What next?"

"Back to Ridhurst," Arnold replied. "We've got to do something about that skeleton. And I expect the sergeant will have got a doctor to see to that other body by this time."

Once more they drove to the police station, and this time Merrion went in with Arnold. "This is my friend Mr. Merrion, Sergeant," said the latter. "He was good enough to drive me down here. You've got the body in the mortuary?"

"Yes, sir," the sergeant replied. "And I've asked Dr. Wiston to examine it. He's there now, and he promised to come on here and tell me the result. And there's another thing, sir. I've rung up my superintendent and reported the matter. He can't come here this morning, but I was to ask you if you'd take charge, as you were already on the spot."

"I'll do all I can to help," said Arnold. "But I don't propose to interfere in your affairs. Arid there's another problem for you to solve. There's a second body, or rather skeleton, in that boat-house."

"A skeleton, sir?" the sergeant repeated incredulously. "A human skeleton, you mean?"

Arnold nodded. "I do, indeed, and it can't be moved. We broke open the door and it can't be fastened again. I suggest you send a man up there to keep guard. We don't want any one interfering with the place."

Matthew Wiston came in while the conversation was proceeding. The sergeant introduced Arnold to him, while Merrion remained in the background. Wiston glanced at him, then looked again more closely. "Why, bless my soul!" he exclaimed. "Mr. Merrion! I didn't expect the pleasure of meeting you here."

"Being a very old friend of Arnold's he asked me to drive him down," Merrion replied evasively.

Arnold came to the rescue. "I'm glad I did. I've always valued Merrion's opinion. What have you to tell us, Doctor?"

Wiston frowned. "One of the most unpleasant tasks I have ever been called on to undertake. Not only is the body in a state of decomposition, but it has been most horribly gnawed by rats. I need not go into revolting details, but identification by the features is quite impossible. The only thing that could be recognised is the hair, dark brown and cut closely in the form of an Eton crop."

"That's something at least to go on," Arnold remarked. "Can you give us any further particulars?"

"Not very many, I'm afraid," Wiston replied. "The body is that of a woman, aged about forty, more or less. I have not discovered the cause of death, and under the circumstances I think it would be impossible to do so. Nor can I determine with any accuracy the time when death took place. Having regard to the state of decomposition and the heat of the weather lately, I am of the opinion that it must have taken place five or six days ago."

Arnold turned to the sergeant. "Has any one been reported missing locally?" he asked.

"No, sir," the sergeant replied. "And I don't know of any one about here with hair cut like the doctor says."

"Well, I'm grateful for what you have been able to tell us Doctor," said Arnold. "And now we shall have to trouble you for your opinion on another matter. There's a human skeleton in that boat-house."

"Good heavens!" Wiston exclaimed. "Your discoveries are most amazing. Inspector. I must examine it, of course."

"My car is outside," Merrion remarked. "I am at your service if you would like me to drive you there."

Wiston accepted this offer, and they went out, leaving Arnold in consultation with the sergeant. They drove to the spot, to find the constable who had been dispatched already on duty at the boat-house. He made no difficulty about letting them go in, and Wiston knelt down on the debris to examine the bones. "It's a woman, again," he said. "Of middle age, to all appearances. And this skeleton seems to have been lying here for a long time. But I think a more expert opinion should be sought. If your friend Mr. Arnold agrees, I will ring up a friend of mine in London and ask him to come down. He will be better able to give a detailed report than I am."

"That would seem a good idea," Merrion replied. "You must know pretty well all the people round about, Doctor. Have you any sort of suspicion as to the identity of the body in the mortuary?"

"Not the slightest," said Wiston emphatically. "I feel sure that the dead woman was a complete stranger to me. Nor can I imagine how her body came to be found in this almost inaccessible boat-house. I do not wish to ask indiscreet questions. But it can scarcely have been found here unless it was being searched for."

Merrion was not prepared to explain how it had been found. "We must allow Arnold to keep his own counsel about that. This place is not very easy to get at, certainly. Who does it belong to?"

"Sir Julius Blackrock, I suppose," Wiston replied. "You'll remember that I spoke of him to you the other day. It appears to stand on the edge of his property. But I feel sure that he has never used it, for many years at least."

"You spoke to me of a housekeeper and a gardener," said Merrion. "Is there any other staff at The Retreat?"

"Not now," Wiston replied. "Before the war Sir Julius kept a cook and house-parlourmaid, but they left and have never been replaced. The housekeeper, Mrs. Moffatt, does all the indoor work. The greater part of the house is shut up and disused, I understand. And Sir Julius never has any one to stay with him."

Merrion drove the doctor back to Ridhurst, and then went to the police station, where he found Arnold. "Medical evidence is to the effect that the skeleton is that of a middle-aged woman," he said. "The doctor proposes to get more expert opinion upon it. Meanwhile, I expect you'll concentrate on the other one?"

"I've been examining the clothes she was wearing," Arnold replied. "Or, rather, what the rats have left of it. It's quite plain and of rather cheap quality, and not marked in any way. The shoes are rough and heavy, and very much worn. But there's one thing that may help us. The dress she was wearing was open in front, and this was fastened with a brooch. There it is." He pointed to the object lying on the desk. It was a silver safety-pin, with a single small opal set in the middle of it. Not, in fact, a very distinguished piece of jewellery.

"Opals are said to be unlucky," Merrion remarked. "And I don't think this one is likely to bring you much luck. The pin isn't sufficiently remarkable for any one but the owner to have noticed it particularly. Well, having introduced you to the puzzle, I'll leave you to it. I have matters that can't be put off to attend to this afternoon."

And in spite of Arnold's protests, he insisted upon going. Until evening, the affair of business upon which he was engaged monopolised his attention. Not until he sat down to dinner, alone in his rooms, did he find time to concentrate upon the Fernbrake Forest adventure.

At the back of his mind from the first had been an unspoken question. Could there be any connection between the gruesome discovery in the boat-house and the experiences of those two young people the previous Wednesday? The theory that David had attempted the life of Mrs. Lavant might, for the moment, be relegated to the background. In the simplest terms the question was this. Could the body now in the mortuary be the one which David and Annabel saw, or believed they saw?

For the affirmative there were these points. The body was that of a woman. Dr. Wiston estimated that she had been dead for five or six days, a period which covered the previous Wednesday. The distance between the lawn at The Brake and the boat-house was short enough to present no insuperable difficulty to the transport of a body.

The objections for the negative were these. The body, or alleged body, seen by David and Annabel was that of an elderly woman. This term, though vague, certainly exceeded Dr. Wiston's estimate of forty, more or less. It had been richly dressed, and adorned with expensive jewellery. This was in strong contrast to the plain clothing of the boat-house body and the cheap opal-mounted safety-pin. Since all the inmates of The Brake had been accounted for, the body in the hammock could not have been any of theirs. It was, of course, just possible that an afternoon visitor to The Brake had died suddenly. But it was not easy to understand why, in such a case, the body should have been transported to the boat-house. Had she been murdered by Mrs. Lavant or her entourage, her body would not have been left alone in the hammock for all the world to see.

There was the further problem of entrance to the boat-house. Merrion had fully satisfied himself that, dead or alive, the woman could have got in only by the landward door. If dead, she must have been carried in. But the door had very definitely been locked, with the key on the inner side. How then had those who carried her in made their departure?

On the whole, then, it seemed that the woman must have entered the boat-house alive. For what purpose? It was far from an inviting place to choose for a quiet rest. Could she have been seeking refuge from some pursuit or other? She had certainly locked herself in. Dr. Wiston had employed the epithet inaccessible. The boat-house undoubtedly offered a sanctuary which might well be undiscovered. But what then? Had she died there of exhaustion?

A more likely theory seemed to be suicide. The unhappy woman had crept into the boat-house to die. The thorough search made by Arnold and Merrion had disclosed no weapon. Not even a handbag, which was rather curious. But she might have swallowed poison which she had brought with her. Her reason for choosing this hidden spot might have been a desire to disappear from this world without leaving a trace behind her.

But how had she found it? Surely not by chance. Fembrake Forest was to a great extent unfenced, and open to any one who cared to wander through it. The litter at the southern end of the footpath was evidence that people did so. But the boat-house was buried in undergrowth difficult to penetrate. It was not likely to be discovered by any one unaware of its existence. The inference was that the woman had been someone familiar with the neighbourhood. But the sergeant had been positive that no one living round about was missing.

Merrion finished his dinner and sat down to enjoy a cigarette. His thoughts returned to The Brake, and the many odd things he had been told about the house and its tenant. If his theory was correct that the woman whose body he had discovered had committed suicide, her act was not without precedent locally. Some three years ago Mrs. Lavant's foreign companion had been driven mad enough to commit suicide. Could there be any connection between the two events? It seemed hardly possible. The woman of the boat-house had certainly not been Mrs. Lavant's companion. According to Dr. Wiston, the only female companion she had had of recent years was Mrs. Lingfield, and she had been seen alive and well subsequent to Wednesday.

According to Dr. Wiston. That thought gave Merrion pause. The sergeant, presumably of his own volition, had called upon Dr. Wiston to view the body. There was nothing in that, for he seemed to be the doctor regularly employed by the local authorities. The coroner had requested him to examine the body of Madame Tallinn, for instance. It was absurdly illogical to suggest that Dr. Wiston had his suspicions as to the identity of this latest body. But Merrion would never have found that body if he had not set out to explore the possibility of David Wiston having attempted to murder Mrs. Lavant.

All this, Merrion told himself, was sheer nonsense. But his thoughts persisted in revolving round the event, remotely and without much approach to logic. David had been in the vicinity of the boat-house on Wednesday. His actions that afternoon during the period that his companion was asleep were unconfirmed. Had he any knowledge of the existence of the unknown woman, or of the circumstances which had led to her death?

VIII

It may have been because Merrion had had no sleep the previous night that his thoughts drifted into incoherency. He threw away the end of his cigarette and was dozing off in his chair when he was aroused by the entrance of Newport, who announced that Inspector Arnold had called to see him. "Come along in," said Merrion, as Arnold appeared. "Sit down, and I'll pour you out a drink. You look as if you wanted one."

"I could do with one," Arnold replied. "I've just got back from Ridhurst, and I looked in to give you the latest news."

"And ask for my opinion, I dare say,' said Merrion. "My brain is a bit torpid, but fire away."

"I'll begin at the wrong end," Arnold replied. "Dr. Wiston rang up his pathologist friend, and he drove down late this afternoon. He gave me a lift back, by the way, or I shouldn't be here now. I took him first to see the skeleton, which had not been disturbed. He agreed that it was a woman's, and he said that she must have been little over fifty when she died. The bones show no signs of violence. As to when she died, the pathologist was naturally very cautious. Some years ago, possibly up to five or ten, probably not more than that. There was nothing about the bones of any use as a clue to identity. No teeth with dentist's work on them, for instance.

"Then I thought he'd better have a look at the other body, so I took him to the mortuary. He couldn't tell me much more than Dr. Wiston already had. He found a good set of teeth, with only three or four missing, but again no dentist's work. At Dr. Wiston's suggestion, he brought some of the remains away with him for analysis.

"So much for him. Now, to go back. Early this afternoon the superintendent in charge of the district came over. He didn't ask any awkward questions, and was quite ready to lay all the responsibility on the shoulders of the Yard. He said it would probably turn out to be our job in any case, for if the woman was a stranger, she probably came from London. I rang through to the Chief, who agreed that I should undertake the investigation."

"That's all to the good," Merrion remarked. "Have you done anything about it?"

Arnold laughed. "I've taken a fortress by storm, or something like it. Obviously the first thing to do was to make inquiries about the boat-house. So the sergeant and I drove to The Retreat to interview Sir Julius Blackrock. When we got to the entrance gate we found it locked, and nobody about to open it for us. So we left the car outside and climbed the gate, not without a lot of trouble, for it had barbed-wire on the top.

"But that was only the first line of defence. We walked up to the house and rang the bell. The door was opened by a woman of uncertain age, who glared at us as though we'd been pickpockets. It's true that the sergeant had torn a great rent in his trousers climbing over the gate, and was doing his best to hide it. We asked to see Sir Julius, and she told us that he never on any account saw visitors unless he was expecting them."

"I've been told that he prefers a life of solitude," said Merrion. "However, you saw him, I suppose?"

"Oh, yes, we saw him," Arnold replied. "The sergeant was in uniform, of course, and I produced my official card. The woman didn't seem very much impressed, but we persuaded her to tell Sir Julius we were there, and she went off, leaving us on the doorstep. After a while she came back and took us into a big room, which I suppose was the lounge. But we could not see much of it, for all the curtains were drawn, and in the middle of the afternoon, too."

"Sir Julius is nearly blind, I believe," said Merrion. "I dare say he finds that a glare hurts his eyes."

"Oh, so that's it," Arnold replied. "He's an old man, and seems rather infirm. He didn't get out of his chair while we were there, but he was quite ready to talk to us. We didn't tell him what had been found in the boat-house, but asked him if it was his. He said that it was, but that he hadn't been there for many years.

"Then we asked him when it had last been used. He told us that during the war a searchlight detachment had been in camp in the Forest, not far away. The officer in charge had called on him and asked if his men might be allowed to bathe in his lake. Sir Julius had told him they were welcome to. He had gone on to say that they would find an old skiff in the boat-house which they could have the use of.

"Just before the troops left the district, the officer called again to thank him. He brought back the key of the boat-house, which Sir Julius passed on to his gardener. He was the only person who was in the least likely to have gone there since then. To the best of his recollection, this had been shortly before D-day."

"D-day was five years ago," said Merrion thoughtfully. "It's not very likely that the troops deposited the skeleton in the boat-house before they left. If it had been there while they were using the place, they would have been bound to find it and would presumably have reported having done so. We can take it, I think, that the skeleton, possibly then clothed in flesh, found its way there during the last five years."

"That's about it," Arnold agreed. "We didn't ask Sir Julius any more questions. Of course he wanted to know why we were interested in the boat-house. I told him that we had our suspicions that it had been used for unlawful purposes, which wasn't very far from the truth. He'll hear all about it before very long. He rang for the woman to show us out, and we asked her if the gate couldn't be unlocked. She said she'd have to go and find the gardener, as he was the only person who had the key.

"After a while the gardener turned up, an elderly chap and nearly stone-deaf. However, by shouting at him we made him understand what we were talking about. He remembered Sir Julius giving him the key of the boat-house. The troops had made full use of the permission they had been given, for there were always some of them bathing or skylarking about in the skiff. After they had gone he went to the boat-house to see what damage they had done. He found they had knocked it about a bit, and broken the old skiff all to pieces. They hadn't left anything behind, as far as he could see. To the best of his recollection he had left the key in the door, for there was nothing there worth any one's while to steal. He hadn't been there since, for he'd had no occasion to.""So the boat-house has been derelict for at least five years," Merrion remarked. "That is, if we accept the statements of Sir Julius and his gardener. You saw no one else at The Retreat, except the housekeeper?"

"Not another soul," Arnold, replied. "Now, look here. Do you think it likely that nobody at The Retreat knows anything about the affair?"

Merrion shrugged his shoulders. "You should be the best judge of that. Just now I'm so drowsy that even my imagination is asleep. You run along, and if you care to call here in the morning I'll drive you down to Ridhurst."

A night of sound sleep restored Merrion to normal. As soon as he woke up his mind reverted to the case. This was a wonderful opportunity of satisfying his curiosity. Ever since Henry Dorset's visit he had been anxious to make the acquaintance of Mrs. Lavant. And to make inquiries at The Brake would be no more than a natural matter of routine.

As he had expected, Arnold came early, and they set off together in the car. "I've been thinking over what you told me yesterday evening," said Merrion. "In the course of your conversation with Sir Julius, did he mention his neighbour, Mrs. Lavant?"

"No, he didn't," Arnold replied. "There was no reason why he should that I can see."

"I'm given to understand that she is one of the few people he receives," said Merrion. "She and Dr. Wiston. I dare say she knows as much as anybody of what goes on at The Retreat. It might be worth our while to call on her."

Arnold agreed to this, but without much enthusiasm. They drove first to Ridhurst police station to hear the sergeant's report, but this was entirely negative. In spite of the most searching inquiries, he could hear of no one being missing. A photograph had been taken of the opal-mounted pin, and this, with a short description, was to be inserted in the next issue of the Pembroke Forest Standard. The coroner had arranged to hold inquests, on the body and skeleton, at half-past two that afternoon, and the jury had been summoned. "You'll give evidence of finding, sir?" the sergeant added.

"Yes, I'll do that," Arnold replied. "Well, then, I'll go and have another look round." He and Merrion left the police station.

"Well, the news will be all round the town by now," said Merrion when they were seated in the car. "We shan't give anything away by asking questions. So let's go and call at The Brake. There are two entrances, for the drive runs the whole length of the isthmus. At the lower end of it is a lodge in which a keeper lives. A bit of a tough customer, from all accounts. But the upper end is unguarded, so it may save us trouble to go in that way."

They reached the upper gate, opened it and drove towards the house. Before they reached it they saw on their left, between the drive and East Moon, a vegetable garden, in which an elderly man was working. "I know who that must be," said Merrion, bringing the car to a standstill. "Let me see now, what did the doctor say his name was? Edgefield, that was it. He's the gardener, but he doesn't live on the premises. We'll have a word or two with him."

They got out and walked towards the man, who regarded them with some astonishment. "Good morning, Edgefield," said Merrion. "This is Inspector Arnold, from Scotland Yard. You've heard of the body that's been found, I expect?"

"Aye, I've heard about that," Edgefield replied. "I was round at the Verderers' Arms last night, and they were all speaking of it."

"And there was a good deal of guessing who the body belonged to, I dare say?" Merrion suggested.

"There was that," Edgefield agreed. "They say the rats had been at it, so there was no telling whose it was. The sergeant has been round asking a lot of questions. But it's nobody from round about, that's a sure thing."

Arnold jerked his head towards the wall, a section of which was visible. "You know the gardener next door, I take it?"

"Old Amos Wanstead?" Edgefield replied. "I can't say that I know him overwell. He keeps himself to himself pretty much, and he's that deaf it's hard to make him understand sense. But he looks into the Verderers' now and again."

"Was he there yesterday evening?"Arnold asked.

Edgefield shook his head. "Can't say as he was. Not while I was there, that is."

"You know the boat-house where the body was found, I expect?" Arnold suggested.

"Why, yes," Edgefield replied. "I remember well enough when it was built. That was when I was a young chap. There was a large family living at The Retreat then, and I used to work for them. The young ladies and gentlemen were always rowing about on the lake. Why, I helped to clear the ground where the boat-house was to be."

"Has it been used much since that family went away?" Arnold asked.

"That I couldn't say," Edgefield replied. "You mightn't believe it, but I haven't been inside the grounds since Sir Julius bought The Retreat. But while the war was on the soldiers used to use it, I do know that. Sir Julius told them they might, so I understood at the time. I don't reckon it's been used since then."

Merrion put in a word. "Has Mrs. Lavant heard about the body being found?"

Again Edgefield shook his head. "That I couldn't say. But I can tell you this. I told the missus, and it wouldn't be like her to keep such a thing to herself. She's up at the house now, and it's likely she's told Mrs. Lingfield. And I shouldn't wonder if Mrs. Lingfield hadn't passed it on to Mrs. Lavant by now."

Merrion thought this highly probable. He complimented Edgefield upon the appearance of his garden, then he and Arnold turned away. As they regained the car, they became aware of a man walking swiftly from the direction of the house towards them. "This will be Mr. Lingfield," Merrion had time to whisper before he came up.

He eyed them with some disfavour. "Good morning, gentlemen," he said acidly. "Will you be good enough to tell me your business?"

Arnold presented him with an official card. "I am here on duty," he replied stiffly.

"Forgive me," said the other, glancing at the card. "I saw your car standing in the drive, and wondered whose it could be. My name is Lingfield, and my wife and I live here with Mrs. Lavant, who rents the property. No doubt your duty is in connection with the dreadful discovery of which I only heard this morning. May I ask if the body has been identified yet?"

"It's past identification," Arnold replied. "And there is nothing distinctive about the clothing. The only clue, and that a slender one, is that the woman was wearing a silver safety-pin with a small opal in the centre. Do you remember seeing any one about here wearing such an ornament?"

"A silver pin with an opal," Lingfield repeated thoughtfully. "A fairly common object, I should imagine." He stood frowning at the ground at his feet for several seconds. "It's rather curious, all the same," he added.

"What is curious, Mr. Lingfield?"Arnold asked encouragingly.

"Oh, there's probably nothing in it," Lingfield replied. "But I do remember a pin such as you describe. It belonged to my half-sister, Loretta Sowley, who lived with us here for a while. Not very long before she left she lost the pin, and was very upset about it. Not on account of its value, which was trifling, but because it had been given her by a very dear friend of hers, who was killed during the war. Loretta is inclined to be temperamental, and she made a great fuss. She declared that the pin must have been stolen from her dressing-table."

In telling Arnold the story of The Brake, Merrion had thought Loretta too minor a character to be worth mentioning. "I understand you to say that your half-sister has left here," Arnold said. "Where is she now?"

"In Australia," Lingfield replied. "We had a letter from her only last week. I'll tell you all about her shortly. My father died when I was hardly more than a baby, and my mother married a second husband. Loretta is the only child of that marriage. She entered the theatrical profession, in which she became quite successful. In 1945 she had a severe breakdown, and a long and complete rest was prescribed. Mrs. Lavant, who is always most generous towards any one connected with the stage, invited her to come here and stay as long as she liked. She did, and was with us over a year."

"She left here three years ago?" Arnold suggested. "Of her own accord?"

"Why, certainly," Lingfield replied, in a slightly shocked tone. "I shouldn't like you to think that Mrs. Lavant drove her away, or anything like that. She was given the opportunity of joining a touring company which was going to Australia, and as by then she had completely recovered her health, she thought it only right to accept the offer."

Merrion thought it might be as well to hear Lingfield's version of what Dr. Wiston had told him. "Your half-sister's decision was not influenced in any way?" he asked. "By friction with any one here, for instance?"

Lingfield frowned. "The gossip current at the time has evidently been repeated to you. There was no real friction, only the irresponsible conduct of a poor demented woman. Mrs.

Lavant had taken compassion upon a refugee from abroad, who was then living here as her companion. She brooded so upon her exile that eventually she went out of her mind. She took an unaccountable dislike to Loretta, and was always being rude to her and annoying her in other ways. As a matter of fact, Loretta believed that it was this woman who had spitefully stolen the pin I was speaking of just now. As you have probably heard, she drowned herself in the lake very soon after Loretta left."

"Yes, we've heard about that," said Merrion. "Your half-sister has never suggested coming back to England?"

"Not within the last year or two, at all events," Lingfield replied. "She appears to have made a host of friends in Australia. In one of her letters she said that she had made up her mind to settle there after her retirement. She has never married, but from hints she has dropped in her letters recently my wife and I both believe that she may be contemplating marriage at last. It would be an excellent thing, if she has found the right man."

"You say at last," Arnold remarked. "Are we to infer that Miss Sowley is no longer young?"

Lingfield smiled. "Still young enough to marry. She is ten years younger than I am, which would make her thirty-eight this year. She has never been beautiful, but she has a fine figure and a mass of fair hair of which she is immensely proud."

"About that pin," said Arnold. "You are quite sure that it really was lost or stolen?"

"Loretta left us in no doubt about that," Lingfield replied. "We're none of us likely to forget the fuss she made. And I'm sorry to say that I think she was right about Madame Tallinn having taken it. During the last few weeks of her life that unhappy woman developed a habit of picking up things and either hiding them or throwing them away, into the lake as often as not. I shouldn't wonder if that's where Loretta's pin is."

"Not necessarily," said Arnold. "If this lady you speak of had picked it up and thrown it away, someone else might have found it and kept it, not knowing who it belonged to."

Lingfield shook his head. "That's hardly possible. You see, Madame Tallinn never went out anywhere. The only time she ever left these grounds was to go to The Retreat. Sir Julius had taken a great fancy to her. She could only have thrown the pin away here or there. And nobody who came to either place could have been ignorant of whom it belonged to, after all the fuss Loretta had made. For days we were hardly allowed to think of anything else."

"Was a doctor ever called in to give an opinion upon Madame Tallinn's state of mind?" Merrion asked.

"Unfortunately not," Lingfield replied. "The fact is, Mrs. Lavant has a violent mistrust of doctors. She never has a day's illness herself, and is firmly convinced that they usually do more harm than good. Not long before the end my wife did suggest that a doctor ought to be called in, but Mrs. Lavant wouldn't hear of it. She said that he would be sure to certify poor Madame Tallinn and carry her off to an asylum, and she couldn't bear to think of that."

"Mrs. Lavant was genuinely fond of Madame Tallinn?" Merrion suggested.

"There can be no doubt about that," Lingfield replied. "So much so that she closed her eyes to her eccentricities. She was inclined to be just a trifle impatient with Loretta when she complained about her. Again, I must repeat that there was no question of Mrs. Lavant driving Loretta away. So far from it that she was very sorry when she went, and missed her for quite a while."

But Arnold's mind was still on the same track. "Do you think Miss Sowley can have lost the pin at The Retreat?" he asked.

"That it wasn't stolen at all, but just dropped out of her dress?" Lingfield replied. "Well, I suppose that's possible. But if she dropped it at The Retreat, Mrs. Moffatt, Sir Julius's housekeeper, would have found it. And she knew well enough that Loretta had lost just such a pin. She would have brought it back at once."

Merrion glanced at the wall. "Climbing over that obstacle to do so?" he suggested easily.

Lingfield smiled. "That obstacle is unclimbable. But there's a door in it, which is kept locked. Sir Julius has the key, and Mrs. Moffatt would have asked him for it. She wouldn't have come all the way round."

Merrion glanced at Arnold. "Do you think we might see Mrs. Lavant, Mr. Lingfield?" he asked.

"Well, not just now," Lingfield replied. "Mrs. Lavant is in bed.

She very rarely gets up before lunch. But if you care to call again this afternoon, I will warn her that you are coming, and I am sure that she will be delighted to see you."

They took their leave of Lingfield, having promised to call again about four o'clock, and got into the car. Merrion drove to the sweep outside the entrance to the house, swung round, and left the place by the way they had come. "We've no time to waste with the keeper now," he said. "We'll see what the hotel at Ridhurst can do in the way of lunch, and after that you'll have to attend the inquest. The sergeant will find me a seat somewhere, I dare say."

IX

The inquests were held in the Town Hall and as might have been expected attracted what for Ridhurst was a large crowd. However, the sergeant found Merrion a seat from which he could follow the proceedings without difficulty.

The coroner began with the body, and called first upon Arnold, whose opening evidence was slightly sensational. Certain official investigations in which he was engaged had brought him to Fernbrake Forest. Without actually saying so, he let it be understood that the Yard were engaged in some mysterious quest in the neighbourhood. Happening to pass the boat-house, a suspicious smell had attracted his attention to it. He had burst open the door and found the body.

He followed this with a detailed description of how he had found it, and of the steps he had taken. He laid emphasis on the fact that the door had been locked, with the key on the inner side of the lock. He had satisfied himself that there had been no other means of entry, the doors opening on the lake not having been unfastened for years.

The sergeant gave evidence concerning the removal of the body, and then Dr. Wiston was called. He described the state of the body, which was evidently due to it having been gnawed by rats. This destruction had gone so far that it had not been easy for him to form an opinion. All he was prepared to say was that deceased was a woman aged about forty and that death had probably occurred during the early or middle part of the previous week. Identification of the body by inspection was impossible. He had been unable to ascertain the cause of death, but certain organs had been removed for analysis.

The coroner intimated that at this stage he would call no further witnesses. Inquiries were being made with a view to discovering the identity of the deceased and the cause of her death. Sufficient time must be allowed for those inquiries to bear fruit. He would therefore adjourn the first inquest and pass on to the second.

Again Arnold was the first witness. In the course of his

examination of the boat-house he had found the skeleton. It had been buried under an accumulation of mould and dead leaves. In reply to a question by the coroner, Arnold explained that he did not mean it had been buried deliberately. He had formed the impression that the debris had drifted over the skeleton in the course of time. He had not disturbed the remains.

The pathologist followed. His evidence was highly technical, but it amounted to no more than he had already told Arnold. In his opinion the skeleton was that of a woman aged about fifty. It was impossible to determine with any degree of accuracy when she had died. The rate of decay of the soft tissues depended upon many factors. The presence of rats in the boat-house would accelerate the disappearance of these tissues. He thought it unlikely that death had occurred more than ten years ago. Owing to the peculiar circumstances it might have taken place at a considerably later date than that. He had found no indications to allow him to form an opinion as to the cause of death.

The coroner pointed out that in this case it was unlikely that any further evidence would be forthcoming, and he proposed to ask the jury to consider their verdict. This they did without delay. The skeleton was that of an unknown woman, and there was no evidence to show how or when she had died. The coroner expressed himself satisfied with this and issued burial certificates in both cases.

Merrion joined Arnold outside the Town Hall. "No more inconclusive than inquests so often are," he remarked. "It's already past half-past three, and we may as well make a start for The Brake. Come along."

They drove off, and this time Merrion approached the house by the gateway on the southern lane. When they reached this they found the gate shut, and Merrion touched the button of his horn. At this summons Hopton appeared from his lodge. He did not open the gate sufficiently to let the car through, but only enough to permit his own egress. He came out into the roadway and spoke, respectfully but firmly. "Beg pardon, gentlemen, but I've got my orders to ask people their business before I let them in. Does Mrs. Lavant know you're coming?"

"Mrs. Lavant is expecting us," Arnold replied. "I am an officer from Scotland Yard."

Hopton straightened himself and touched his forelock. "That'll be all right, sir," he said smartly. He turned and pushed the gate wide open, holding it so until the car had passed through. "Not half so savage as I was given to understand," Merrion remarked as they proceeded up the drive. "In fact, I thought he seemed rather a decent young chap. He calls himself the keeper, but I haven't seen any signs of game being preserved. I fancy his principal job must be to act as lodge-keeper and bar the way to unwanted visitors. Mrs. Lavant doesn't like people dropping in unannounced, I'm told."

"Well, it's a lot easier to get in here than it is next door," Arnold replied. "The sergeant and I had a devil of a job climbing over that gate yesterday. I'm wondering why Sir Julius barricades himself in like that."

They reached the house and rang the bell. Almost immediately the door was opened by a woman, plainly but neatly dressed, who smiled at them welcomingly. "My husband told me you were coming," she said. "Mr. Arnold, isn't it? Will you come in? Mrs. Lavant is in the drawing-room, and is expecting you."

They found Mrs. Lavant sitting in her chair, with Lingfield standing beside her. He took a step forward as they entered. "Ah, here you are!" he exclaimed. Then, turning with a slight bow, "This is Mr. Arnold. Mrs. Lavant, and—"

Merrion completed the introduction for him. "Mr. Merrion, Mr. Arnold's colleague."

Mrs. Lavant was dressed for the occasion, wearing her white dress and a dazzling array of jewellery. The rings on her fingers sparkled as she waved her hands gaily towards her visitors. "I'm so glad to see you," she said effusively. "People don't often take the trouble to call on an old woman like me. But it was quite different once upon a time, I can tell you. Then I was quite the rage, and people tumbled over one another to see me. Why, I remember once at the Theatrical Garden Party I had to have a regular guard. But do sit down, won't you?"

Arnold thought it best to state his business while he could get a word in edgeways. He had brought the pin with him, and now produced it. Lingfield and his wife had taken up positions one on either side of Mrs. Lavant's chair, rather like a lord and lady-in-waiting on a queen, Merrion thought. Arnold handed the brooch to Lingfield. "That's the pin I was talking to you about this morning," he said. "Do you recognise it?"

Lingfield took the pin and turned it over in his fingers. "It's difficult to say," he replied. "It looks very like the pin Loretta lost. But that was so long ago now that I don't remember exactly what it looked like."

Mrs. Lavant clearly did not appreciate any conversation in which she did not take a leading part. "Let me see it, Lance!" she exclaimed imperiously, almost snatching the pin from his hand. "I remember Loretta's brooch perfectly well. A nasty cheap thing, with a horrid little opal set on it. I've always hated opals, they're so terribly unlucky. I had a friend once who was given an opal ring and the very first day she wore it she fell downstairs and broke her leg. It was weeks before she was able to get about again. I never would let my husband buy me opals."

At last she condescended to inspect the pin, holding it at a distance as though she feared that its maleficent influence would infect her. "Of course I remember Loretta's pin very well," she went on. "I've got a wonderful memory, all my friends tell me so. I always wondered how she could bring herself to wear such a tawdry-looking thing. I offered to let her have any of my brooches she cared to choose, but she said she preferred her own. This isn't it, though."

The finality of this last sentence was unmistakable. "Are you quite sure it isn't the one, Mrs. Lavant?" Arnold asked.

"I'm quite certain it isn't," she replied. "I tell you, I have a wonderful memory, especially of jewellery, of which I'm very fond. And I know this isn't Loretta's, for the bar of hers was broad and flat, while this one is round. And this opal is round too, while hers was oval. You must remember that, don't you, Lin. Take it and look for yourself."

Mrs. Lingfield, thus appealed to, took the pin from her hand. "Yes, I remember it very well, now that you remind me," she replied meekly. "You're quite right, Mrs. Lavant. This isn't the pin Loretta lost."

As she handed it back to Arnold, Merrion reflected that her opinion was of little value. He had already formed the impression that if Mrs Lavant were to maintain that black was white, both Mrs. Lingfield and her husband would support her stoutly. But in this case Mrs. Lavant was probably right. The profusion she was wearing gave grounds for the assumption that she might be accepted as an authority on jewellery.

Arnold pocketed the pin. "No doubt, Mrs. Lavant, you have heard of the discovery that was made yesterday?" he asked.

She folded her arms upon her bosom with a dramatic gesture. "Yes, they told me about it. It's too dreadful. And they say that nobody knows who she was. She must have been some poor woman who had got herself into trouble and crept into that horrid place to die. I don't like to think of it. It reminds me too much of the death of a very dear friend of mine."

Arnold turned to Lingfield. "You didn't see any strangers about here last week?" he suggested.

Lingfield shook his head. "I can't say that I did. I don't remember seeing any one I didn't know."

But Mrs. Lavant interposed vigorously. "Nonsense, Lance! There were strangers about last week. And they had the impertinence to come here, on to the lawn. The day that I gave an interview to the local newspaper. You must remember."

"Oh, yes, of course," Lingfield replied guiltily. "I'd forgotten about them for the moment."

"You're always forgetting things," said Mrs. Lavant severely. "You forgot to tell Edgefield this morning to mow the lawn, and now it will have to wait till the next time he comes. I remember those people perfectly well, two men and a woman, I'm sure they were. Just inquisitive idlers. How they got in I don't know. Hopton must have been neglecting his duty. They came out of the shrubbery while I was talking to the newspaper men, and I sent them away."

It was quite clear that Mrs. Lavant had not recognised the intruders, one of whom at least she knew, if only slightly. "I expect they came from Ridhurst," said Merrion lightly. "Perhaps they had heard that you were giving an interview that afternoon, and thought they would take the opportunity of catching a glimpse of so famous a lady."

Mrs. Lavant smiled, obviously gratified by the compliment. "Well, perhaps you're right. But they had no business here at all. Two men and a woman. I think you and Mr. Arnold ought to try to find out who they were. They may have been up to mischief of some kind. I shouldn't be surprised if the body found yesterday wasn't that woman's."

"We shall do our best to find out who they were," Merrion replied gravely. "I saw your photograph in the Pembroke Forest Standard, and see now what an excellent likeness it was. Didn't you find giving the interview very tiring?"

"Oh, dear me, no," Mrs. Lavant replied airily. "I have given so many interviews in my time to newspaper men that I'm quite used to it. They were both very nice, well-mannered young men, and I really enjoyed talking to them. Besides, before they came I had a most refreshing sleep in my hammock on the lawn, as I always do after lunch when the weather is warm enough. I was still asleep when you came back, wasn't I, Lance?"

"Yes, you were," Lingfield replied. "We had to wake you, for it was very nearly the time that you had told the newspaper men to come. Lin and I were back later than we had meant to be."

"You went out, leaving Mrs. Lavant alone on the lawn?" Merrion remarked conversationally.

"Of course they did," Mrs. Lavant replied indulgently. "I'm quite capable of looking after myself, and I don't like having people at my elbow all the time. They went for a walk and called in at The Retreat on the way back to see Mrs. Moffatt."

"Yes, and that's what made us late," Lingfield agreed. "We couldn't get away from her."

"And you felt no ill-effects from this sudden awakening?" Merrion asked politely.

"Oh, none at all," Mrs. Lavant replied. "You and Mr. Arnold will stay and have tea with us, I hope?"

Merrion rose from his chair, glancing at Arnold, who followed his example. "That's very kind of you, Mrs. Lavant," he said. "But I'm afraid we can't. We have already taken up far more of your time than we intended. By the way, as we passed through the hall just now we saw a telephone there. Might I put a call through to Ridhurst?"

"Oh, the telephone!" Lingfield replied with a slightly forced laugh. "I'm afraid it would be no good to you, Mr. Merrion. You see, it's not connected to the exchange, it's only a private line to The Retreat. We very rarely use it, though, for if we do, it doesn't usually happen that either Sir Julius or Mrs. Moffatt hears it. But Sir Julius finds it convenient. He uses it to invite Mrs. Lavant to go and see him."

"Oh, I see," said Merrion. "We must hurry off, then." They

took their leave of Mrs. Lavant, who inclined her head
graciously. Lingfield escorted them to the car, and they drove
off. "That's a queer household, "Merrion remarked. "Entirely
dominated by the old lady, as any one can see. I think we'll stop
and have a word with that young keeper as we go out."

But when they reached the entrance, there was no sign of
Hopton. The gate was open and fastened back, evidently to save
them the trouble of opening it, and the door of the lodge was
shut. "Well, never mind," said Merrion. "I suppose he has other
things to do than hang about here all the time. You can see him
some other time. My curiosity is satisfied, and you're assured
that the pin isn't the one that was lost or stolen. And it's pretty
clear that those people don't know anything about the boat-
house affair. In spite of Mrs. Lavant's dark suggestion that the
body might be that of the woman who intruded on her privacy
last Wednesday. Which it certainly isn't."

"You're quite sure of that?"Arnold asked doubtfully.

"As sure as I can be of anything," Merrion replied. "The
female intruder was Annabel Dorset, and if she were missing her
father would have told me. Besides, she must be in her twenties,
and therefore does not conform to the medical evidence. I don't
remember the colour of her hair, but if it was dark brown and
cut short, Dr. Wiston, who knows her well, would surely have
noticed the coincidence. But one point in her story is explained,
anyhow."

"What's that?"Arnold asked.

"The telephone," Merrion replied. "She says that when she
was at The Brake on Wednesday she tried it and couldn't get
any reply. We know how that came about now. Lingfield said
that the people at The Retreat rarely heard it. And, as the
Lingfields were out, there was no one in the house to hear the
racket she kicked up."

"I'm glad your curiosity is satisfied," said Arnold. "But that
doesn't get us any nearer to identifying the body. I'm still not
certain about Sir Julius. I've got an idea that he, or some
member of his staff, knows something about it."

"You haven't tackled Mrs. Moffatt yet," Merrion replied.
"You've got an excellent opening, for you can ask her if she
knows what time the Lingfields left The Retreat last Wednesday.
From that you can go on to any inquiries you like. And, if I were

you, I'd have a talk to Mrs. Edgefield, the gardener's wife, who works at The Brake in the morning. I shall have to leave you to it, for I've got to be back in London by seven o'clock."

Having dropped Arnold in Ridhurst, Merrion drove back to London to keep his appointment. This involved dining out with a business acquaintance. Later in the evening he returned to his rooms, where he sat down at leisure to review the events of the day. If he had accomplished nothing else, he had made the acquaintance of a remarkable woman.

He felt able to appraise Mrs. Lavant impartially. Henry Dorset was prejudiced by his resentment at her longevity. Dr. Wiston knew her only very slightly, and had perhaps paid too much attention to the stories he had heard. Merrion had perceived for himself that she was inordinately vain and inclined to be domineering, but this without malice. And she certainly was a wonder. Her manner was lively and vivacious, and she was in full possession of her mental faculties. Her elaborate make-up almost but not quite hid all sign of wrinkles, and her wig was a masterpiece of art. Her stage training enabled her to control her voice, which betrayed no note of senility. True, she probably conserved her energies for special occasions, and this was probably the reason why she refused to see any one without previous appointment. She had no intention of being caught without her war-paint. Otherwise she took things easily enough, relaxing whenever possible. She spent the morning in bed, and indulged in a siesta after lunch.

Beside her, the Lingfields paled into insignificance. Their complete subservience suggested that they were entirely dependent upon her. Merrion had been amused by the contrast between Lingfield's manner in the morning and in the afternoon. In the morning, by himself, it had been natural and easy. In the afternoon, in Mrs. Lavant's presence, it had been dumb and submissive. Mrs. Lavant called him Lance, and his wife Lin. Dr. Wiston had said that they had once been a music-hall turn. Lance and Linette. Merrion dimly remembered these coupled names. He might even have seen their performance. But, if so, it had not been sufficiently striking to leave any record in his memory.

At all events, they seemed quite resigned to Mrs. Lavant's autocratic rule. It might have been otherwise with the two women who had previously lived at The Brake. There might be some truth in the rumour that the true reason for Madame Tallinn's suicide had been that she couldn't stick it but had nowhere else to go. And Merrion could well imagine that Loretta Sowley had not found The Brake altogether a bed of roses. Lingfield had described her as temperamental. If she was a woman of spirit, she might well have seized the first opportunity of getting away.

The subject of Loretta led naturally to the pin. Merrion was quite satisfied that it was not the one about which Loretta had made such a fuss. If every one at The Brake had flatly denied all knowledge of such a thing, he might have had his doubts. But nothing of the kind had happened. Quite unprompted, Lingfield had volunteered the information that his half-sister had possessed such a pin. Mrs. Lavant also remembered that fact, in far greater detail. She had been able to describe it, and so to point out the differences between it and the one produced.

Was then the pin entirely without significance? The rational answer was that such pins were common enough, and that the unknown woman might well have possessed a pin bearing a superficial resemblance to the one lost by Loretta. But Merrion's imagination could never rest content with the merely rational. Given that the pin found was not Loretta's, could there be any hidden reason for the dead woman having worn it?

This opened the portal of the realms of fantasy, and Merrion allowed his imagination to wander there at large. It seemed that for sentimental reasons Loretta had valued the pin, and had worn it if not constantly at least very frequently. And that presumably, not only at The Brake. It must have been familiar to her friends before she retired there after her breakdown. Any one of these wishing to pass herself off as Loretta would naturally wear a similar pin as part of the disguise. It was at least possible that such a person was not aware that Loretta had gone to Australia, and believed her to be still living at The Brake.

From that, Merrion's mind jumped to the more immediate problem. The state of the boat-house and its fastenings were not consistent with any theory of murder. It was not easy to visualise how a murderer could have locked the door behind him, leaving the key on the inside. The alternatives were suicide or accident. The unhappy woman might have locked herself into the boat-house and there swallowed poison. The pathologist might have something to say about that in due course. If no trace of poison were found, could death have been accidental?

It was difficult to imagine what fatal accident could have occurred in such a place. A long-disused boat-house was not very likely to contain anything lethal, and if it had some evidence of this would have remained. Merrion was about to dismiss all possibility of accident when a sudden inspiration came to him. Snakes!

With that one word the whole scene sprang vividly to his imagination. It was a matter of fairly common knowledge that there were adders in Fernbrake Forest. The woman had intended to pass herself off as Loretta, returned unexpectedly from Australia. Just why was rather obscure, but that might pass for the moment. She could hardly have hoped to impose upon the Lingfields, or upon Mrs. Lavant for that matter. But at The Retreat, Sir Julius, with his failing sight, would be an easy dupe.

But there was Mrs. Moffatt to be reckoned with. It would never do to confront her in broad daylight. The unknown woman had arrived in the neighbourhood before sundown and, seeking for a place in which to hide till dark, had discovered the boat-house. It was to be supposed that the key was then where Wanstead said he had left it, in the lock on the outside. She had entered, locked herself in, and sat down on the soft carpet of leaves. In so doing she had disturbed an adder, or possibly a whole nest of adders. Their bites had been fatal.

Merrion smiled to himself as he threw away his cigarette. Extravagant though the theory seemed, there might be something in it. Meanwhile, now that he had made the acquaintance of Mrs. Lavant, it was time to invite himself to dinner with the Dorsets. He would ring up Henry Dorset in the morning.

X

Arnold, left to himself, decided that he would put up that night at the hotel in Ridhurst. He had taken Merrion's suggestions to heart, and intended to interview the people he had mentioned. And it seemed to him that the evening would afford the best opportunity of doing so.

Having fortified himself with a meal, he borrowed a bicycle from the sergeant and set out soon after eight o'clock. The evening was cloudy, and comparatively dark for the time of year. The Edgefields' cottage lay between Ridhurst and the Moon isthmus, and the sergeant had given him directions how to find it. It formed, as Arnold discovered, one of a scattered group, among which was a small and unpretentious public house. The Verderers' Arms. He knocked on the door, which was opened by a tall, gaunt woman who eyed him curiously. "You want to see my husband?" she asked.

"Well, as a matter of fact I should like a few words with you, Mrs. Edgefield," Arnold replied. "I met your husband this morning."

"Oh, so that's who you are," she said. "My husband told me that two gentlemen had been speaking to him, and you'll be one of them, no doubt. I don't know what you want to talk to me about, I'm sure. But you'd best come in."

She admitted him to the kitchen, where Edgefield was sitting in an armchair, apparently doing precisely nothing. His remark showed that he recognised Arnold. "So you haven't brought the other gentleman with you, then?"

"Not this time," Arnold replied. "This is what I want to ask you, Mrs. Edgefield. Do you remember Miss Loretta Sowley?"

Mrs. Edgefield shook her head. "I never saw her. I've often heard Mrs. Lingfield speak of her, but she had left The Brake before I went there to work. And that was getting on for three years ago. That's right, isn't it, Fred?"

"Yes, that's right," Edgefield replied. "You see, it was this way. I started jobbing at The Brake soon after Mrs. Lavant went there. There was four of them then, Mrs. Lavant, Mr. and Mrs.

Lingfield, and a foreign woman. Tally or some such name. Then Miss Loretta came and that made five. I can't say that I ever saw much of the womenfolk, for it was always Mr. Lingfield who gave me my orders and paid me my money."

"There were changes at The Brake some three years ago, weren't there?" Arnold prompted him.

Edgefield nodded. "That's right. And that's how the missus come to go there. You see. Miss Loretta went away, and not long after that the foreign woman went and drowned herself in the lake. And a while after that Mrs. Lingfield came out and spoke to me. She said that now she was left alone to do all the housework she'd want some help, and did I know of anybody. So I told her I'd speak to the missus."

"And so he did," Mrs. Edgefield chimed in. "I was working in Ridhurst two or three days a week, but I'd thought of giving it up before then. It was too far to go all that way and back, especially when the weather was bad. So when my husband told me what was wanted, I said I'd be willing to help in the house in the mornings. That's how I came to go there."

"So of course you never met Miss Loretta," said Arnold. "But I dare say your husband remembers what she looked like?"

"Can't say that I do," Edgefield replied. "As I've told you, I never used to see much of the womenfolk, no more than I do now. I only go to work there in the mornings, and then they were mostly indoors. All I remember of Miss Loretta was a likeness between her and Mr. Lingfield. She was his half-sister, so they said."

"Do you remember hearing that she had lost a brooch, not long before she left The Brake?" Arnold asked.

"I don't remember hearing that she'd lost anything," Edgefield replied. "But I might have known at the time. It wouldn't have concerned me, and if I'd been told it would have gone in at one ear and out of the other."

So far the Edgefields had not been very helpful, and Arnold tried a fresh tack. "Who lives in the lodge at The Brake?" he asked.

"Young Tom Hopton," Mrs. Edgefield replied. "He hasn't been there very long, not above six months ago. I don't see much of him, for he doesn't often come up to the house. He looks after himself at the lodge, and I've always found him nicely spoken.

Mrs. Lingfield told me that Mrs. Lavant took him on because she wanted a watchman about the place. She'd got it into her head that folk came prowling round the grounds. An old woman's fancy, I say."

"He's all right," Edgefield remarked. "He'll come and give me a hand sometimes if I ask him. Quiet sort of chap, not one of those who wag their tongues all the time. He's never told me much about himself, only that his last place was in Scotland somewhere. He said he was there quite a while after he was demobbed, and left because he didn't like it."

"And how do you get on with Mrs. Lavant, Mrs. Edgefield?" Arnold asked.

"Well enough, because it isn't often that I see her," she replied. "Mostly she stays in bed all the morning, and that's the only time I'm there. She does get up sometimes before I've left, but not very often. I don't know that I've seen her for a fortnight or more. It's Mrs. Lingfield who works with me about the house, and Mr. Lingfield too, as often as not. Like this morning when they was with me both, and Mrs. Lavant was upstairs in bed. I helped get her breakfast tray ready and Mrs. Lingfield took it up to her. And that's how it usually is."

"There have been no visitors staying at The Brake this last week or so, I suppose?"Arnold suggested.

Mrs. Edgefield shook her head. "No, nor ever have been since I've been working there. Mrs. Lavant is too old a lady to entertain company for long. Mrs. Lingfield has told me that she likes to see people now and again as long as they don't outstay their welcome. A grand-niece of hers came to see her one afternoon last week, so Mrs. Lingfield told me. The first I'd heard of her having any relations. And of course she's very chummy with old Sir Julius next door."

Arnold chatted for a few minutes longer, without eliciting anything of interest. Then he left the cottage, and started off again on his bicycle. He had firmly made up his mind to make no further attempt on the locked gate of The Retreat. Merrion had discovered an overgrown path leading from the boat-house. It would surely be easier to negotiate that than tackle the barbed wire.

So he rode round until he reached the lane skirting the northern end of the two lakes. Lifting his bicycle over the stile, he hid it in the undergrowth, and made his way towards the boat-house. By now the track had been so well trodden that he found the going easy enough. Nor did he hear any scurrying, for the rats, deprived of their prey, had deserted the place. But, from the boat-house onwards it was a different matter. He found the remains of a path, but this had been invaded not only by stout saplings, but by a profusion of trailing brambles. He had not forced his way more than a yard or two along it before he became convinced that no one had followed this route for a long time.

At last, scratched and dishevelled, he emerged from the wilderness. In the deepening twilight he saw before him a stretch of flower garden, with the glass-topped wall on the left and the house beyond. He made his way first to the wall, in which a narrow postern was visible. On trying this he found it securely locked. Then he went on to the house, from which gleams of light shone from behind the drawn curtains, and rang the front-door bell.

For some considerable time this produced no effect. Then he heard the sound of heavy footsteps and the drawing of bolts. The door opened slowly and cautiously, to reveal a figure outlined against the faint radiance in the hall. He held a heavy stick in his uplifted hand, and his attitude was distinctly menacing. His features were indistinguishable, and for an instant Arnold wondered who he could be. Surely not Sir Julius? Then he remembered the existence of Wanstead, the deaf gardener.

There was no light over the doorway, and they confronted one another in the semi-darkness. Wanstead could hardly be expected to recognise the visitor. "Who may you be, and what do you want?" he growled.

Arnold bawled at him. "I'm Inspector Arnold. You remember me. I was here with the sergeant yesterday afternoon."

But Wanstead continued to bar the passage. "Aye, I remember," he replied. "But you can't see Sir Julius at this time of night. He wouldn't have it, and that's flat. You'd best come back in the morning."

"I don't want to see Sir Julius," Arnold shouted. "I want to speak to Mrs. Moffatt."

"Well, I dunno," said Wanstead doubtfully. "I'll go and see what she says about it." He was about to shut the door in

Arnold's face, but he was saved the trouble. Mrs. Moffatt, summoned by Arnold's bawling, appeared in the background. "Whatever's all this?" she exclaimed sharply. "You mustn't make a noise like that. Sir Julius will hear it in the library."

"Good evening, Mrs. Moffatt," Arnold replied in his normal voice. "I came to ask if you could spare me a few minutes."

Mrs. Moffatt touched a switch, illuminating the hall more brightly. "Why, you're the gentleman who was here with the sergeant yesterday!" she exclaimed. "Yes, I'll spare you a minute, if it's me you want to see. Will you come along to my sitting-room?"She wasted no breath shouting at Wanstead, but merely tapped him on the shoulder and nodded. At this he stood aside and slouched off, muttering something incomprehensible.

She shut the door behind Arnold and bolted it. While she was doing so Arnold glanced about him. At his first visit he had not noticed the telephone, but he saw it now, standing on a table in the hall. This, no doubt, was the one connected by a private line to The Brake. And Lingfield's remark about the difficulty of getting an answer was explained. Sir Julius, sitting in his library with the door shut, would never hear it. Nor probably would Mrs. Moffatt from her sitting-room. As for Wanstead, the sound would not penetrate his ears if he were standing beside it.

"I wasn't expecting anybody," said Mrs. Moffatt. "So when the bell rang I sent Amos to see who it was. I'm a bit nervous after what happened yesterday. Let me see, Mr. Arnold, isn't it? Will you come this way?"

She led him along a passage to a comfortably furnished room. Arnold noticed that it had one point in common with the drawing-room at The Brake, for the walls were hung with signed photographs. Among them was one which he had no difficulty in recognising as Mrs. Lavant in her younger days. The signature "Claire Gabriel " verified this. Mrs. Moffatt invited him to sit down. "Now, whatever can it be that you want to talk to me about, Mr. Arnold?" she asked.

"Nothing very alarming," Arnold replied. "I want you to try to remember last Wednesday afternoon."

Mrs. Moffatt frowned thoughtfully. "Let me see, now. That's the day the butcher brings out the meat ration. Last week he brought a bit of beef, and the weather was so hot that I had to cook it that same evening. But it was so tough that Sir Julius couldn't eat it. I don't recollect anything particular happening that afternoon. Only that Mr. and Mrs. Lingfield looked in to see me. I've known them ever so many years, since the time they were on the halls. I was a dresser you know, before Sir Julius asked me to come as his housekeeper. I got to know pretty well everybody who was on the stage in those days. And ever so many of them gave me their photographs to keep." She waved her hand proudly towards the wall.

"And of course you hung them up where you could always see them," said Arnold. "You're sure it was Wednesday that Mr. and Mrs. Lingfield were here? I always find it so difficult to remember which particular day anything happened."

"I'm positive it was Wednesday," Mrs. Moffatt replied. "They told me Mrs. Lavant had made an appointment to be interviewed by the Standard at four o'clock."

"Yes Wednesday was the day of the interview," said Arnold. "How did the Lingfields get here? By the door in the wall?"

Mrs. Moffatt shook her head. "Oh, no. It s only Sir Julius who ever unlocks that. They were passing the gate, and saw Amos weeding the border just inside. So they thought it would be a good chance of coming in to see me, and they got him to open the gate for them. I brought them in here and we had a chat together."

"Do you remember what time they left?" Arnold asked.

"I couldn't say exactly," Mrs. Moffatt replied. "It must have been after three. The three of us were sitting in here when Sir Julius's bell rang. I went along to the library, and Sir Julius kept me a few minutes. And when I came back here Mr. and Mrs. Lingfield had gone. They had to be home before four o'clock, you see."

This confirmed the account Arnold had already heard. In any case the incident was of no importance, and had merely served as an introduction. Arnold felt that he could now venture upon more pertinent topics. "So Mr. and Mrs. Lingfield are old friends of yours," he said conversationally. "Then you must know Mr. Lingfield's half-sister. Miss Loretta Sowley?" ,

"She was with them at The Brake for a while, Mrs. Moffatt replied. "But I can hardly say I know her. I never met her in the old days, for she must have been too young to be on the stage then. When she was at The Brake I don't remember her coming here more than once or twice, and it's only once in a blue moon that I go over there. I don't think I should know her again if I saw her."

"She went to Australia about three years ago, I believe." Arnold remarked.

Mrs. Moffatt nodded. "That's right. Mrs. Lingfield has read me her letters from there, and she seems very happy. And that I fancy was more than she was when she was at The Brake."

"She didn't get on with Mrs. Lavant?" Arnold suggested.

"I don't know that it was that, quite," Mrs. Moffatt replied. "But there was another lady there then, Madame Tallinn. She was a foreigner, though you'd never have thought it to hear her speak. She used to come here often enough, for Sir Julius took to her, though he usually only cares to see people who can talk to him about the stage. And so far as I could make out from a word or two dropped by Mrs. Lingfield, she and Miss Loretta didn't hit it off. And that of course upset Mrs. Lavant. In the end the poor lady went dotty and drowned herself in the lake."

"So I've been told," said Arnold. "Not very long after Miss Loretta had left The Brake. It must have been a great blow to Mrs. Lavant."

"It was!" Mrs. Moffatt agreed heartily. "She hadn't minded Miss Loretta going, or so Mrs. Lingfield told me. But Madame Tallinn's death was a terrible loss to her. She was ill at the time, but I mustn't say that for she would never admit it for a moment. But she had a heavy cold and was keeping to her room, so that she couldn't come over here to see Sir Julius. But when she was told what had happened, she insisted on doing everything herself. She went to Ridhurst to give evidence at the inquest, and she arranged a wonderful funeral for the poor lady. I know that, for Sir Julius hired a car to go to it, and took me with him."

"I expect Mrs. Lavant got over the shock fairly soon?" Arnold asked.

Mrs. Moffatt smiled. "Mrs. Lavant is one of those that nothing worries for very long. But it took her a while to get over Madame Tallinn's death. When Sir Julius rang her up the day after the funeral she told him that she didn't feel up to seeing anybody, even him. And when she did come, which wasn't till a week later or more, I could tell that she was still feeling her loss. She looked older, and her voice wasn't as loud as usual. Sir Julius told me after, she'd gone that he'd never known her so upset about anything. But after a bit she became herself again."

"She had another upset not long afterwards, didn't she?" Arnold suggested.

"Oh, you mean that shocking business of her husband's grandson," Mrs. Moffatt replied. "Well, to tell the truth, that didn't seem to upset her nearly as much as the other. When the police fetched her to see the body, Mrs. Lingfield went with her, and she told me all about it afterwards. She said that Mrs. Lavant behaved splendidly. She recognised the body, of course, but she didn't break down, or anything like that. She told the police quite quietly who he was and what she knew of him. There had been some trouble with him before, it seems, and she hadn't seen him since then. Perhaps that's why she didn't feel it so much. And, after all, the young man was no real relation of hers."

Arnold's reason for encouraging Mrs. Moffatt to talk was the hope that she might let drop something that he would find useful. "You see a good deal of Mrs. Lavant, I expect?" he remarked.

"Well, I wouldn't say that," she replied. "Sir Julius sees a lot more of her than I do. He rings her up every other day or thereabouts, to ask how she is and whether she would care to come and talk to him. If she does come, he unlocks the gate in the wall himself. Either Mr. or Mrs. Lingfield nearly always comes with her. And when Sir Julius has taken Mrs. Lavant to the library, whichever it is comes in here to talk to me. Often enough I don't see Mrs. Lavant at all. And as I say, it's very rarely I go to the Brake. And when I do it's only to see Mrs. Lingfield about something."

"Mrs. Lavant and Sir Julius are old friends?" Arnold suggested.

"Why, bless you, yes!" Mrs. Moffatt exclaimed. "They must have known one another ever since Mrs. Lavant started acting as a girl. Sir Julius wasn't an actor himself, but his father was a manager and producer and when he died Sir Julius followed in his footsteps. Claire Gabriel, as she was then, often appeared as his leading lady. And he has a very high opinion of her, too. He said to me once that it was a thousand pities that she left the stage when she got married. Though of course her husband was a rich man and she had no need to go on working."

"Sir Julius must be very glad to have her living next door," said Arnold.

"I'm sure he is," she replied. "And she must be, too, for they've so much in common to talk about. She's known him ever so much longer than she has Mr. and Mrs. Lingfield. And, besides, they were only on the halls. It was a great sorrow to Sir Julius when he had to retire, but his eyesight wouldn't let him go on. Although he doesn't like people to know it, he's nearly blind now, and he's getting an old man. He said to me more than once that he wished he knew Mrs. Lavant's secret for keeping young. And it's true enough that she never seems to grow a day older."

Arnold smiled. "Her make-up has a lot to do with that, I dare say."

"Well, that may be," Mrs. Moffatt admitted. "But there are other things besides. The way she moves about, as though she'd never begun to feel a touch of rheumatism. And her voice, which even though it may have changed a bit is as strong and clear as ever it was. No, as everybody says, she's a wonder."

"And strong-minded at that, I imagine," said Arnold. "By the way, Mrs. Moffatt, I wonder if you remember something. Not long before Miss Loretta left The Brake she lost a brooch, didn't she?"

Mrs. Moffatt shrugged her shoulders. "Very likely, though I don't recollect it. Mrs. Lingfield used to tell me she was very careless. Between ourselves, I fancy Mrs. Lingfield found her a bit of a trial. She was all moods, and very often sulky ones at that. She'd hide herself away in her room for days at a time, so they say. The artistic temperament, Mr. Lingfield put it down to. In my opinion it was a relief to them all when she left."

"Perhaps it was," said Arnold. He paused, then went on. "I mustn't take up much more of your time, Mrs. Moffatt. You've heard, of course, what was found in the boat-house yesterday?"

"I didn't hear until after you and the other gentleman had been," she replied. "Then I knew why you'd been asking questions. You may take it from me that nobody in this house has been to the boat-house for ever so long."

"And you haven't the slightest suspicion whose the body may

have been?" Arnold asked.

"No, that I haven't!" Mrs. Moffatt exclaimed firmly. "It can't have belonged to anybody about here. Lots of folk come from all parts to the Forest, especially at this time of year. That's why Sir Julius is always so particular about having the gate kept locked. He's afraid people might get in and do damage. He was very much annoyed when I told him what had happened."

A man might well be annoyed to learn that not only had a dead body been found on his property, but a skeleton into the bargain, Arnold thought. But was Sir Julius's annoyance due not so much to the existence of these unpleasant objects as to their discovery? But Arnold did not put this question into words.

"Well, Mrs. Moffatt," he said. "I'm much obliged to you for sparing me so much of your time. I'll be getting along now."

"It's been a pleasure, Mr. Arnold," she replied. "Now, I'm one who knows better than to ask too many questions. I don't know how you got in, but I'm going to tell Amos to walk down to the gate with you and let you out."

Arnold could hardly raise any objection to this. Amos was summoned, and Mrs. Moffatt made him understand what was wanted. As they walked down the drive, Arnold tried to engage him in conversation. But Amos seemed so deaf that evening as to be utterly irresponsive. Perhaps this was merely surliness, due to being dragged out at that hour.

Arnold parted from him at the gate, and, turning to the right, followed the lane until he reached the stile at the lower end of the footpath to the west of the lake. With the aid of his torch, he made his way the length of the path to its upper end, where he found the bicycle as he had left it. Riding back to Ridhurst he came to the same conclusion that Merrion had reached independently. The woman whose body had been found had had some connection with the inmates of one of the two houses on the isthmus. The Brake, possibly, but more probably The Retreat.

XI

The following evening found Merrion at the Dorset's house in Surbiton. He had rung up Henry Dorset in the morning, and been cordially invited to dinner. The inquest of the previous day had been briefly reported in the newspapers, and during the meal the conversation had turned largely upon the mystery. But, in the presence of Irene Dorset and Annabel, Merrion had discreetly made no mention of the part he had himself played. Now they had left the dining-room, and he found himself alone with Henry Dorset. "I had a most interesting conversation with Mrs. Lavant yesterday," he remarked.

Dorset stared at him. "What!" he exclaimed. "You've actually met the old woman? How did that come about?"

"We were talking about the inquest just now," Merrion replied. "I was present, as an interested spectator. You saw in the account of it that the discovery was made by an inspector from Scotland Yard. That inspector happens to be a very old friend of mine, and he allowed me to accompany him on his investigations, which included a visit to The Brake."

"Well, I'm blest!" Dorset exclaimed. "I always knew you had a most uncanny knack of getting at the heart of things, but I didn't expect that. And how did you find the old woman?"

During the course of the day Arnold had called at Merrion's rooms and given him an account of his conversations with the Edgefields and Mrs. Moffatt. One of Mrs. Edgefield's remarks had struck Merrion as particularly curious. "I found Mrs. Lavant in the best of health and spirits," he replied. "'You've had news of her quite lately, haven't you?"

Dorset's amazement was ludicrous. "Now, how the devil do you know that! Did the old girl tell you herself?"

Merrion smiled. "No, I only heard of it by chance. It is true, then?"

"Yes, it's true enough," Dorset replied. "Last Friday afternoon Annabel took it into her head to pay a call at The Brake, without saying a word to her mother or me of what she was up to. She seems to have had some romantic idea that she might be able to bridge the family gap. But the bridge she built wasn't very substantial. She was told that she might call again, upon giving proper notice. And she brought us back a photograph of her great-aunt as a keepsake."

"Did she go alone this time?" Merrion asked. "Or did David Wiston go with her?"

"She went alone," Dorset replied. "She and David seem to have parted brass-rags for the time being. She hasn't seen or heard of him since they went on that expedition together, and that's a week ago to-day."

"His father gave the medical evidence at the inquest," Merrion remarked. "Your daughter will have given you an account of Mrs. Lavant's entourage. Two other people frequent The Brake, the gardener and his wife, but your daughter won't have met them, for they only appear on the scene in the mornings. Last Wednesday afternoon Mrs. Lavant was quite alone, for the Lingfields were next door, paying a call on Sir Julius's housekeeper."

"Eh?" Dorset replied. "The old woman mentioned that name to Annabel. Who is this Sir Julius?"

"Oh, of course you wouldn't know," said Merrion. "Sir Julius Blackrock lives at The Retreat, the house on the farther side of that formidable wall which no doubt has been described to you. He is a retired theatrical manager, and is, I gather, one of Mrs. Lavant's oldest and dearest friends. They meet quite frequently."

"Good heavens!" Dorset exclaimed. "You don't think there's any chance of his marrying her, do you?"

Merrion was amazed at this fresh evidence of his obsession. If Mrs. Lavant were to marry again, her husband would presumably continue to enjoy her share of the trust income during his lifetime. "Sir Julius must be several years younger than Mrs. Lavant," Merrion replied maliciously. "And she strikes me as a woman who would not shrink from any adventure, even a second experience of matrimony. But I think you can set your mind at rest. For one thing, if they had ever contemplated marriage, they would have brought it off long before now. And for another, apart from Sir Julius being nearly blind, he is a confirmed recluse. But we were talking of the Lingfields. As they were at The Retreat that afternoon, the fact that your daughter could make nobody hear is explained. I'd very much like to hear her account for myself."

"No difficulty about that," said Dorset. "Finish your glass of port and we'll go along to the lounge."

They found Annabel and her mother talking together. "I've got a bit of news that will interest you both!" Dorset exclaimed as they entered the room. "Merrion was at The Brake yesterday afternoon and saw Claire Gabriel."

"You did, Mr. Merrion?" Annabel inquired eagerly. "Did she tell you that I'd been to see her?"

"No, she didn't tell me that," Merrion replied, sitting down beside her. "But she told me a lot of other things. I was very glad to find you safe and sound this evening. Mrs. Lavant had a dark suspicion that the body might be yours."

Annabel laughed merrily. "Mine! Whatever made her think that?"

"When you went to see her on Friday, she didn't recognise you as one of the group who appeared on her lawn on Wednesday," Merrion replied. "She supposed, and still supposes, that the group was composed entirely of strangers. Her deduction is that if the body is that of a strange woman, the stranger must have been the one she saw. I'm very much intrigued by what happened that Wednesday. Particularly your adventure with the telephone. Tell me about that."

"I couldn't get it to work," Annabel replied. "The wretched thing must have been out of order. I don't mind confessing that I was in a state of complete dither. I thought Auntie was dead, and it seemed so horribly uncanny that the house should be deserted. I think I must have picked up the telephone and just shouted into it. I don't remember exactly what I said. Something about an urgent call and that I wanted to be put through to Dr. Wiston. But I couldn't get an answer."

Merrion smiled. "I can tell you why that was. It's only a private line to The Retreat, and more often than not the people there don't hear it when it rings. Do you know what time it was when you tried to get through?"

Annabel shook her head. "I was much too flustered by then to think about the time. All I can tell you is that when it was all over and I was having tea with Dr. Wiston, the clock struck five."

"I don't wonder you were flustered," said Merrion. "You honestly thought that Mrs. Lavant was dead?"

"I was sure of it," she replied. "So sure that I didn't stop to find out. But, of course she wasn't, only fast asleep. And Auntie must sleep pretty soundly, for all the noise I made didn't wake her."

"She was still asleep when the Lingfields came back, and they had to wake her," said Merrion. "She told me that she always has a siesta after lunch, in the hammock, if the weather is fine enough. And you can't be blamed for thinking Mrs. Lavant was dead, since David Wiston thought so too."

Annabel frowned slightly at the mention of David's name. "Oh, David!" she replied scornfully. "He was as flustered as I was. He'd had a row with Tom Hopton, the keeper, in which he came off second-best. He was feeling so ruffled that he hardly knew what he was doing. He must be ashamed of himself for having been so silly."

"The keeper was definitely rude to you both, wasn't he?" Merrion asked.

"Oh, it wasn't his fault!" she exclaimed. "David took the wrong line with him from the start. After all, his orders are to keep people out, and he was naturally annoyed that we had got in without his knowing. It's no use pretending that we weren't trespassing. I saw him again when I went to The Brake on Friday, and he's quite nice, really."

"He was respectful enough when I saw him," Merrion remarked. "Now, let's go back a little. When you and David Wiston left the car, you followed that footpath to the west of the lake. Before you got to the other end of it, he left you to have a bathe, and you went to sleep under the trees. How long do you suppose you were asleep?"

"I know I must have gone to sleep, for I woke up dreaming," Annabel replied. "But I'm sure I don't know how long it was. It can't have been very long, not more than half an hour at most."

"When you woke up, you kept on along the path," said Merrion. "Not very long before you got to the end of it, did you see the boat-house at the head of the lake?"

Annabel nodded. "Yes, we saw it, but it never occurred to us to go to it. I don't know how we should have managed it if we'd wanted to. At least not without breaking our way through the bushes which had grown up all round it. They were so thick that we could only just see the boat-house from the path."

"You didn't see any broken branches, as though any one had forced a way through?"Merrion asked.

"No, we didn't," she replied. "I don't think any one can have been that way for a long time. Even the path itself was so overgrown that I began to think that we should never be able to get through."

"I don't think the path can be often used," said Merrion. "Did you notice any animals about?"

"I don't remember seeing any," Annabel replied. "A few birds, but that was all."

"And you met nobody until you got to the lawn at The Brake, and peeped at Mrs. Lavant asleep in the hammock?"

"Not a soul!" she replied. "We saw nobody, from the time we left the car till then."

"Well, I'm very glad to have had the details at first hand," Merrion remarked lightly. "When your father told me of your adventure, it sounded so queer that all my curiosity was aroused. But I never thought I should be given the opportunity of visiting The Brake for myself. When you went there on Friday, you saw no one in the house but Mrs. Lavant and the Lingfields?"

"I saw no one else," she replied. "I don't think there can have been any one else, for the Lingfields brought in tea themselves."

"The Lingfields have been living at The Brake for a long time," said Merrion. "Before that, they used to appear on the music-hall stage as Lance and Linette. I seem to remember their names, but I've forgotten what their turn was."

"Lance and Linette?" Dorset repeated. "Yes, I have a vague recollection of them. But that was some time ago, before the war. I suppose Claire Lavant likes to surround herself with stagey folk. Birds of a feather, you know."

Merrion shook his head. "There's not much similarity in the plumage. Rather, I should say, a bird of paradise and a pair of barn-door fowls. Mrs. Lavant is very much the dominant partner. The Lingfields know their place and keep to it. It's rather significant that while Mrs. Lavant associates with Sir Julius, they hobnob with his housekeeper."

"She'd dominate over any one dependent on her," said Dorset. "Annabel can please herself, but Irene and I aren't making any advances. I don't want to seem callous, but I shouldn't have broken my heart if that body had been hers."

"Well, it wasn't," Merrion replied. "Whether it ever will be identified is rather doubtful. It isn't even known yet how the unfortunate woman met her end. It doesn't look like murder, and it may have been accidental."

"Then look here," said Dorset. "A woman dies by accident, which means that no one has any reason for concealing the fact that she is missing. Nearly all of us have friends, or even creditors, who have some interest in our existence. How is it that the disappearance of this woman from her usual haunts has not been reported to the police?"

"It may never be reported," Merrion replied. "People do disappear from their usual haunts without, apparently, their friends and acquaintances, or even their relatives, bothering much about them. It isn't until some member of their family is in extremis that an attempt is made to trace them. The constant S O S messages we hear on the wireless is sufficient proof of that."

"You think that this poor soul must have been a stranger to the neighbourhood?" Irene Dorset asked.

"In the sense that she didn't live there, yes," Merrion replied. "But I think she must have known her way about there. Would a complete stranger ever have found the boat-house? You heard what your daughter told us a minute ago. The boat-house is by no means conspicuous from the path and to reach it from any direction entailed forcing a way through the undergrowth. My own view is that she had previous knowledge of the boat-house, and selected it as a secure hiding-place."

"And who do you suppose she was hiding from?" Dorset asked. "That we may never know," Merrion replied. "It may be that she was not hiding from any one in particular, but because she did not wish her presence to be disclosed till the appropriate moment."

"Meaning that she was up to no good?" Dorset suggested. "A female burglar, after Claire Lavant's jewellery, perhaps?"

"Something of the kind, I dare say," said Merrion. "But we might guess all night without hitting on the truth. We shall have to leave it to my friend Inspector Arnold. He'll ferret out the mystery, if any one can."

Shortly after this Merrion took his leave. As he made his way

back to his rooms he reviewed his conversation with the
Dorsets. That he had learnt anything of any consequence
seemed more than doubtful. Annabel's account of her
adventures conformed with the statements he had heard at The
Brake, and with what Mrs. Moffatt had told Arnold. The times
could not be established within fairly wide limits. But the course
of events might well have been this. The Lingfields had left The
Retreat immediately after Mrs. Moffatt's summons to the library.
A minute or two later, Annabel had made her fruitless attempt
to summon aid. At that moment, the Lingfields having left the
house, and both Sir Julius and Mrs. Moffatt being in the library,
the telephone bell would not have been heard.

That seemed a satisfactory explanation, and Merrion was
going on to the next point, when an idea struck him. The
Lingfields had not returned to The Brake by the door in the wall.
The only person who ever unlocked that was Sir Julius, and at
that time he was in the library. They must have walked down to
the gate, which no doubt Amos Wanstead had opened for them,
thence along the lane to the entrance of The Brake, and up the
drive to the house.

But what about Annabel and David? Immediately after she
had left the telephone, they had met on the lawn. Following a
short discussion, they had walked down the drive, and thence
along the lane to where they had left the car, passing the gate of
The Retreat. They had, in fact, followed the route taken by the
Lingfields, but in the reverse direction. How was it that the two
couples had not met?

Well, it was a matter of no great importance. Rather more
helpful had been Annabel's evidence regarding the boat-house
and the bushes surrounding it. One might assume that had a
passage been forced through these she would have noticed the
traces which had been left. These traces had been dearly visible
to Merrion when he had visited the spot. The strong probability
then was that the unknown woman had not reached the boat-
house by the middle of Wednesday afternoon.

But what interested Merrion most was David Wiston's
behaviour. Once again he asked himself what David's true
motive for absenting himself from Annabel might have been. She
could not tell how long this absence had lasted, but it was fairly
safe to assume that it was long enough to have allowed him to

go some little distance. It was not impossible that during this period he had met the woman who had subsequently entered the boat-house.

There might be nothing in the fact that since that afternoon David had kept out of the way. On the other hand, it might be due to a desire not to be questioned. Having told Annabel that he had been bathing, he could hardly admit now that he had been elsewhere and met the woman. But why the deception? Had he been up to something he didn't want Annabel to know about? And had this woman been in some way connected with this action?

Even Merrion's imagination could find no thread to lead him through this labyrinth. He reached his rooms with his mind still absorbed in the problem of the boat-house. Leaving the more recent body aside, what could be the explanation of the skeleton? Regarding this, the evidence was clear enough up to a point. It was not an anatomical specimen, abstracted from some medical school and dumped there for no apparent purpose. Merrion had seen for himself, and Dr. Wiston had confirmed his observation, as had the pathologist, that the bones had been lying, not jumbled together, but in their correct positions. It was therefore unlikely that the skeleton, as such, had been transported. When it reached the boat-house, it must have been clothed in flesh. In other words, its owner must either have died there, or been carried there after death.

This could not have occurred while the troops were using the place. While they were doing so, the boat-house must have been more accessible than it was now. Their constant passage to and fro would have kept the undergrowth at bay. Only gradually, after their departure, would it have encroached as it had now. For at least a year or two it would have been perfectly easy to reach the boat-house from the footpath, or alternatively, in all probability, from The Retreat.

There was nothing about the skeleton to suggest that it was the remains of a murderer's victim. But there was the possibility that someone, having an inconvenient corpse on his or her hands, had deposited it in a spot where it was unlikely to be found. But whose corpse could it have been? Since the departure of the troops, only one death had been recorded at either The Brake or The Retreat, that of Madame Tallinn. And she had been buried with considerable pomp in Ridhurst cemetery.

Of course, there was no reason to suppose that the skeleton had originated from either of those houses. As Merrion had already argued, the boat-house must have been easily accessible for some time after the departure of the troops. They had presumably reached it from the upper lane, and any one else might have done so. Remembering that Amos Wanstead had said that he had left the key in the lock, a theory could be advanced. A woman, not necessarily a local woman, had been lured into the boat-house and there murdered. That type of crime was by no means unknown.

Merrion lighted a fresh cigarette. The temptation to look nearer home was irresistible. Could Mrs. Lavant, or any of her entourage, have wished to dispose of a body? Merrion's imagination pictured how this might have been the case. It was admitted that there had been ill-feeling between the half-demented Madame Tallinn and Loretta Sowley. Loretta was said to have gone to Australia. But had she? Was it not dimly possible that Madame Tallinn had murdered her in an access of maniacal frenzy? Merrion could picture Mrs. Lavant's reaction to such an event. If it were to be disclosed, the unhappy Madame Tallinn would certainly be confined in a criminal lunatic asylum, if nothing worse happened to her. It had been precisely because Mrs. Lavant had dreaded the idea of her certification that she refused to allow a doctor to be called in. The event would have been known to the Lingfields, but they could be counted upon to obey Mrs. Lavant's behests. Loretta's body had been conveyed to the boat-house, and the story of her having gone to Australia put about to account for her disappearance. Even a pathologist might be mistaken in a woman's age merely from her bones.

This was plausible enough, but Merrion was rarely content with a single theory. His thoughts roamed from The Brake to The Retreat, and he asked himself a similar question. Could any one in that establishment have wished to dispose of a body? Though Merrion had many contacts, none of these were with theatrical circles. He remembered the name of Sir Julius Blackrock as being connected with the theatre, but he could not have said what his activities had been. Now that Arnold had repeated his conversation with Mrs. Moffatt, Merrion's memory began to stir. In the distant past he had heard Sir Julius spoken of, not always in terms of approval. Professionally, he had been highly successful, to such an extent that he had been rewarded with a knighthood. But there had been queer and unsavoury stories about his relations with women. It had been rumoured that it was on account of his infidelities that his wife had left him. It was not impossible that he had indulged in intrigue after his retirement, and that this had ended fatally for the woman. And was Sir Julius's eyesight so defective as was alleged?

XII

Whatever her parents might think, Annabel was determined
not to abandon her attempt to establish friendly relations with
her great-aunt. It seemed to her ridiculous that pride, or
obstinacy, or whatever it was, should be allowed to prevail. At
least, that was what she told herself. Actually her curiosity, and
perhaps something else as well, drove her irresistibly in the
direction of The Brake. The prospect of another visit was
exciting.

So, on the morning after Merrion's visit, she wrote a note,
affectionate but dutiful. Aunt Claire—she dropped the "great,"
thinking this might be taken as a compliment—had said she
might come and see her again if she gave due notice. She would
be in Ridhurst next day, Friday, and would call and pay her
respects. As she posted this, she congratulated herself on her
cunning. The notice was too short for Auntie to write a refusal
in reply. Unless, of course, she sent a peremptory telegram
forbidding her to come. And it wasn't very likely that she would
do that.

Annabel travelled to Ridhurst by the train she had taken
before, and set out on foot for The Brake. As she had expected,
she had received no prohibition from Auntie. It was, of course,
just possible that Tom Hopton had been given orders not to
admit her, but she would have to risk that. And if he had? Well,
she would see.

When she reached the gate she was vaguely disappointed
that Tom Hopton was not there to greet her. But the door of the
lodge was ajar, so he was presumably within. In opening the
gate, she purposely fumbled with the latch, making a much
noise as she could. This promptly brought Tom out. He
recognised her at once, and his face lighted up with an engaging
grin. "Why, good afternoon, miss!" he exclaimed. "I wasn't
expecting to see you again so soon."

"Good afternoon," Annabel replied demurely. "I wrote to Mrs.
Lavant telling her I was coming. Didn't she let you know?"

Hopton shook his head. "Mrs. Lavant wouldn't do that. She

wouldn't think it was any concern of mine. And if you're going to see her you'll find her alone. Mr. and Mrs. Lingfield are out in the car. I let them through the gate only a few minutes ago. And I'm sure Mrs. Lavant will be as pleased to see you as I am myself."

"It's nice of you to say that," Annabel replied. "And I'm sure I'm pleased to see you again myself."

"Thank you, miss," said Hopton respectfully. "It doesn't often happen that a young lady thinks of sparing a word for a rough chap like me. It's a lonely job this, I've taken on, but it's better than being right away in Scotland. That's where I was until I came here, ever since I was demobbed."

"So you were in the Forces too?"Annabel asked. "So was I. I served in the Wrens."

"Yes, miss," said Hopton. "I was in the Army. I joined up before the war, and I was in the Commandos by D-day."

"Oh, how exciting!" Annabel exclaimed. "You must find it lonely here after that. But I expect you've got friends or relations who come to see you sometimes?"

Hopton shook his head. "No, miss, I'm alone in the world, as you might say. I've lost touch with all my friends, drifted apart from them, like. And the only relation I've got that I know of is a second cousin, a girl of very much the same age as you, miss. But we were never together, and she wouldn't know me if we was to meet."

"But you could get in touch with her, surely?" Annabel replied. "You know where she lives, I expect?"

Hopton's eyes twinkled strangely. "No, miss, I don't know where she lives, but I don't doubt I could find out. Maybe I'll make myself known to her before very long. She might be glad to hear from a second cousin of hers."

"I'm sure she would be," Annabel replied. "Is she married?"

"No, miss, she's not married," Hopton replied slowly. "She had a young man once, but he wasn't much of a chap, or so I've heard. I'll have to be looking after myself. I shouldn't be kept on here if anything was to happen to Mrs. Lavant."

Annabel found this train of thought rather obscure. "When I saw Mrs. Lavant last week, it didn't seem that anything was likely to happen to her for several years yet," she replied.

"You never can tell, miss," said Hopton darkly. "There's such a thing as accidents. And if anything was to happen I should be looking for another job. You'll be going along to see Mrs. Lavant now? I'll be here to let you out when you come back."

"Thank you so much," Annabel replied. She went on her way up the drive, feeling just a trifle resentful. Tom Hopton and his affairs could be nothing whatever to her. He would probably seek out this second cousin of his and marry her. It was to be hoped that she would make him a good wife. Annabel wondered what she was like, and whether she was good enough for him. Tom might describe himself as a rough chap, and in some ways, his appearance, for instance, he conformed to that description. But when he allowed himself to be natural, he showed definite signs of good breeding, and his voice was cultured. He might be better born than he cared to admit. An illegitimate son, perhaps. Annabel almost began to picture him as the prince transformed by a malignant fairy into a common labourer.

She reached the house, to find the front door shut, and came to a stand outside it in some perplexity. Tom had told her that the Lingfields had gone out, and that Mrs. Lavant was therefore alone. Should she ring the bell? Auntie would not care to be disturbed to the extent of getting up to admit her visitor. Especially as it was very likely that she was in the hammock on the lawn. After some hesitation, Annabel decided that her best course was to look for her there. After all, Auntie must be expecting her, since she hadn't given Tom orders to keep her out.

She walked round the house, through the shrubbery, and on to the lawn. The hammock was in its usual place, but it was unoccupied. However, in it were a few rumpled cushions and a copy of the current issue of the Fernbrake Forest Standard. Annabel supposed that Auntie had gone indoors for something. No doubt she would come back presently. The obvious thing for Annabel to do was to wait where she was.

It was a fine summer afternoon, very still, with not a breath of wind stirring. She strolled idly across the lawn to the edge of the lake, and glanced at the unruffled surface of the water. Upon it floated a few fragments of toast, and the small fishes nibbling at them darted away as her shadow fell on them. Everything was very peaceful and quiet. Not a sound came from the house, only, far away, the faint whistle of a train. Annabel turned away, and strolled back to the hammock.

The minutes passed, and still Mrs. Lavant did not appear. Another idea occurred to Annabel. Perhaps Auntie was waiting for her in the drawing-room. Ought she to have rung the bell after all, instead of behaving in this unceremonious fashion? All the windows were open, including the french window of the hall. In some trepidation she approached this and entered. Everything was as she remembered it, and the door of the drawing-room was ajar. She rapped upon it softly, but received no reply. Then she tiptoed through the doorway and looked swiftly round. The room was empty.

This came as a shock to her. She remembered her first uncanny experience of finding The Brake empty, and failing to make any one hear. Where could Auntie be? Not upstairs in bed, surely. The Lingfields would never have gone out, leaving her alone there. There was only one other possibility. She had gone to The Retreat to see Sir Julius.

Only then did it dawn upon Annabel that this was Auntie's method of administering an effective snub to her persistent great-niece. She could come to The Brake if she liked, but she would find no one there to greet her. Annabel had an uneasy feeling that she had brought the rebuff upon herself. She was furious. It could not be that Auntie had never received her letter. She had meant to teach her a lesson not to intrude where she wasn't wanted.

As she marched indignantly through the hall, the telephone caught her eye. She had half a mind to ring through to The Retreat and tell Auntie what she thought of her behaviour. But Mr. Merrion had said that a call from The Brake was very rarely answered, and, besides, it would be beneath her dignity. She opened the door and walked out on to the drive.

There she paused. After all, she might have jumped to conclusions too readily. Perhaps she hadn't been expected quite so early. Auntie would come back from The Retreat any moment now. Or the Lingfields would return with some satisfactory explanation. She walked a little way along the drive, towards the northern entrance. To her left was the wall, and in it she caught a glimpse of the doorway, half-hidden by the trees. She stopped and stood watching it, expecting it to open and Mrs. Lavant to appear, escorted by Sir Julius.

But nothing of the kind happened, and Annabel's indignation boiled up afresh. There was no longer any room for doubt that she had been made a fool of. She could only take herself off with what dignity she could. She turned and walked swiftly down the drive towards the lodge. Tom had certainly been on the look-out for her, for he appeared before she reached the gate. "Why, you're soon back, miss," he said. "You found Mrs. Lavant quite well, I hope?"

Annabel had no intention of exhibiting her discomfiture. "I found nobody at home," she replied lightly. "Mrs. Lavant must have mistaken the day I said I was coming and gone next door to see Sir Julius."

"Yes, that may be," said Tom. "But you'll be coming back another day, miss?"

Annabel's annoyance got the better of her. "I shall never come here again!" she exclaimed violently.

"I shouldn't take it like that, if I was you, miss," said Tom in a soothing tone. "Mistakes are bound to happen now and again. Would you like me to tell Mrs. Lingfield when she comes back that you've been here? She'd pass it on to Mrs. Lavant."

"No, I shouldn't," Annabel replied with immense determination. "I'd rather you said nothing about it, if you don't mind."

"Oh, no, I don't mind, miss," said Tom. "I'd do anything you asked me, and glad to. And perhaps, before very long, you might be willing to do something to help me. I'd be in a bit of a fix if anything happened to Mrs. Lavant."

The idea of losing his job seemed to be on Tom's mind, Annabel thought. "Of course I'd do anything I could to help you," she replied. "You'd want another job something like the one you've got now, I suppose?"

"I might have a chance of bettering myself," said Tom slowly. "And that's where you might help me. If anything was to go amiss here, it would mean a lot to me. And to you too, miss, if I may say so without offence."

This was rather startling. "Now, what in the world do you mean by that?" Annabel demanded.

But Tom shook his head. "Time enough when it happens, miss. We shall see for ourselves then, both of us. You're sure you wouldn't like to wait till Mr. and Mrs. Lingfield come back?

You could sit down in my lodge yonder."

"Thank you very much," Annabel replied. "But I won't wait. I'll get along now. Good afternoon."

"Good afternoon," said Tom. Then, meaningly: "You'll be back again before very long, I don't doubt."

He opened the gate and Annabel passed through. As she walked away down the lane she wondered vaguely what Tom had been talking about. There was something fascinating in his deference and his child-like belief that she could help him in some way. She didn't at all like the idea of never seeing him again, but she was fully determined to keep away from The Brake in future. Her resentment returned in full force, inflamed by the thought that her parents had been right after all. Auntie was not the sort of person to accept the proffered olive branch. In this case at least she had rejected it with contumely. If Annabel told her parents of this humiliating experience, they would merely reply "We told you so." She would keep the matter strictly to herself.

As she reached the outskirts of Ridhurst she heard a car coming up behind her. It drew up with a squeaking of brakes, and a well-known voice hailed her. "Hallo, Annabel! What in the world are you doing here?"

David was the very last person she wanted to see just then, "That's got nothing to do with you," she snapped.

"Well, if you care to put it that way, I suppose it hasn't," David replied equably. "I'm on my way to see my father. We haven't met since that day last week when you and I saw him together. Jump in and come along too, and later I'll drive you home."

But Annabel shook her head. If she accepted the invitation she would be bound to offer some explanation of her presence in Ridhurst. "Thanks very much," she said coldly. "But I'd rather make my own way home by myself."

She turned away without further farewell, and David drove on. Matthew Wiston was pleased to see him, and naturally their conversation reached the subject of the discoveries in the boat-house. "Of course the police are on to it," said Matthew. "Not the least extraordinary part of it is that the discoveries were made by a man from Scotland Yard who was apparently here upon some totally different business. Quite a good fellow of the name of Arnold. I'm afraid he hadn't much to go upon, for it was impossible to identify either the body or the skeleton. Or to establish the cause of death, either. The pathologist rang me up this morning to tell me he had found no evidence of poisoning in the organs he has examined."

David merely nodded. His thoughts seemed to be elsewhere. Probably reflecting upon his unexpected meeting with Annabel, of which he had not spoken. And his father went on: "And there's a most extraordinary coincidence. With Inspector Arnold on Monday was a Mr. Merrion, an old friend of his. Now I've known this name for some time. Henry Dorset has often spoken of him. He met him during the war, at the Admiralty, and has a great admiration for him. The curious thing is that when I met Merrion on Monday, he was no stranger to me, for he had been here to see me this day last week."

"Had he?" David replied without much interest. "To consult you professionally on Dorset's recommendation?"

"No, it wasn't that," said his father. "He came here because he was interested in Mrs. Lavant and her environment. Henry Dorset had told him of that odd adventure you and Annabel had had a couple of days before."

David frowned. "I hate to be reminded of that. I wish now I'd never gone near the place. But I suppose any one might make a mistake like that, once. I hadn't a stethoscope with me, you know."

"I'm not blaming you," Matthew Wiston replied indulgently. "In the case of old people sleep is apt to simulate death very closely. And Mrs. Lavant is certainly no chicken, though she does her best to look like one. I wonder that she finds all the trouble she must take worth while. So used to making up for the stage that she can't give it up even now, I suppose. But it is queer that not very long after you thought she was dead, a genuine corpse was found not far away."

"Oh, dash it all!" David exclaimed. "You're not suggesting that the corpse was Mrs. Lavant's, are you?"

Matthew Wiston laughed. "My wits aren't so far gone as that. Mrs. Lavant, I'm told, must be eighty at least, and the corpse was that of a comparatively young woman. And, even if you couldn't trust your own eyes, there is ample evidence that Mrs. Lavant was alive as recently as yesterday. I had made an appointment to see Sir Julius in the afternoon. I was rather afraid that this boat-house business would have upset him. As it turned out he wasn't upset in that sense, only highly indignant that such a thing should have happened on his carefully enclosed property.

"He told me that he had been talking to Mrs. Lavant only a few minutes before I came. He had asked her to come and have a chat, and had met her at the door in the wall. She didn't stay with him very long, for when she heard I was expected she insisted on going home. She told Sir Julius that she really didn't feel up to meeting people just now. The affair seems to have shaken her pretty badly, for Sir Julius said that she sounded tired and worried. She told him that she had visions of them all being murdered in their beds any night now."

David shrugged his shoulders. "I don't see what she's got to be afraid of. The body had nothing to do with her, had it?"

"If you don't already know what old women are like, you'll learn before you've been in practice very long," his father replied. "No, the body had nothing to do with her. It didn't come from The Brake, for all the people there are accounted for. But one can understand a woman of Mrs. Lavant's age not relishing a discovery of that kind almost on her doorstep. There's no evidence of murder so far, but no doubt that is the conclusion Mrs. Lavant has jumped to."

Meanwhile, Annabel was in the train on her way home. To the humiliation of her snub was added the annoyance of meeting David. She asked herself whether that meeting had been so accidental as it seemed. Was it possible that David had been watching her movements, and had had the impertinence to follow her? It seemed incredible, for apart from the letter she had written, she had told no one of her intentions. But in her present state of aggravation anything seemed possible. It might almost be that David had been in the secret, and had accosted her to enjoy her discomfiture.

Of one thing she was fully determined. Wild horses would not drag her to The Brake again. Even though this meant that she would entirely lose touch with Tom Hopton and his mysterious hints. If anything went amiss there, it would mean a lot to him, and to her. That was what he had said. To him, yes, for Mrs. Lavant's death would mean the loss of his job. But to her? Did he guess that she would inherit her great-aunt's money?

That was all he could have meant. Mrs. Lavant's keeper could hardly be expected to have an intimate knowledge of her family circumstances. Perhaps he had some wild vision of Annabel succeeding Mrs. Lavant in the occupancy of The Brake. That would explain his suggestion that she might be able to do something for him. He would ask to be retained in his present employment. Of course, that must be it, fantastic though his vision might be. When eventually he did find himself out of a job, she would do her best to find him another. Even if he did marry that second cousin of his.

XIII

It had long been arranged that Joe Edgefield and his wife should go to work at The Brake on Saturday mornings. It was nice to have the place tidied up for the week-end. Edgefield doing what was necessary out of doors, and his wife indoors. They were always paid that morning, the former by Lingfield, and the latter by Mrs. Lingfield.

So, on the Saturday morning, the day following Annabel's futile visit, the Edgefields set out as usual on their bicycles a little before eight o'clock. They reached the gate of The Brake, and as Edgefield opened it, Hopton emerged from his lodge. "Good morning!" he called out cheerfully. "Going to be warm later on."

"Good morning," Edgefield replied. Then to his wife, "You go on. Missus. I want a word with Tom."

Mrs. Edgefield cycled up the drive to the house. The so-called back door was at the southern side, nearest the lodge. She had no key, for this was unnecessary, as one of the Lingfields unlocked the door before she came. This morning she found it unlocked as usual, and entered. She put her bicycle against the wall of the wide passage and went on to the kitchen.

Immediately she was struck by something unusual in the atmosphere, which seemed to lack its habitual friendly warmth. The reason of this was not far to seek. The Aga was out, and practically cold. So was the boiler which supplied the hot-water system. This was entirely new to her experience, for Mr. Lingfield always made up both last thing at night. Finally, there was no sign of the pot of tea which Mrs. Lingfield invariably made before she came.

This was odd, and Mrs. Edgefield felt completely at a loss. She might tackle the boiler, for that was straightforward enough. But, never having found the Aga out before, she had no idea how to relight it. Mr. or Mrs. Lingfield must be about somewhere, or the back door would not have been unlocked. She went through into the hall and listened. Everything was perfectly still, and she could hear no movement, upstairs or down. Then she noticed that the french window leading on to the lawn was open. She looked into the drawing-room. Nobody was there, but to Mrs. Edgefield's surprise the curtains were drawn back and the windows were open.

The explanation that occurred to her was that the Lingfields had got up earlier than usual and gone out into the garden. But that, by itself, did not account for the state of affairs in the kitchen. How was she to set about getting breakfast? The only alternative to the Aga was an oil-stove in the scullery, which to the best of her knowledge had never been used, and was probably out of order. And if Mrs. Lavant's breakfast tray wasn't taken to her sharp at nine, there would be ructions.

Mrs. Edgefield went out on to the lawn and looked about her, failing to see or hear any sign of any one about. The hammock was in its usual place, and the cushions had not been brought in overnight. They were soaking with dew, as was a newspaper lying with them. It became more than ever clear to her that something very much out of the ordinary must have happened. She returned to the house and went upstairs. The door of the Lingfields' bedroom was wide open. The room was in some disorder, and both single beds were made up and had apparently not been slept in.

This was so amazing that Mrs. Edgefield uttered an involuntary exclamation. Then she remembered Mrs. Lavant. The suite she occupied, bedroom, dressing-room and bathroom was across the landing, and shut off from it by a door. This was shut, and, greatly daring, Mrs. Edgefield knocked upon it. There was no reply, and after an interval she opened it softly and entered the lobby beyond. The doors of all three rooms opening off it were open. The bedroom was in even greater disorder than the Lingfields. The big bed in it was made up and undisturbed. Mrs. Lavant was not in it.

Something very like panic seized upon Mrs. Edgefield. She ran downstairs, across the hall to the front door. This was not bolted, as it invariably was at night. She opened it and ran out on to the drive. Approaching her was her husband, wheeling his bicycle, and Hopton walking beside him. Mrs. Edgefield gave a gasp of relief and rushed towards them. "Joe!" she exclaimed breathlessly. "They're gone!"

Edgefield stared at her in stolid surprise. "Why, Missus,

whatever's come over you? What's gone?"

"All of them!" she replied frantically. "There's nobody in the house, and the fires are out."

But Edgefield was not so easily stampeded. "If they're not in the house, they'll be outside somewhere," he said in a matter-of-fact tone. "And if the fires are out you'd best light them. Tom and I are going along to the orchard. He's going to give me a hand picking them early plums there."

Hopton seemed to share Edgefield's complacency. A momentary flash of astonishment had lighted up his eyes at Mrs. Edgefield's dramatic announcement, but now he appeared to have lost all interest in the matter and stood feeling in his pockets one after the other. "Left my pipe behind," he muttered. "Shan't be a minute, Joe. Find you in the orchard." And he slouched off towards the lodge.

Mrs. Edgefield hardly noticed his departure. "They're not there, I tell you, Joe!" she exclaimed angrily. "I've been upstairs and looked in the rooms, and they haven't been slept in all night."

"Maybe, being a warm night, they thought they'd like to sleep out of doors," her husband suggested tranquilly.

"They'd never do such a thing!" Mrs. Edgefield replied. "At least, Mrs. Lavant wouldn't, that's a sure thing. Besides, I've been out on the lawn and there's nobody there. Where else would they sleep, outside?"

Something of her consternation began to infect Edgefield. "Well, it does sound a bit queer," he said. "We'd better have a look round." Then a bright idea occurred to him. "We'll see if the car's in the garage."

The garage stood a short distance from the house, towards the northern entrance. As they reached it, they saw that the doors stood wide open and that the garage was empty. Edgefield pushed back his cap and scratched his head. "Well, that's a rum 'un, that is," he growled. "If they've gone away, who's going to pay us our money?"

That aspect of the matter had not hitherto dawned upon Mrs. Edgefield. "Why, they'll come back, surely! But I don't like it, Joe, not after the dreadful things that happened hereabouts last week. And they've left the house wide open, for any one to walk in and take whatever they wanted. The sergeant ought to know about it, in my opinion."

Edgefield seemed rather doubtful about this. "It's no business of ours, properly speaking. Suppose we was to tell the sergeant, and they was to come back presently? What then? Mrs. Lavant wouldn't be best pleased."

"We could say it was because we found the house open," Mrs. Edgefield replied firmly. "Now, just you hop on your bike and get back to the Verderers'. There's a telephone there, and you can ring up the sergeant. All you need say is that we found the house open and nobody there, and ask him what we'd best do about it."

It usually happened that Mrs. Edgefield had the last word. Her husband mounted his bicycle and rode off grumbling. She returned to the house and entered the kitchen. Feeling that she must find something to do, she began to tackle the oil-stove. She filled it up with paraffin, and after some coaxing got one of the burners to light. She put on a kettle, and busied herself making a cup of tea. Thus engaged, she felt less lonely in the oppressive stillness of the house. The kettle boiled and she filled the teapot. Looking for the milk, she found a full jug left over from yesterday. The milkman wasn't due for another hour yet. She found herself wondering whether she'd better take any when he came. She poured herself out a cup of tea, adding milk in quantity to make it cool enough to sip. As she drank it, she began to feel capable of dealing with whatever might happen next.

She had barely finished her cup, when she heard her husband's voice at the back door. "You there, Missus?" She joined him, looking at him inquiringly. "I spoke to the sergeant and told him what you said," he went on. "He said he'd come out right away and see how things were for himself. And he said we was to wait here till he comes."

"Then we'd best go outside and meet him as he comes along," said Mrs. Edgefield. "I know we've done the right thing, Joe. If we'd said nothing and anything was found missing, they'd say we'd taken it."

They went to the drive in front of the house, and in a very few minutes a car came along. It stopped, and the sergeant got out of it. "Well, what's all this?" he demanded. "Nobody here, and the house left open? How did that come about?"

"That's more than we can tell. Sergeant," Mrs. Edgefield replied. "Maybe you'll come inside and look round?" The three of them entered the house by the back door, and so to the kitchen, where the teapot stood upon the table. "You'd like a cup, Sergeant, I dare say," Mrs. Edgefield went on. "It's fresh made." She picked two cups off the dresser and, having poured out one each for the sergeant and her husband, refilled her own.

The sergeant sat down at the table, produced his note-book and laid it before him. He gazed doubtfully at the point of his pencil, then licked it. "Now then," he said amiably, "let's hear what you have to say."

Mrs. Edgefield responded to this with a clear if voluble account of her adventures. "I knew there was something wrong as soon as I saw the fires were out," she concluded. "But what possessed them to go away and leave the house wide open? I've never known them to do such a thing before, and nor's my husband. Have you, Joe?"

Edgefield shook his head forebodingly. "There's something behind it, you mark my words," he muttered.

The sergeant scribbled a few notes in his book. "When did you last see any of these people?" he asked.

"Not yesterday, for Friday's not our morning," Mrs. Edgefield replied. "We were here the day before, though, and everybody was about as usual then. I spoke to both Mr. and Mrs. Lingfield, and they didn't say anything about going away. I didn't see Mrs. Lavant, for she was in bed all the morning. But I saw Mrs. Lingfield take her tray up to her."

"There's a man works on the place, isn't there?" the sergeant asked. "A keeper, or something of that?"

"That's right," Mrs. Edgefield replied. "Didn't you see him down by the gate as you came through?"

The sergeant shook his head. "There was nobody there. I had to open the gate for myself."

"Tom wasn't there when I came back, neither," Edgefield remarked. "Maybe he's gone along to the orchard. I asked him to give me a hand there picking some plums as the missus and I came along in."

"Well, we'll look for him presently," said the sergeant. "From what you say it looks as if these people had gone off on a sudden. An urgent message, perhaps. Do you know any one who's likely to have sent them one?"

"Can't say that I do," Mrs. Edgefield replied. "Wait a bit, though. A great-niece of Mrs. Lavant's came to see her one day last week, or so Mrs. Lingfield told me. Or they might know something next door, over at The Retreat."

The sergeant grunted. He had a vivid memory of his last visit to The Retreat, and of the rent in his trousers. "It's not so easy to get in there," he said. "The gate's always kept locked."

Mrs. Edgefield glanced at the clock. "Amos Wanstead will be there to open it and let the milkman in before very long."

"Well, perhaps I'll get him to let me in too," the sergeant replied. Now, about that young lady you spoke of that came here. Do you know her name, and where she lives?"

"Mrs. Lingfield didn't tell me that," Mrs. Edgefield replied. "It was the first time she'd been here, she said."

The sergeant closed his note-book and finished his cup of tea. "I'd like to have a look round the house now," he said.

Mrs. Edgefield conducted him through the rooms, upstairs and down. He made no detailed examination, contenting himself with glancing round each room in succession. There was every evidence of a hasty departure. In the bedrooms and dressing-rooms drawers and wardrobes were open. In the Lingfields' room, a dress which Mrs. Edgefield recognised as the one Mrs. Lingfield had been wearing when she last saw her was lying unfolded on the bed. And in the dining-room were the remains of a meal, which had not been cleared away.

"We'll leave everything as it is," said the sergeant. "Now I'll try to find this keeper. What's his name, by the way?"

"Tom Hopton," Mrs. Edgefield replied. "He hasn't been here so very long. Came from Scotland, I understand. My husband's gone along to the orchard I expect, and maybe Tom's there with him. I'll show you where it is, if you like."

The orchard lay between the drive and the lake, beyond the vegetable garden. When they reached it they found Tom ensconced among the boughs of a plum-tree, picking the fruit and passing it down to Edgefield, who stood on the ground beneath him. At the appearance of the sergeant Tom climbed down and looked at him rather vacantly.

"Well, Hopton, you live in the lodge by the gate, don't you?" said the sergeant. "When did you last see any of the people who live in the house here, Mrs. Lavant or Mr. or Mrs. Lingfield?"

"It's quite a while since I've seen Mrs. Lavant," Hopton replied unhesitatingly. "But I saw both Mr. and Mrs. Lingfield yesterday afternoon. They came down the drive in the car and I opened the gate to them. I didn't notice the time particularly, but it must have been round about half-past two?"

"They were alone in the car?" the sergeant asked. "Mrs. Lavant wasn't with them?"

Hopton shook his head. "There was nobody else in the car but them two. I've never known Mrs. Lavant go out in the car all the time I've been here. They didn't speak to me, but I thought they must be going along to Ridhurst to do a bit of shopping, as they do now and again. But they didn't turn to the left along the lane. They went the other way."

"Didn't you think it queer that they didn't come back again?" the sergeant asked.

"Well, I can't say that I gave it a thought," Hopton replied. "You see, they might very well have come back without my knowing. If they'd come round by the top lane and in by the gate at the other end of the drive, that is."

This was reasonable enough, and the sergeant nodded. "Did you go to the house at all yesterday afternoon or evening?"

"No, for I had no occasion to," Hopton replied. "I don't go to the house until I'm sent for. I didn't go near it until Mr. Edgefield came along this morning and asked me to lend him a hand with these plums."

"Did any one come here before Mr. and Mrs. Lingfield left?" the sergeant asked.

"Not that I know of," Hopton replied. "Nobody came by the lodge gate. But they might have come the other way."

The sergeant turned away, beckoning to Mrs. Edgefield. "I'm going to see if I can get into The Retreat," he said. "I'll ask you to stop in the house while I'm gone, just to see that nothing is interfered with." They went together as far as the house, which Mrs. Edgefield entered. The sergeant continued down the drive and along the lane to the gate of The Retreat. The chain and padlock had been removed, and Amos Wanstead was at work with a hoe on a border nearby.

The sergeant opened the gate and walked in. Knowing that it was not much use bellowing at Amos, he merely nodded and pointed up the drive. Amos in return bade him a surly good morning. As the sergeant went on his way he met the milkman returning from the house on his bicycle, his bottles rattling as he came. The sergeant reached the door, and Mrs. Moffatt appeared in answer to his ring. "Good morning. Sergeant,' she said. "And what brought you here?"

"I'm just making a few inquiries," the sergeant replied. "Have you seen any one from next door lately?"

"Not since the day before yesterday," Mrs. Moffatt said. "Mrs. Lavant came across that afternoon, but I didn't see her myself. But I saw Mr. Lingfield, who came with her. He stopped and chatted with me."

"Did Mr. Lingfield say anything to you about going away?" the sergeant asked.

"Going away?" Mrs. Moffatt replied. "What, from The Brake, you mean? No, that he didn't. Neither he nor Mrs. Lingfield would ever dream of leaving Mrs. Lavant, I'm sure of that, they're much too fond of her. Why, when he was here the day before yesterday he was telling me that they were both rather anxious about her. That affair you know of had got on her mind proper, and she kept on saying that she was sure something terrible was going to happen to her."

"Mrs. Lavant was so frightened that she might suddenly take it into her head to go away?" the sergeant suggested.

"Well, I don't know about that," Mrs. Moffatt replied. "There's no telling how a thing like that might affect some people. But Mrs. Lavant can't have said anything to Sir Julius about going away, for if she had, he'd have told me."

It had been the sergeant's intention to ask to see Sir Julius, but on looking at his watch he decided that he had not the time to spare. On the previous evening he had received a message that Inspector Arnold would come to Ridhurst on Saturday morning, arriving there between ten and eleven. It was a quarter to ten already. The sergeant thanked Mrs. Moffatt and hurried back to The Brake, where he found Mrs. Edgefield pottering rather aimlessly about the kitchen. "Has any one been here while I was away?" he asked her.

"Only the milkman," she replied. "He came very soon after you'd gone. But I didn't take any, for I thought it wouldn't be wanted."

"I don't expect it will," the sergeant agreed. "Now look here, Mrs. Edgefield, I've got to get back to Ridhurst sharp. This is what I want you to do. Go round the house and shut and fasten all the windows. When you've done that, see that the front door is bolted. Go out by the back door, lock that, and take the key with you. Tell Hopton that if Mrs. Lavant or the Lingfields should come back, they can get the key from you. But don't let any one else have it."

Mrs. Edgefield agreed to do this, and the sergeant drove back to Ridhurst. A few minutes after he had reached the police station a car drove up with Merrion at the wheel and Arnold as a passenger. Arnold and Merrion came in, and the former acknowledged the sergeant's salute. "Good morning, Sergeant. I thought I'd run down and hear how you're getting on. Have you anything fresh to tell me?"

"Not about that body, sir," the sergeant replied. "The woman didn't come from anywhere round about, I'm sure of that."

"We've had a report that makes it pretty certain she wasn't poisoned," said Arnold. "And we've circulated what few particulars we've got about her. All we can do now is to sit tight and hope for the best."

"Yes, sir," the sergeant replied. "There's one thing I ought to tell you. Mrs. Lavant has left The Brake."

"Has she?" said Arnold. "What made her do that? Where has the old lady gone to?"

The sergeant replied with a brief account of his visit to The Brake and his conversations there. "I went on to The Retreat, sir, and saw Mrs. Moffatt," he continued. "Mrs. Lavant and Mr. Lingfield were there on Thursday, but it seems that neither of them said anything about going away. The only thing is that Mrs. Lavant was very nervous over what had happened."

Arnold turned to Merrion. "What do you make of that?" he asked.

"Not very much, so far," Merrion replied. "The departure of the Lingfields seems to have been rather hasty. Mrs. Lavant was not in the car with them. Where did they leave her? If at The Brake, where did she go to? A woman of her age could not be expected to go very far on foot. There is at least one possible answer to that question."

"Well, and what is it?" Arnold asked impatiently.

"That in fact she didn't go very far," Merrion replied. "No farther than through the doorway in the wall."

"But Mrs. Moffatt told the sergeant that Mrs. Lavant hadn't been to The Retreat since Thursday," Arnold objected.

"Exactly," said Merrion. "Have you spoken to any one who has seen Mrs. Lavant since Thursday, Sergeant?"

"No, sir," the sergeant replied. "The Edgefields didn't go to The Brake yesterday. And Hopton says he doesn't often go up to the house, so he wouldn't have seen her."

Merrion nodded. "So that it's quite possible that when the Lingfields left, Mrs. Lavant was no longer at The Brake. She may never have gone back there after her visit to The Retreat."

"But if she's still there, Mrs. Moffatt must know," Arnold insisted.

"Perhaps she has been told to hold her tongue," Merrion replied. "But there's still another possibility. Do you consider it your duty to follow up this rather odd disappearance?"

"I'm going to get you to drive me to The Brake," Arnold replied. "I'd like to have a look round for myself."

"By all means," said Merrion quietly. "But, before we do that, how would it be to have another look inside that boat-house?"

XIV

The three of them left the police station in Merrion's car and drove straight to the stile at the northern end of the footpath. By this time the approaches to the boat-house were so trodden down that they had no difficulty in reaching it. The door had been repaired sufficiently to allow it to be locked, but the sergeant had brought the key and unlocked it. Arnold entered first and looked round. "There's nothing here!" he exclaimed.

Merrion followed him, and saw at once that the boat-house was indeed empty. The debris on the floor lay just as it had after the removal of the skeleton. As Merrion stirred it with his foot, a leaf fluttered down through the aperture in the roof where the wooden shingle had fallen away. By the end of autumn, a fresh layer would be added. Merrion reflected that very few autumns would have been sufficient to hide the skeleton entirely.

Arnold probed about until he had satisfied himself that no third body could be hidden. "Well, your imagination was at fault that time," he said. "You'll have to guess again. Now we'll try The Brake, and see what we can find there."

They drove first to the Edgefields' cottage and collected the key. When they reached the lodge gate they found it shut, and no sign of Hopton. "I left him picking plums in the orchard, sir," the sergeant explained. "I expect he's still there."

"We'll look for him presently," Arnold replied. "First of all, you shall take us over the house." They went on up the drive, and entered by the back door. The sergeant took them first to the dining-room, and displayed the table laid with the remains of a meal. Three places had been laid, and at each of these was a plate with fragments of food still upon it. Arnold pointed this out. "They had lunch before they left, three of them, Mrs. Lavant and the two Lingfields."

"That's what it looks like," Merrion agreed. "But perhaps it was meant to look like that. However, let's suppose for the moment that Mrs. Lavant did have lunch here yesterday. What then?"

"There's a hammock out on the lawn, sir," the sergeant

suggested. "With cushions and a newspaper in it."

Merrion nodded. "After lunch Mrs. Lavant went and lay down in it for her siesta. The Lingfields left her there and went out. That had happened before, as we know, on Wednesday of last week. But on that occasion they returned. This time they didn't, and after they had gone, Mrs. Lavant vanished. Let's go upstairs."

They entered Mrs. Lavant's suite, which Merrion proceeded to examine minutely. The drawers and wardrobes were packed with clothing, dresses and underclothes in the utmost profusion. Only a few of the articles were in disorder, the rest were neatly folded or arranged on hangers. In the dressing-room a heavy curtain hung over a recess. Merrion drew this aside, to reveal a fair-sized safe. The door was wide open, and it was empty.

"That's where she kept her jewellery, no doubt," Merrion remarked. "Wherever she's gone, she's taken it with her, every bit of it. I haven't seen as much as a brooch lying about anywhere. But she doesn't seem to have taken many clothes with her. There are enough here to stock a shop. All right, let's look into the Lingfields' apartment."

They crossed the landing, and Merrion proceeded to examine the Lingfields' bedroom. Here he found conditions rather different. Apart from the frock lying on the bed, very little clothing was to be found. Only a few articles remained, and among these nothing of value. "That's rather curious, when you come to think of it," Merrion remarked. "The Lingfields left, taking with them most of their possessions. Mrs. Lavant left, taking with her only her jewellery. While we're on this floor we'd better look into the rest of the rooms."

There were half a dozen other rooms. Of these, only two were furnished, but they did not appear to have been used for a long time, and there were no sheets or blankets on the beds. The remaining rooms were empty, except for a small one fitted with shelves which were stacked with household linen.

From the house the sergeant led them to the orchard. The plums had all been picked, and Edgefield and Hopton were loading baskets of fruit on to a wheelbarrow. The sergeant beckoned to the latter, who came forward sheepishly. Recognising Arnold and Merrion, he raised his hand in salute. "Good morning, Hopton," said Arnold. "I'll ask you to repeat to us what you told the sergeant just now about yesterday afternoon.'

Hopton gave his account clearly enough. In reply to Arnold's question, he expressed his certainty that Mrs. Lavant had not been in the car. He hadn't actually looked into it, but if she had been there he must have seen her. Unless she had been crouching on the floor at the back, and she would never have done a thing like that.

"I don't suppose she would," Arnold agreed. "Now, about this car. It belongs to Mrs. Lavant, I suppose?"

"I expect it's hers, sir," Hopton replied. "But I've never seen any one but Mr. Lingfield driving it."

"Can you describe it?" Arnold asked.

Hopton hesitated. "Not very well, sir. I don't know much about motor-cars, and I've only seen this one as it passed by. my lodge. It's a biggish car, and looked pretty old, but it always seemed to go all right. And it was painted black. I never thought to notice the number, sir."

"You saw it about half-past two." said Arnold. "Did any one come here yesterday afternoon after that?"

Again Hopton hesitated, and this time apparently did a bit of rapid thinking. "Well, yes, sir," he replied reluctantly. "Someone did come, not long after. But she didn't stop very long, and she asked me not to say that she'd been."

"Did she?" Arnold asked. "Do you know who this person was?"

"Oh, yes, sir," Hopton replied. "I shouldn't have let her in else. I saw her twice last week, and she told me that Mrs. Lavant was her great-aunt. Yesterday when she came back from the house she told me that she hadn't found any one there."

"You had seen the Lingfields go out," said Arnold. "But didn't you think it queer she hadn't found Mrs. Lavant?"

"Why, no, not particularly, sir," Hopton replied. "The young lady herself said that Mrs. Lavant must have gone across to The Retreat."

Merrion caught Arnold's eye. "I don't think Hopton can tell us much more just now," he said. He turned away, followed by Arnold and the sergeant. "The young lady was, of course, Annabel Dorset," he went on, when they were out of earshot. "It strikes me as quite likely that she knows something about all this. Just as well not to let Hopton think that we are interested in her visit, for it's just possible that they are in communication. I was talking to her on Wednesday evening, when Hopton was mentioned. It struck me then as rather curious that she knew not only his surname, but his Christian name as well."

"Have you got it at the back of your mind that Miss Dorset kidnapped her great-aunt?" Arnold asked dryly.

"Not for a moment," Merrion replied. "Annabel can wait for a bit. What are you going to do about tracing that car?"

"If it is licensed in Mrs. Lavant's name, we can get a description of it by sending a circular to the various registration authorities," Arnold replied.

"No doubt you can," said Merrion. "But there ought to be a short cut. Cars don't go farther afield than they can help in these days of shortage of petrol. Where's the nearest petrol pump. Sergeant?"

"There's none nearer than Ridhurst, sir," the sergeant replied. "But there are half a dozen there."

"Then it's a pretty safe guess that when the car wanted petrol it was driven to Ridhurst, and probably always to the same pump. And cars want other things besides petrol, tyres and adjustments, for instance. It's ten to one that somebody in one of the garages in Ridhurst knows all about this car. But that again can wait until this afternoon. We've time to call at The Retreat before lunch."

The sergeant looked doubtful. "I don't know how we'll get in, sir. Wanstead let me out, but he'll have locked the gate again by now."

"There's the telephone," Merrion replied. "It will be rather interesting to see if it's really difficult to get a reply as we've been told it is."

They went back to the house, and Arnold applied himself to the telephone in the hall. It was an old-fashioned instrument, with a handle which when turned rang a bell at the other end. Arnold made several attempts at this, but it was some minutes before he got a reply. Then he heard a female voice. "Who's there? Is that you, Mr. Lingfield? It's lucky I was passing by, or I should never have heard your ring. Is anything wrong?"

"It isn't Mr. Lingfield," Arnold replied. "It's Inspector Arnold. You remember the chat we had the other evening, Mrs. Moffatt.

Now I want to see you again. Will you send Wanstead to the gate to let me in?"

"There!" Mrs. Moffatt exclaimed. "I guessed there must be something wrong when the sergeant came to see me a while ago. I'll go and find Amos and send him down at once."

"Thank you, Mrs. Moffatt," said Arnold. He put down the telephone and turned to the sergeant. "You'd better stop here, just in case any one comes along. If they do, keep them till we get back." He and Merrion walked to the gate of The Retreat, where they found Amos waiting for them. He recognised Arnold and greeted him with a surly nod, but Merrion he eyed with evident disfavour. However, he let them both in, and they walked up the drive.

Mrs. Moffatt, with an anxious expression, was waiting for them on the doorstep. "Whatever is it, Mr. Arnold?" she exclaimed. "It gave me such a turn when you told me who it was on the telephone. I was passing through the hall when I heard it ring, and I made sure it must be Mr. Lingfield. There's nothing amiss at The Brake, surely?"

"There's something that wants explaining," Arnold replied. "And perhaps Sir Julius can help us. Can we see him?"

"He's in the library," said Mrs. Moffatt. "I wouldn't like him upset. But I'll tell him you're here." She went away, and came back in a minute or two. "Sir Julius will see you, and the other gentleman too." She led them to the library which, as the curtains were almost drawn together, was in semi-darkness. On the table at which Sir Julius sat was a reading-lamp, so shaded that it cast only a circle of light downwards. He was wearing powerful glasses, and in the circle of light was a pack of full-sized cards laid out in a game of patience. He bent down and very deliberately moved one of the cards before he spoke. "Sit down, Mr. Arnold. And the friend I'm told you have with you, too. Have you come to talk to me again about those gruesome discoveries you made in my boat-house?"

"Not this time. Sir Julius," Arnold replied. "I've come to ask you if you can tell me where Mrs. Lavant is."

"Mrs. Lavant!" Sir Julius exclaimed. "Why, at The Brake, presumably. Where else should she be?"

"Mrs. Lavant is not at The Brake," said Arnold. "The house was found empty this morning. My information is that Mrs.

Lavant was here on Thursday afternoon. Is that the case?"

"It certainly is," Sir Julius replied. "She came at my invitation, and sat for a while in this room, talking to me.

"Would you mind telling me the exact circumstances, Sir Julius?"Arnold asked.

Sir Julius's mind seemed still to be half-occupied with his game of patience, for he moved another card before he replied. "There is little or nothing to tell. Claire Lavant is a very old friend of mine, and she is good enough to come here and talk to me. I am unable to read, except with the greatest difficulty, and I find that time hangs heavily on my hands. I had not seen Claire Lavant for some days, not in fact since Monday of last week. On Thursday, the day before yesterday, I rang her up and begged her to come over, if she could make it convenient to do so. She promised to come, and she did."

"You let Mrs. Lavant in through the doorway in the wall, didn't you?" Arnold asked.

"That is correct," Sir Julius replied. "It is my usual custom to do so. We arranged that she should be at the door at a quarter to three. Lingfield came with her, but not Mrs. Lingfield. I brought Claire Lavant in here, and Lingfield went to find Mrs. Moffatt. Claire Lavant was with me for I dare say half an hour."

"Did you find Mrs. Lavant upset by what had happened earlier in the week?" Arnold asked.

It almost seemed that Sir Julius had not heard the question. He peered intently at his cards, and moved one or two of them before he replied. "My sight does not enable me to perceive any one at all clearly. I am unable to say whether her expression revealed that she was upset. But failing sight is apt to render the other senses more acute. As Claire Lavant sat here talking to me, the tone of her voice and the sound of her nervous movements told me that she was in a state of great mental stress."

Merrion had not yet spoken. "A stress due to fear?" he now suggested.

At the sound of his voice Sir Julius turned his head in the direction from which it came. "Apprehension would perhaps be a better word. We have known one another long enough to justify me in asking her what was the matter. She told me that she hadn't been able to sleep since she had heard of that dreadful body having been found. She was not afraid for herself, for she was an old woman, and in any case she could not have much longer to live. But it would be too awful if anything happened to Lance or Lin, as she calls Mr. and Mrs. Lingfield. I had never heard her talk like that before. Some subtle and distressing change seemed to have come over the woman I have known so long."

He paused, peered again at his cards, and then went on:

"Jumpy perhaps expresses the state that she was in. It happened that I was expecting Dr. Wiston at half-past three that afternoon. Not infrequently Claire Lavant has been here when he came and has remained to talk to him. But when I told her of his impending visit she almost leapt from her chair. She said she couldn't possibly see any one in the state her nerves were in, and begged me to take her to the door before he came. As we went out, Lingfield was in the hall, and he joined us. I let them both into The Brake through the doorway."

Arnold had no reason to doubt the truth of what Sir Julius had said. "As I have told you. Sir Julius, neither Mrs. Lavant nor the Lingfields are at The Brake now, and there is evidence of their hasty departure. Do you think that Mrs. Lavant's apprehension can have become so strong that she decided to leave?"

"I cannot imagine her doing so without letting me know," Sir Julius replied. "Even if she had not come herself, she would surely have sent Lingfield or his wife to tell me that she was going, and where. There could be no reason whatever for her withholding that information from her oldest friend."

"I'm bound to ask you this question. Sir Julius," said Arnold. "Do you know where Mrs. Lavant is now?"

"Most certainly I do not," Sir Julius replied sharply. "In fact, what you tell me causes me considerable anxiety. Knowing Claire Lavant as I do, I cannot believe that she left The Brake under the influence of panic."

"The whole thing is most mysterious," said Arnold. "The Lingfields were seen to leave The Brake in the car yesterday afternoon, but Mrs. Lavant was not with them."

This time Sir Julius was thoroughly roused. He took off his glasses and swept the cards aside impatiently. "But that is most extraordinary!" he exclaimed. "The Lingfields would never have left Claire Lavant alone in the house for more than an hour or so. Since they have given up their profession, they have been entirely dependent upon her. She could not be left to look after herself, for in spite of her vivacity, she is unable to walk far or do any work. She told me that she was alarmed not for herself but for the Lingfields. It is, I suppose, just faintly possible that she insisted they should go away. But, in that case, where can she have gone to herself?"

"The most natural thing would be for her to seek refuge with you. Sir Julius," Arnold replied meaningly.

Sir Julius frowned. "I quite appreciate, Inspector, that you feel it your duty to find Claire Lavant, and I am very glad that is so. But she is not here. You have my full permission to make as exhaustive a search of the premises as you please."

"I'll take your word for it, Sir Julius," said Arnold. "We needn't trouble you any longer. It's quite possible that you will hear from Mrs. Lavant, telling you where she is. If you do, may I ask you to communicate with the sergeant at Ridhurst?"

"I will certainly do so," Sir Julius replied, ringing the bell. "In return, may I ask you to let me know if you have any news of her?"

Arnold promised to do this. Mrs. Moffatt appeared, and having bade farewell to Sir Julius, Arnold and Merrion followed her from the room. "You didn't see Mrs. Lavant when she was here on Thursday?" the latter asked.

"No, I didn't," she replied. "Sir Julius let her in himself, and let her out again. I only saw Mr. Lingfield, who came with her. Mrs. Lavant had gone by the time I showed Dr. Wiston into the library."

Arnold and Merrion left the house. "The only person here who saw Mrs. Lavant that afternoon was Sir Julius," Merrion remarked, as they walked down the drive. "Or rather, he didn't see her, only sensed the jumpy state she was in. And that, when you come to think of it, is rather curious. When we were with her on Tuesday she had already heard about the boat-house body, and didn't seem unduly disturbed about it."

"Do you think that Sir Julius was spinning us a yarn, then?" Arnold asked.

"No, I don't," Merrion replied. "I think he told us what appears to him to be the exact truth. But I'm beginning to feel that the disappearance of Mrs. Lavant will turn out a pretty sticky business. Never mind, let's get back to Ridhurst and have lunch."

At The Brake they picked up the sergeant, who had nothing to report. They left the house, locking the back door and taking the key, which Arnold entrusted to the sergeant. On their way to Ridhurst in the car, they called on Mrs. Edgefield and informed her that any one seeking admittance to The Brake must be told to apply at the police station.

After lunch, they set out to make inquiries about Mrs. Lavant's car. At the sergeant's suggestion, they started with Parbeck's Garage, the most important in the town. They hit the target at once, for Mr. Parbeck, the proprietor, was able to give them all the information they required. "Mrs. Lavant, of The Brake?" he replied to Arnold's question. "Yes, I know her car well enough. Mr. Lingfield, who always drives it, has dealt with us for some years now, and Mrs. Lavant has an account with us. It's an old black Daimler saloon, about 1935, I should say. I saw it only yesterday."

"How was that?" Arnold asked.

"It stopped here in the afternoon for petrol," Mr. Parbeck replied. "Mr. Lingfield was driving, and Mrs. Lingfield was sitting beside him. And there was another lady sitting in the back, but I don't know who she was."

"Could this lady have been Mrs. Lavant?" Arnold asked.

Mr. Parbeck shook his head. "Oh, no, she wasn't Mrs. Lavant. There's no mistaking her. I saw her about three years ago, when she hired cars from us for a funeral. An old lady dressed in black, and hung all over with pearls. And her picture was in the Standard last week, looking just as I remember her, only she was in white this time. No, this lady wasn't her. Somebody much younger, round about forty, I dare say."

"Have you any idea what time it was when the car stopped here?" Arnold asked.

"I couldn't say, exactly," Mr. Parbeck replied. "But I had an appointment over the road at three, and it wasn't very long before I went to keep that. Say a quarter to three, nearabouts."

When Mr. Parbeck had looked up the number of the car, ZZZ 352, they went back to the police station. "The mystery deepens," said Merrion. "Who was this other lady, and where did the Lingfields pick her up? I think we can be quite confident that she wasn't Mrs. Lavant. Well, that's up to you two. I'm going to Surbiton, to find out what's to be learned there."

XV

When Merrion arrived at the house in Surbiton, he inquired for Henry Dorset, and was told he was at home. He was shown into the lounge, where Dorset, who was alone, greeted him with some astonishment. "Hallo, Merrion, I'm delighted to see you. Irene and Annabel are out, but they'll be back before very long. What brings you here?"

"I've come to tell you something you ought to know," Merrion replied. "That is, if you don't know it already. Mrs. Lavant has disappeared from The Brake, without leaving any indication of where she has gone."

Dorset stared at him. "That's news to me. What do you mean by disappeared?"

"Exactly what I say," Merrion replied steadily. "And, if it's news to you, it won't be to your daughter."

"Annabel!" Dorset exclaimed. "What are you driving at now? Claire Lavant hadn't disappeared when Annabel saw her last week."

"Your daughter has been to The Brake since then," said Merrion. "She was there yesterday. Didn't she tell you?"

Dorset .shook his head. "Not a word. Look here, you're not supposing that Annabel knows what's become of the old woman?"

"It will be interesting to hear her own account of her visit to The Brake," Merrion replied. "Meanwhile, I'll tell you how things were found there this morning."

Dorset listened in astonishment to Merrion's account of the situation. "Well, that's amazing!" he exclaimed. "But there's this about it. Wherever she's gone, she'll have to let the trustees know, or rather, their solicitors. She won't draw her interest next quarter unless she does that."

This was yet another indication of Dorset's obsession with Mrs. Lavant's money. "How is the interest paid to her?" Merrion asked.

Dorset shrugged his shoulders. "In the same way that it is paid to Irene, I suppose. The solicitors send her a cheque every quarter. With it is a form of receipt which has to be signed in the presence of two witnesses. The idea being, I take it, that the receipt serves as a certificate that the beneficiary is alive."

There was a sound of voices in the hall, and a moment later Irene Dorset and Annabel entered the room. Henry Dorset allowed no opportunity for greetings. "Eh, what's this, Annabel?" he demanded. "Mr. Merrion tells me that you were at The Brake yesterday afternoon. Why didn't you say anything about it to your mother and me?"

Annabel turned on Merrion. "How did you know?" she demanded petulantly. "Did David tell you he'd seen me?"

It struck Merrion as significant that David Wiston's name should crop up again at this juncture. "No, Hopton, the keeper, told Mr. Arnold. He obviously didn't want to, for you had asked him to tell nobody that you had been to The Brake. But you mustn't blame him, for obviously he couldn't withhold information from the police."

"But, my dear child, why all this secrecy?" Irene Dorset asked.

"Because I didn't want any one to know I'd been made a fool of," Annabel replied tempestuously. "I'd written to Auntie, telling her I'd call yesterday afternoon. And when I got to The Brake there was nobody there. The Lingfields had gone out in the car, and Auntie must have gone to The Retreat to see Sir Julius."

Merrion shook his head. "She hadn't. You found the house open?"

"Oh yes, wide open," Annabel replied. "And I knew that Auntie could only just have gone. Her hammock was on the lawn, with the cushions and a paper in it. And there were even some bits of toast scattered on the lake for the fish to feed on. I looked into the drawing-room, but there was nobody there."

"Did you look into any of the other rooms?" Merrion asked.

"No, I didn't," she replied. "I only looked in the hall and the drawing-room. But there was nobody in the house, I'm sure of that. The only person I saw about the place at all was Tom Hopton. And that was by the lodge."

"You said just now that David Wiston had seen you," said Merrion. "Where was that?"

"In Ridhurst, while I was on my way back to the station," Annabel replied. "He was in his car and pulled up when he saw me. He said that he was on his way to see his father, and asked me what I was doing, but I didn't tell him." Merrion stayed to tea, in the course of which Annabel gave a fuller and more detailed account of her visit to The Brake. But she said little of Tom Hopton, merely that it was he who had told her that the Lingfields had gone out in the car. She was quite sure that she hadn't met the car as she walked out from Ridhurst.

Merrion drove back to his rooms, intent upon the puzzle. He was pretty well satisfied that all the statements he had heard that day could be accepted at their face value. On that assumption, what could be the explanation of Mrs. Lavant's disappearance? Had it been voluntary or involuntary?

Considering first that it had been voluntary, that Mrs. Lavant had been so perturbed by the discoveries in the boat-house that she had been impelled to run away from The Brake and hide somewhere else. So acute had been her desire for concealment that she had not confided even in Sir Julius. By what means had she left The Brake? Certainly not with the Lingfields in the car on Friday afternoon. And she was incapable of walking any distance.

Then a plausible answer dawned on Merrion. Nobody but the Lingfields had seen Mrs. Lavant at The Brake since Thursday afternoon. That evening, Lingfield had driven her away in the car, using the northern entrance to avoid Hopton's eye, and returning the same way. He had deposited her in some place of comfort and security, probably a hotel at some distance. On Friday afternoon he and Mrs. Lingfield had joined her there.

Somehow this didn't seem very satisfactory, and Merrion turned to the alternative. If Mrs. Lavant's disappearance had been involuntary, that could only mean that she had died or been murdered. It could hardly be supposed that she had been transported like a bundle of washing, alive and protesting. If dead, her body would surely come to light. Bodies had a way of cropping up in that neighbourhood. And Dorset's eagerness for his wife to acquire her aunt's share of the trust income would be satisfied.

And that was what worried Merrion. Of course, a woman of eighty might die, suddenly and naturally. But, when he had seen Mrs. Lavant only four days earlier, she had exhibited every symptom of robust health. Her passing from this world might have been assisted. Merrion still half believed that an attempt of this kind had been made before. But by whom? Surely not by the Lingfields, in spite of their highly suspicious behaviour. Sir Julius had said most emphatically that they were entirely dependent upon Mrs. Lavant. Far from having anything to gain by her death, it would be a positive disaster for them.

The only people who had anything to gain by the demise of Mrs. Lavant were the Dorset family. This statement, so often repeated, rang like a knell in Merrion's brain. Surely it was unthinkable that any one of them would commit, or connive at, murder. But there was that strange persistence on Annabel's part in maintaining contact with The Brake, in the face of the expressed disapproval of her parents. And then, her encounter with David Wiston. Had his sole reason for being in the vicinity been a filial visit to his father?

With some relief Merrion reminded himself that speculation upon a possible murderer of Mrs. Lavant must be unprofitable until her death was established. Meanwhile, there were other facets of the problem inviting thought. The behaviour of the Lingfields, for example. There was no reason to doubt Hopton's veracity. When they left The Brake, Mrs. Lavant had not been with them. It was not unlikely that they had left by the lodge entrance so that Hopton should see them, and so serve as a witness to that fact. They had been located in Ridhurst not much later, having driven there by a devious route, which would account for Annabel not having met the car.

Merrion's study of the local topography enabled him to visualise what this route might have been. Hopton had seen them turn to the right on reaching the southern lane. They could have followed this, past the gravel pit where he had left his car on that memorable night. Not far beyond this the northern and the southern lanes converged. They could have turned sharp right into the northern lane, past the stile leading to the boat-house, and so to Ridhurst.

If the statements as to time made by Hopton and Mr. Parbeck could be accepted, the Lingfields could not have dallied en route. The wholly unaccountable third party seen by Mr. Parbeck in the car must have been picked up on the road. Who she could have been it was impossible to conjecture. Perhaps some casual pedestrian, to whom the Lingfields had offered a lift. Yet Merrion could not fail to be struck by the fact that unidentified women, dead or alive, had a curious knack of turning up in the neighbourhood. The skeleton and body found in the boat-house, and now the woman in the car.

Arnold, weary and disgruntled, arrived as Merrion was about to sit down to dinner. While Newport laid a second place, Merrion regaled his visitor with a stiff drink. "Ah, that's better!" Arnold exclaimed as he gulped it down. "I've been at it the whole afternoon, and, but for one thing which doesn't help much, I've drawn a blank."

"Well, never mind," Merrion replied consolingly. "While we're having something to eat, you can' tell me all about it."

Arnold was ready enough to tell his story. "After you'd gone, the sergeant and I went back to The Brake, taking a couple of his men with us. We set to work first of all on the house, and went over every comer of it, from roof to cellar, without finding any sign of Mrs. Lavant. Then we tried the lodge, which was quite neat and tidy, with no sign of any one but Hopton having been there. That young chap came with us when we started to explore the grounds, and was most helpful. We went over every inch of them, outhouses, shrubberies and all. We even dragged the lake, the one in front of the house, that they call East Moon. All with no result. I'm prepared to swear that Mrs. Lavant, dead or alive, is nowhere on the premises."

Merrion nodded. "I'll accept your oath. But from what you said just now, I gather you found something?"

"Not at The Brake," Arnold replied. "I thought all along that the Lingfields might have come up to London. So after we'd got the number of that car, I rang up the Yard and told them to put a call out. And by the time we got back to Ridhurst police station there was a message waiting for me. The car had been found, all right, standing deserted in one of those parking places on a bombed site, just off Bond Street."

"Quite a fashionable neighbourhood," Merrion remarked. "And the Lingfields, and their passenger?"

Arnold shrugged his shoulders. "Goodness knows! In the drawing-room at The Brake was a photograph of them taken both together. Although it must be some years old, it's a good enough likeness of what I remember of them. I've brought it with me, in case it should be wanted."

Merrion smiled. "In case the Lingfields should be wanted, you mean. But are they wanted, in that sense? So far as I can see, there is no evidence at present of their having transgressed the law in any way."

"There's no evidence of anything," Arnold replied shortly. "But what have they done with Mrs. Lavant?"

"I think you can take it that they haven't murdered her," said Merrion. "In fact, what you tell me of your efforts at The Brake inclines me to think that Mrs. Lavant isn't dead. It seems more likely that she and the Lingfields have gone into hiding—probably together, and possibly in London. But whether their shyness is entirely due to unreasoning alarm on Mrs. Lavant's part, I very much doubt."

"Everything at The Brake suggests that they bolted at very short notice," Arnold remarked significantly.

"Exactly," Merrion replied. "But that appearance may have been created deliberately. What strikes me as curious is the contrast between Mrs. Lavant's self-confidence on Tuesday, when we saw her, and her apprehension, as Sir Julius calls it, two days later when she was at The Retreat. But we've got this to remember. Mrs. Lavant has been an actress all her life. Even after she left the stage she hasn't been able to resist playing a part. She is quite capable of displaying herself in any role, either for our benefit or that of Sir Julius."

"Yes, I dare say," Arnold agreed. "She plays the part of mutton dressed as lamb all right, anyhow."

"She does," Merrion replied. "But I can't help thinking that something must have happened at The Brake quite recently, which defied even Mrs. Lavant's histrionic gifts. My imagination hasn't yet thrown light on what it may have been. I've been groping among fantastic improbabilities ever since I got back from Surbiton. You'd better hear about that, by the way."

Arnold listened to Merrion's account of his conversation with the Dorsets. "So that girl admits she was at The Brake yesterday afternoon," he said. "I dare say she knows more about what's happened than she told you."

"She may," Merrion replied. "But somehow I don't think that she does. It strikes me that there are two significant things in what she said. The first is that she had written a letter saying she was coming, which Mrs. Lavant should have received yesterday morning. And the second is that she unexpectedly met David Wiston in Ridhurst.

"A moment ago I suggested that something out of the ordinary might have happened at The Brake quite recently. If so, I have an idea that it happened on Wednesday of last week, the day that Annabel Dorset and David Wiston visited The Brake together. I have suspected before now that, in the course of that day, an attempt was made on Mrs. Lavant's life."

"Then why did she take it lying down?" Arnold asked. "Why didn't she report it to the police?"

"That, in the literal sense, she took it lying down is very likely," Merrion replied. "Why she didn't report it is another matter. Probably because she was afraid of appearing ridiculous. She didn't know who had made the attempt, and it wasn't till Annabel went to see her two days later that she began to have her suspicions. When she got Annabel's letter yesterday morning, she feared a second attempt, and panicked. It may not have been wholly by chance that David Wiston's appearance in Ridhurst coincided with Annabel's visit to The Brake yesterday."

"You're being pretty obscure, aren't you?" Arnold asked.

"Probably," Merrion replied. "I was thinking aloud, rather than trying to put up any definite theory. Now let's come back to what we know. Everything tends to show that three people had lunch at The Brake yesterday, and I don't see any reason why a false appearance should have been created. Two of these people were certainly the Lingfields. Was the third Mrs. Lavant? I'm inclined to think not."

"Who was it, then?" Arnold demanded. "And if it wasn't Mrs. Lavant, where was she then?"

"I'll try to answer your two questions separately," Merrion replied. "The third person at lunch was the woman whom Mr. Parbeck saw with the Lingfields in the car. Who she may be, I'm not prepared to guess. After lunch, the Lingfields started off in the car, going out by the lodge entrance to draw Hopton's attention to the fact that Mrs. Lavant was not with them. Meanwhile, the other woman walked up to the unguarded entrance. The Lingfields drove round to the northern lane, picked her up and, I imagine, brought her up to London with them.

"Where was Mrs. Lavant, you ask? Already where is she now,

wherever that may be. She was spirited away from The Brake earlier. There wouldn't be the slightest difficulty about that. The Edgefields didn't go to work at The Brake on Friday morning. And Hopton himself says that any one can come or go by the northern entrance without his knowledge."

Arnold considered this for a few moments. "You don't think that Mrs. Lavant is dead, then?" he asked.

"Why should she be?" Merrion replied. "At all events, I'm quite certain that she didn't die at The Brake within the last couple of days. If she had, you'd have found her body. I utterly refuse to believe that the Lingfields murdered her and transported the body elsewhere. And if any one else had murdered her, or she had died a natural death, they wouldn't have bolted like that. It would amount to a public confession of guilt on their part."

"Yes, that seems sound enough," Arnold agreed. "But what next?"

"Well, that rests with you," Merrion replied. "The situation as I see it is this. Mrs. Lavant supposed, possibly with good reason, that she was in danger of being murdered. In order to escape this fate, she made up her mind to hide, with the greatest possible secrecy. As we have seen for ourselves, the Lingfields are ready to do anything she tells them. Lingfield drove her away somewhere, to a London hotel, I expect, probably yesterday morning. For some purpose or other he brought the woman of the car back with him. Between them they packed what would be required, including Mrs. Lavant's jewellery. Then, after lunch, they drove away from The Brake and joined her. The car was abandoned, because if it had been left in a garage it would have provided a clue which might have led to their whereabouts. Are you sufficiently interested in Mrs. Lavant's disappearance to follow up the matter?"

"Well, I don't know," said Arnold doubtfully. "If she's alive, I suppose her tricks are no business of mine. But she's put me to so much trouble already that I'd like to know what's become of her. It's the sergeant's job, really."

"If she's in London, he'll want the help of the Metropolitan Police," Merrion replied. "Now, here's a hint for you. Mrs. Lavant's income is paid to her quarterly by cheque, or so Dorset supposes. That must mean that she has a banking account somewhere, upon which she'll have to draw, sooner or later. Mr. Parbeck told us that she had an account with him, and this, in all probability, is settled periodically by cheque. I expect he'll remember the bank on which those cheques are drawn. Contact the manager, and the next cheque she draws ought to lead you to her."

XVI

Henry Dorset was not greatly perturbed by what Merrion had told him. Claire Lavant's sudden fancies had always been unpredictable. It was quite impossible, and equally unprofitable, to guess why she had left The Brake so suddenly. She might, for instance, have taken offence at something which her old friend Sir Julius had said quite innocently, and cleared out in a huff. And the shock wasn't likely to prove fatal, worse luck.

But Annabel regarded the matter quite differently. She was stricken with remorse for the indignation she had felt at the apparent slight put upon her. It was not now to be supposed that the house had been abandoned merely to teach her a lesson. There must have been some far more potent reason than that.

Was it possible that Tom Hopton guessed what this reason was? His prediction that she would be back at The Brake before long seemed more mysterious than ever. Had he known then that Mrs. Lavant had gone away? It seemed unlikely, for he could have had no reason for concealing the fact, at least from her. Annabel felt an uncontrollable desire to see him again. Between them, they might get to the bottom of the mystery.

This time she made no secret of her intentions. "I'm going to The Brake again to-day," she said defiantly at breakfast on Sunday morning. "I can't believe that Auntie has gone away like that without telling any one where she's gone to. She must have told somebody, and I'm going to make it my business to find out."

"You don't expect us to go with you, I hope?" her father asked mockingly. "I believe in minding my own business."

"Thanks. I'd rather you didn't," Annabel replied. "Besides, it is my business. Auntie was quite nice to me when we did meet, and she said I might see her again. I shouldn't like her to think that I was neglecting her."

Henry Dorset shrugged his shoulders. "You must do as you please. But don't blame your mother or me if you get a rap over the knuckles."

Annabel set off without further discussion of the matter. When she reached the gate of The Brake, Tom Hopton came out of the lodge to meet her. Because it was Sunday, perhaps, he had taken some pains with his appearance, being newly shaved and wearing a dark-brown suit. "Good morning, Miss," he said cheerfully. "I said you'd be here again before long. But I'm afraid I can't let you go up to the house. I've orders from the police not to let any one do that."

"You seem to have a great respect for the police," Annabel replied coldly. "You told them that I'd been here on Friday."

"I'm sorry. Miss," said Tom contritely. "But I couldn't help it. They asked me straight out if any one had been here. How was I to know that they wouldn't ask you and that you'd tell them? I don't want to get myself into trouble."

"Oh, I dare say it wasn't your fault," Annabel replied. "Now then, tell me this. Where is Mrs. Lavant?"

Tom shook his head. "I don't know, Miss," he said gravely. "I wish I did, for it would make things a lot easier for both of us. But I'm sure enough that neither of us will ever see her again."

"Do you mean that she's dead?" Annabel exclaimed incredulously.

Again Tom shook his head. "That I cannot say, Miss. But there's a lot I could tell you. Not out here, though. Being Sunday, there'll be folk going past, and it might be as well if we weren't seen talking together. Would it be too much to ask you to step inside my lodge for a while?"

Annabel hesitated. But, after all, there was no reason why she should refuse the invitation. Tom's manner was perfectly respectful, and in any case she felt fully capable of taking care of herself. "Yes, if you like," she replied.

She walked through the doorway, to find herself in a kitchen, sparsely furnished, but commendably clean. Tom followed her, and to her satisfaction left the door open behind him. "If you'll be pleased to sit down. Miss," he said, drawing forward the only chair the room contained.

Annabel sat down. "Well, what is it you have to tell me?"

Tom perched himself on the edge of the kitchen table. "It's something you ought to know. Miss, for it concerns you as much as it does me. But before I say anything I must ask you to promise that you won't let it go any further."

"If it's got anything to do with what's happened to Mrs. Lavant, you can't expect me to promise that," Annabel replied.

"It's got nothing to do with what's happened to her," said Tom earnestly. "It's something that concerns you. And if it got about it would do me a lot of harm. Now, do you promise?"

Annabel nodded. "Yes. I promise faithfully not to repeat to any one what you care to tell me."

But still Tom seemed not quite satisfied. "What if you should feel it your duty to break your promise?" he asked.

Annabel's curiosity was by now aroused to fever pitch. So much so, that she hardly noticed that the last vestige of Tom's roughness of manner had left him, and that he was speaking as her equal. "I'm not in the habit of breaking my promises," she replied. "I don't know what you mean by my duty. I shan't tell any one else without first obtaining your permission. I can't say anything fairer than that, can I?"

"Very well, then, that's a bargain," said Tom. He settled himself more firmly on the table, and looked at Annabel searchingly. "Did you know Mrs. Lavant before the war?" he asked. "In the days that Mr. Lavant was alive, and they lived in London?"

Annabel shook her head. "No, I never met Mrs. Lavant till the other day. All I know about her is what my parents have told me."

"I thought as much," said Tom. "You've heard that Mr. Lavant's grandson lived with them then?"

"Yes, I've heard that," Annabel replied. "His name was Roy Rayner, and he turned out a pretty bad lot."

"That's what you've been told," said Tom. "But Roy wasn't nearly so black as some people made out. He'd have made good if he'd been given a proper chance. But he never was. His father died before he was born, and his mother when he was quite a kid. And he was left to the tender mercies of his grandfather and his second wife."

"I've been told all that," Annabel replied. "But I can't understand how you know it."

Tom smiled. "I served in the Army, and so, as I expect you know, did Roy. I say he never had a proper chance. His grandfather couldn't be bothered with him, and Mrs. Lavant wasn't fit to bring up any boy. All she thought of in those days were her own pleasures. Roy to her was like a toy to a peevish child, to be played with while the whim lasted, then neglected and ill-treated. It was no wonder he sought his amusements where he could find them."

"There was a scandal of some kind," Annabel remarked. "He stole something, didn't he?"

"It was only a lark," Tom replied. "Nothing would have been heard of it but for Mrs. Lavant. It was a heaven-sent opportunity for her to cast him off and so get rid of him for good. She d got to the stage where she hated him almost as much as he hated her. And when Roy's grandfather died, she saw no reason why she should have anything further to do with him. If Roy had gone and hanged himself, she'd have thought it a good riddance. But he didn't. He enlisted, and turned out a pretty good soldier all through the war till he was demobbed."

"He got into very serious trouble after that," said Annabel. "I read about it in the papers at the time."

"He only did the same as plenty of other young fellows," Tom replied. "Smuggling isn't a disgraceful crime. It's more taking a sporting chance than anything else. Roy was demobbed, and found himself without a job, never having been trained for one. It wasn't likely that he'd have asked Mrs. Lavant to help him, or that she'd have agreed to if he had. You can't blame him if he seized the chance of what looked like easy money. And he brought it off the first time. It was only at his second attempt that the police heard what was in the wind; I've never understood how."

A light dawned upon Annabel. "You!" she exclaimed. "I believe you must have been one of the crew of that fishing-boat!"

"Well, that's as may be," Tom said warily. "You haven't forgotten that promise you made just now?"

"Of course I haven't!" Annabel replied impatiently. "I shan't give you away, you may set your mind at rest upon that. But I don't know why you're telling me all this about Roy. I've heard it all before, though perhaps you're throwing a different light upon it. I tell you, I never met Roy, who was never more than a name to me. Why did you say this concerned me?"

Tom smiled. "Do you remember my telling you on Friday about that second cousin of mine?"

"Yes, I do," Annabel replied. "Why? How in the world does she come into it?"

"She's in it already," said Tom quietly. "She's sitting in this room at this very moment."

Annabel glanced hastily round her. "Sitting in this room? What nonsense are you talking?" Then in a blinding flash his meaning dawned upon her, and she sprang to her feet indignantly. "What!" she exclaimed. "You're trying to pretend that you are Roy Rayner? I never heard anything so ridiculous m my life!"

She made as though to walk out of the lodge. But Tom, without moving from the table, called her back. "Sit down, cousin mine. I am Roy Rayner. And now I've said that, you'd better hear the whole story."

Almost against her will, as though his fascination held her, she returned to her chair. "But you can't be!" she exclaimed. "Roy's body was identified by Mrs. Lavant herself. You're trying to get something out of this."

"Being Roy Rayner, I have no need to try," he replied quietly. "Mrs. Lavant was mistaken in her identification. Or perhaps she thought that Roy Rayner was better dead and buried. I don't know which it was."

Annabel stared at him incredulously. "But it's preposterous! If you're Roy Rayner, why do you call yourself Tom Hopton? Does Mrs. Lavant know?"

He shook his head. "To everybody but you, Roy Rayner is actually dead and buried. Mrs. Lavant has not the slightest suspicion, for since I have been here I have kept out of her way. The Lingfields never knew Roy Rayner. It must have been after war broke out that she picked them up. If you don't believe me, I'll tell you the whole story?"

"How am I to know that if you do you'll tell me the truth?" Annabel asked.

"Oh, come now!" he replied impatiently. "Should I have told you that I was Roy Rayner, a man wanted by the police, if I hadn't been? As for that unfortunate adventure three years ago, I and some other chaps were running a smuggling racket. One night we dropped anchor off what we believed to be a deserted strip of shore, with a valuable cargo on board. We hadn't been there more than a few minutes when off came a boat with a lot of policemen in it. Of course there was a scrap. I had a gun, and

I bagged one of them before they all set on to me. I got a bash on the head, but I managed to struggle clear and jumped overboard. I was feeling pretty dizzy, and I hardly know what happened next, but I must have swam away from the boat. The next thing I knew I bumped into one of the chaps in the water. He was bashed about too, much worse than I was, and was unconscious, if he wasn't already dead. It would have been quite hopeless to try to get his body ashore. So I hung my gun round his neck to make him sink, and swam for it. I never thought I should make it, but somehow I did. And there I found the rest of the chaps, who'd got to shore in the policemen's boat. We cleared off, and with the exception of the poor chap I'd had to leave behind, none of us was caught. We couldn't have saved him if we'd tried. It was the police who killed him. They were out for blood after I had fired that shot. Of course I read all about it in all the papers I could lay hands on. I had wounded the policeman pretty badly, but he recovered, so I'm not a murderer, whatever else I may be."

"You're lucky," Annabel remarked dryly. "You seem to be a pretty desperate character, anyhow."

"I've given all that up," he replied soberly. "I'd learned my lesson that smuggling wasn't such easy money after all. I'd put all I had into the venture, and of course I'd lost everything. I was on the run till I saw to my utter amazement that the dead man had been identified as Roy Rayner. Then I determined to start afresh as the thoroughly respectable and law-abiding Tom Hopton. I went up to Scotland, and very soon got a job as keeper with a charming old boy, who gave me an excellent reference when I left him."

"But why did you come here?" Annabel asked. "Weren't you afraid of being found out?"

"Not if I played my cards properly," he replied. "I knew where Mrs. Lavant lived from reading the report of the inquest. Evidence of identification had been given by Mrs. Lavant, better known to a wide public as Claire Gabriel, of The Brake, Fembrake Forest. So I came here, and hung around a bit. And then I had a stroke of luck. I saw by an advertisement in the Pembroke Forest Standard that Mrs. Lavant wanted a keeper. I applied for the job, saw Lingfield, showed him my reference, and got it. Nobody else wanted it, for the pay wasn't good enough."

"But I still don't see the idea," said Annabel. "You were surely much safer in Scotland."

"I was safe enough here, as long as I didn't show myself too much," he replied. "My dear girl, can't you see? Almost the first thing my mother taught me was the conditions of the will of our mutual great-grandfather. When Mrs. Lavant died, I should inherit her share of the trust income. I knew very well how old she was, and that she couldn't live so very much longer. And I wanted to be on the spot when she died."

"What could you do about it then?" Annabel objected. "You are supposed to be dead."

"I had my plan," he replied. "It wasn't a very cheerful prospect, but I couldn't think of anything else then. I should have given myself up to the police. If they didn't believe I was Roy Rayner, there are plenty of people in London who would recognise me—people who used to come to the house while I was living there. I shouldn't have had the slightest difficulty in establishing my identity. I should have done time, of course. But when I came out, the money would have been mine. That was the only way I could think of. But now things are different."

"You mean now that Mrs. Lavant has disappeared?" Annabel asked.

Roy shook his head. "I didn't mean that exactly. I assure you, perfectly honestly, that I have no idea what has become of her. But you may take it from me that nobody will ever see Mrs. Lavant again, alive or dead. After a while her death will be presumed, and her share of the income will fall to Mrs. Dorset, if she is still alive, and, failing her, to her daughter."

"My mother is very much alive," said Annabel. "But how do you know Mrs. Lavant will never be seen again?"

"I do know," Roy replied shortly. "And you'll see that I'm right. I haven't made away with her, I promise you that."

"You seem to know a lot," said Annabel. "Did you know who I was that day last week, when you were so rude to David and me?"

Roy frowned. "I hadn't the slightest idea. You must have thought me a bit off-hand, but I was upset. If the pair of you had been seen wandering about the place it might have cost me my job, and I didn't want that to happen. Did you find any one up at the house that day when you ran away from me?"

"Only Auntie, asleep in her hammock," Annabel replied. "So fast asleep that we thought she was dead, and we were frightened out of our wits. We went and fetched Dr. Wiston, and when we got back, there she was, sitting up in all her finery, talking to the newspaper men. I never felt so silly in my life."

"You thought she was dead?" Roy asked meaningly. "Perhaps you and your friend hoped she was?"

"Of course we didn't!" Annabel exclaimed. "What do you mean by suggesting such a thing?"

"If you had nothing to gain directly by her death, your mother had," Roy replied. "You were both quite happy in the thought that Roy Rayner was safely under the ground. Is that young man you call David a great friend of yours?"

Annabel shrugged her shoulders in elaborate unconcern. "I've known him all my life. He's Dr. Wiston's son."

"Oh, so that's who he is," said Roy. "And Dr. Wiston is a friend of Sir Julius, so I'm told."

Annabel was not inclined to discuss David with Roy. "Never mind about that," she replied. "Tell me what you're going to do. You say that Mrs. Lavant will never be seen again. If you're so sure of that, are you going to declare yourself?"

Roy shook his head. "I hold you to your promise," he said gravely. "I know a better plan than that. It's very much to your interest that Roy Rayner should not rise from the grave. Well, let him stay there. The Dorsets shall inherit Mrs. Lavant's share of the trust funds, and every one shall live happily ever after."

"You don't propose to be left out in the cold, I take it," Annabel replied acidly. "Your idea, I suppose, is that we should pay you an allowance to keep your mouth shut. Isn't that very much like blackmail?"

"My dear girl!" Roy exclaimed m a shocked tone. "What a preposterous suggestion! You can't really think so badly of me as all that. No, my idea is quite different. Let Roy Rayner sleep peacefully in his grave. Then let Annabel Dorset marry Tom Hopton, and they can share the money between them."

The cool audacity of this literally took Annabel's breath away, and for a moment she could merely gasp at him. "What!" she exclaimed as she recovered herself. "I marry you? Whatever put it into your head that I should dream of such a thing?"

"Common sense," Roy replied coolly. "You'll have to marry me in the end, you know, for if you don't, I shall put my original plan into operation. Then there'll be a convict in the family, and when that convict is released, he'll inherit the money you've been looking forward to all this time."

"I've never looked forward to it!" Annabel protested indignantly. "And I don't care a bit whether you go to prison or not."

Roy laughed. "I admire your independence of spirit," he replied mockingly. "But just you go home and think it over. Apart from the money side of the question, I'm at least as eligible as your precious David Wiston. After all, I am your second cousin, and I've got just as much of the Lavant blood in my veins as you have."

He slid off the table, went to the door of the lodge and looked out. "Come along," he said. "There's nobody about." Annabel followed him to the gate, which he opened for her. "Sorry I can't let you go up to the house. Miss," he continued loudly. "But orders is orders, and there's no mending them." And then, in a lower tone, "And don't forget your promise. If you do, you'll never see Mrs. Lavant's money." And without giving her time to reply, he went back to the lodge.

XVII

On Monday morning Arnold drove in a police car to Ridhurst. He was determined to do his best to trace Mrs. Lavant, and Merrion's hint seemed well worth taking. At the police station he found the sergeant, who had nothing fresh to report. Together they went to the garage, where they spoke to Mr. Parbeck, who was able to give them the required information. "Yes, that's right," he said. "I've always sent Mrs. Lavant's account out quarterly. She posts me back a cheque, or Mr. Lingfield brings it when he next looks in. And the cheques are drawn on the Home Counties Bank in the High Street here."

Arnold and the sergeant went to the bank and asked to see the manager. They were shown into his room, where Arnold introduced himself. "I am making inquiries regarding one of your customers," he said. "Mrs. Lavant, of The Brake. Can you tell me anything about her? In strict confidence, of course."

The manager's expression showed that he guessed that Arnold's inquiries were connected in some way with the discoveries in the boat-house, still a burning sensation locally. "Very little," he replied. "Mrs. Lavant is certainly a customer of ours, of long standing. Her account was transferred here from our Mayfair branch in the early days of the war, when Mrs. Lavant first lived at The Brake. She came to see me then, and a very fine, gracious old lady I thought her. I have not seen her since then, but my clerks have."

"Mrs. Lavant calls here occasionally?" Arnold suggested.

The manager shook his head. "No. Mrs. Lavant told me at our first and only interview that she found driving in a car most exhausting, and avoided doing so whenever possible. She explained to me that every quarter she was called upon to sign a form of receipt, in the presence of two witnesses. She thought it better that one of these witnesses should not be a member of her own household, but an independent person holding a position of trust. With that end in view, Mrs. Lavant asked me if one of my clerks could attend at The Brake quarterly. Though the request was rather unusual, I felt able to agree to it, and the practice has endured ever since. Whichever of the clerks who happens to be available goes to The Brake. I will call the one who went last quarter, a month ago."

The clerk appeared, and at the manager's instigation told Arnold the facts. "I drove to The Brake on Saturday afternoon, June 25th," he said. "Mrs. Lavant was there, and Mr. and Mrs. Lingfield were with her. Mrs. Lavant signed the receipt in our presence, and Mr. Lingfield and I witnessed it. Mrs. Lavant asked me to stay to tea, and told me a lot about her life on the stage. Her memory is remarkable for so old a lady. It must be eight years now since I first went to The Brake, and she never seems to grow any older."

"You've been there fairly often, I gather," said Arnold. "Who else have you met at The Brake?"

"I must have been there about a dozen times in all," the clerk replied. "Latterly, besides Mrs. Lavant, I have seen only Mr. and Mrs. Lingfield. But some years ago I remember seeing Mrs. Lavant's foreign companion; the poor woman who drowned herself in the lake. And once, about the same time, I saw another lady who was staying at The Brake. I forget her name, if I ever heard it, but she was a relation of the Lingfields, I believe."

"You know Mr. and Mrs. Lingfield quite well?" Arnold suggested.

"I know Mr. Lingfield best, for he comes here nearly every week to cash a cheque of Mrs. Lavant's for household expenses," the clerk replied. "He did so last Friday afternoon. The cheque was for a hundred pounds. Mr. Lingfield told me that it was more than usual, for Mrs. Lavant intended to go to London for a day or two."

Arnold thanked the clerk, who went back to his work. "Mrs. Lavant has left The Brake, and so have the Lingfields," Arnold said to the manager. "I am rather anxious to know where they have gone, because I want to keep in touch with them. If any further cheques are drawn on Mrs. Lavant's account, would you be good enough to let the sergeant know?"

The manager promised to do this, and Arnold and the sergeant left the bank. From there they drove to The Brake, pulling up outside the gate and sounding the horn. At this summons Hopton appeared from the lodge, and touched his forehead. "Good morning, Hopton," said Arnold. "Have you seen anything of Mrs. Lavant or the Lingfields?"

"No, sir," Hopton replied. "They haven't come back. I was up to the house half an hour ago, and it's just as you left it."

"Has any one else been here?" Arnold asked.

"Only the young lady who was here on Friday, sir," Hopton replied. "She came again yesterday and asked me if Mrs. Lavant was back. I told her she wasn't, and I was sorry I couldn't let her go up to the house. That's all, sir."

Arnold nodded. "All right. Keep your eyes open and see that no one interferes with anything." They drove on towards the entrance of The Retreat. "I'd like a word with Mrs. Moffatt," said Arnold. "But how we're to get in I'm blest if I know. I don't feel inclined to do any more climbing. Perhaps we shall find old Amos about."

They reached the gate, to find it as usual securely locked. But, some little way up the drive, Amos was hoeing in the border. The problem was to attract his attention, for in his case the horn would be no use. Arnold manoeuvred the car till the front of it was pointing up the drive, then repeatedly flashed the headlights on and off. Fortunately the sky was overcast, and after a while Amos became aware of something unusual. He looked round, and Arnold and the sergeant beckoned to him urgently. He shambled towards the car, and, on recognising its occupants, opened the gate.

Mrs. Moffatt answered their ring. "You're back, then?" she inquired. "You don't want to worry Sir Julius again, surely?"

"No, we needn't worry him," Arnold replied. "You can tell us what we want to know, I expect. It's about Mr. and Mrs. Lingfield. They've gone to London, it seems. Do you know if they have any friends there?"

"They had plenty of friends there at one time," said Mrs. Moffatt. "People who were on the halls the same as they were. But whether they've kept up with them all this time, I can't say. But there's Mrs. Lingfield's sister. She's often talked to me about her, and she lives in London."

"I'd be grateful if you'd tell me what you know about this sister," said Arnold.

"I've never met her," Mrs. Moffatt replied. "I only know what Mrs. Lingfield has told me about her. She's a younger sister, and a widow, so I've been given to understand, and her husband left her quite a bit of money. Mrs. Lingfield always speaks of her as Sophie, and she's got a flat of her own somewhere near Notting Hill Gate. I can't for the moment recall her husband's name, though I'm sure I've heard it. Wait a minute, it's coming back. Jack Neston, that was it."

"Was Mrs. Neston ever on the stage, like her sister?" Arnold asked.

Mrs. Moffatt shook her head. "Not that I ever heard of. And Mrs. Lingfield wasn't properly on the stage, only on the halls. She and Mr. Lingfield used to do a turn together. Acrobats, they called themselves, and clever enough they were. I remember one of their tricks well enough. He'd stand with his hands open above his head, and she'd climb up till she stood on them. Then, what with her jumping and him throwing her, she'd go right over a trapeze, ever so high it was."

But Arnold, having secured a possible clue in Mrs. Neston, was not interested in the Lingfield acrobatics. He thanked Mrs. Moffatt and drove away with the sergeant. "I'm going to look for this Mrs. Neston," he said. "It's more than likely that she'll know where the Lingfields have got to. And when I've found them, it won't be long before I know what's become of Mrs. Lavant. I'll drop you in Ridhurst, and then get back to London."

The discovery of Mrs. Neston's address proved a very simple matter. The telephone directory contained the name of Mrs. Sophie Neston, living in Bamey Gardens, which Arnold knew to be just off Pembridge Road. Having had lunch, he took the Underground to Notting Hill Gate, and thence walked to the address, which turned out to be a house converted into flats. At the entrance were four brass plates, each with a bell-push beside it. One of the plates bore Mrs. Neston's name, and Arnold rang the appropriate bell.

It was some little time before this produced any response. Then the door opened, and Mrs. Neston appeared. That it was Mrs. Neston, Arnold had no doubt. Her likeness to Mrs. Lingfield, whom he had seen at The Brake, was too striking for that. She started at the sight of this stranger, but very soon recovered herself. "Yes?" she asked. "Who do you want? Have you rung the wrong bell by mistake? People are always doing that."

"I haven't," Arnold replied. "You are Mrs. Neston, I think. May I come in and speak to you?"

"No, you mayn't!" she exclaimed primly. "I'm alone in my flat, and I never let strangers in, especially men."

Arnold thought it better not to reveal his identity. "Oh, it doesn't matter," he said casually. "I only want to ask you a simple question. I'm trying to get in touch with your brother-in-law, Mr. Lingfield. Can you tell me where he is?"

Her hesitation and the look of apprehension which came into her eyes gave her away. And when she spoke, Arnold knew very well that she was prevaricating. "My brother-in-law and my sister live at The Brake, Fembrake Forest."

"They did live there, I know," said Arnold quietly. "But they've left. Where have they gone to, Mrs. Neston?"

"How should I know?" she replied, almost hysterically. "They aren't here, if that's what you think. I haven't seen either of them for ever such a long time. If they've left The Brake as you say I really don't know where they've gone to."

Arnold knew that he could not force his way into the flat without a warrant. And in any case the last thing he wanted was to alarm his quarry. "I'm sorry to have troubled you, Mrs. Neston," he said politely. "It's only a trifling matter of a sum of money owing, which I've been asked to collect. Good afternoon." And he turned away, leaving her gaping after him on the doorstep.

From Netting Hill Gate Station he rang up Merrion's number, to find that he was at home. Asking Newport to tell his master that he was coming, he made his way to the rooms. Merrion welcomed him with cheerful interest. "I can see by your face that you've something fresh to tell me," he said. "Sit down and let's hear all about it."

Arnold told him of the conversations he had had with the bank manager and his clerk, with Hopton, with Mrs. Moffatt, and finally with Mrs. Neston. Merrion listened with the closest possible attention and, apparently, with growing satisfaction. "That's all very illuminating," he said at last. "And it fits in with what I had already begun to believe. So Lance and Linette were an acrobatic turn, were they? Just repeat what Mrs. Moffatt told you about that trick of theirs."

Arnold did so, and Merrion laughed. "Well, you see the full

significance of that, don't you?" he asked.

"No, I don't," Arnold replied irritably. "The only significant thing Mrs. Moffatt told me was about Mrs. Neston."

"We'll come to her presently," said Merrion. "Let's deal with the Lingfields first. A trapeze, ever so high! Why, man alive, if a trapeze, why not that wall? It would present no obstacle to the Lingfield acrobatics. The lady could be caused to sail over that with the utmost grace and facility. And that's not all, by a long way."

"Oh, come on!" Arnold replied. "What else have you imagined? Let's hear it."

But Merrion shook his head. "Not yet. You've got a most amazing tangle to unravel, and unless you stick to one thread and follow it through you'll never do it. Mrs. Neston, now. What struck you about her?"

"The first thing that struck me about her was her extraordinary likeness to her sister," Arnold replied. "Not only her appearance, but her voice, her manner, and everything, reminded me of Mrs. Lingfield as we saw her at The Brake that day. And the second thing that struck me was that she knew very well where the Lingfields were."

Merrion laughed. "And I have an idea that she knew very well who you were. I don't think that matters; on the contrary, it may turn out all to the good. But the ultimate object of your search is Mrs. Lavant. What exactly do we know about her? We have at last an entirely disinterested witness, in the person of the bank clerk. He has seen Mrs. Lavant at intervals for many years, the last occasion being towards the end of last month."

Merrion paused, to light a fresh cigarette. "It's going to be very difficult to make you, or any one else, for that matter, see exactly what's in my mind. The only hope is for us to examine the facts, or what we believe to be the facts. I have no hesitation in accepting Annabel Dorset's account of her experiences on Wednesday afternoon, the week before last. I'm going to take the moment she saw Mrs. Lavant asleep in the hammock, and believed her to be dead, as my starting point. For the sake of brevity, we'll call that moment zero hour.

"Now, since zero hour, who has seen Mrs. Lavant? The Lingfields, of course, but who else? Let's try to catalogue these people, in chronological order. First, the two young men from the Pembroke Forest Standard. They were strangers to The Brake, and it is not likely that they had seen Mrs. Lavant before.

"Next, Annabel Dorset, David Wiston, and his father, simultaneously. They were only allowed a fleeting glance of her, from some little distance. The first two had never seen her before. Mrs. Lavant was apparently too much occupied in posing to the camera to pay much attention to them. But one might have expected her to have recognised Dr. Wiston, whom she had seen at least half a dozen times in the library at The Retreat.

"Here I may as well interpose a negative. Neither of the Edgefields has seen Mrs. Lavant since zero hour, the reason being that they only work at The Brake in the mornings, and recently, at all events, Mrs. Lavant has not got up before lunch. The nearest either of them got to seeing her was when Mrs. Edgefield prepared a breakfast tray, which Mrs. Lingfield took up to her room.

"Then we come to Annabel's visit to The Brake, two days after zero hour. She broke the rules of the establishment by calling without previous notice. The first person she saw was Lingfield, who asked her to wait in the drawing-room. A little later, she saw Mrs. Lavant and the two Lingfields together in that room. She had not before seen Mrs. Lingfield, who had not been present on the lawn during the interview.

"Next, our two selves, six days after zero hour. When we saw Lingfield that morning, he told us that if we wanted to see Mrs. Lavant we had better come back in the afternoon. We did not then see Mrs. Lingfield. In the afternoon we saw Mrs. Lavant, who was easily recognisable as the original of the photograph published in the newspaper. We also saw Mrs. Lingfield, whom neither of us had ever seen before. You may recollect that she took very little part in the conversation, and that when she did she was prompted either by her husband or Mrs. Lavant.

"Finally, Sir Julius, eight days after zero hour. Now, consider very carefully what he told us. He had not seen Mrs. Lavant since Monday of the previous week, two days before zero hour. He rang up on the private telephone and asked her to come to The Retreat. She did so, accompanied by Lingfield, but not by his wife, and Sir Julius let them in. He took Mrs. Lavant to the library, while Lingfield went to talk to Mrs. Moffatt. Later, Sir Julius let Mrs. Lavant and Lingfield off the premises. Mrs.

Moffatt has not seen Mrs. Lavant since zero hour.

"Sir Julius is a very old friend of Mrs. Lavant, and must be familiar with all her ways. He is too blind to see much more than her vague outline, but his other senses are keen enough. And I dare say you remember his remark to us. He said that some subtle and distressing change seemed to have come over the woman he had known so long. Further, as soon as Mrs. Lavant heard that Dr. Wiston was expected, she insisted upon taking her departure before his arrival. We may conjecture upon her true reason for this. Was it that she was in too distressed a state to be able to bear a meeting with a comparative stranger? Or was it because she was afraid of Dr. Wiston seeing her, no longer in a fleeting glimpse from a distance, or in a newspaper photograph, but actually face to fact, at close quarters?"

Merrion paused. "Now then, sum all that up for yourself," he said.

"I've done that," Arnold replied. "I see what you're driving at. But I'd like to hear your explanation of how it could be possible."

"Back to zero hour, then," said Merrion. "That's where the only plausible explanation can begin. I'm quite ready to believe that Annabel Dorset, inexperienced in such matters, might have been mistaken in believing Mrs. Lavant to be dead when she was merely asleep. But that David Wiston, a qualified doctor, with a post in a big hospital, should have shared her mistake seems to me extraordinary. Unless, of course, he bad some reason of his own for knowing that if she wasn't dead yet she very soon would be. I believe now that she was dead when Annabel snatched the newspaper from her face.

"Now, compare Annabel's account of her adventure with the telephone with what Mrs. Moffatt told you. Unfortunately we have no exact time-record. But I think we can safely assume that both Mr. and Mrs. Lingfield were at The Retreat when Annabel went to the telephone. The exact moment, I think, was just after Mrs. Moffatt had been summoned to the library and the Lingfields were passing through the hall on their way out.

"What happened then is worth following very closely. Since the only connection was with The Brake, and they had left Mrs. Lavant alone there, they could only suppose that she had rung it. One or other of them picked up the instrument, to hear to their amazement a perfectly strange and agitated female voice. To the best of her recollection, Annabel said this was an urgent call, and she wanted to be put through to Dr. Wiston.

"Now I'm pretty sure that the Lingfields had nothing to do with whatever happened at The Brake. But this mysterious call from an unknown voice was enough to tell them that something must have gone very wrong. Until they knew what it was, they had better keep it to themselves. One of them must get back at once, but it wouldn't do to ask Sir Julius to let them through the doorway in the wall. To hunt up Amos, get him to unlock the gate, and then to walk all the way round would take far too long. But they had another card up their sleeves, the old acrobatic trick of their music-hall days. Lingfield projected his wife over the wall, then went back himself by the normal route. You can verify that part of it by talking to Amos, if you can make him understand what you mean. He let both of them in. Did he let both of them out, or only Lingfield?

"Incidentally, that explains another minor point. Very shortly after the telephone incident, Annabel and David walked past the entrance of The Retreat on their way back to the car. I've wondered how it was that they did not meet the returning Lingfields. Because she had flown over the wall, and he had not yet reached the entrance.

"What did Mrs. Lingfield find when she alighted on The Brake side of the wall? Possibly she caught sight of two young strangers hurrying down the drive. Certainly she went to the lawn where she had left Mrs. Lavant. Mrs. Lavant was dead, and the newspaper men were expected in half an hour. There was only one thing for Mrs. Lingfield to do, and that was to take Mrs. Lavant's place.

"Mrs. Moffatt may say that Mrs. Lingfield was never properly on the stage. But her career on the music-halls must have taught her acting and the art of make-up. It was not difficult for her to impersonate someone whose constant companion she had been for many years. Convincing enough to satisfy those who had never known the original. And almost convincingly enough for Sir Julius, whose failing sight could not detect difference in appearance."

XVIII

Merrion threw away his cigarette and lapsed into silence. Arnold, striving to arrange his thoughts in some kind of logical order, had as yet nothing to say. There were objections, of course, even impossibilities. But before he could frame these in words, Merrion went on quietly and in a tone of increasing confidence.

"From the Lingfields' point of view, the afternoon passed off very satisfactorily. The newspaper men were no doubt charmed by the manner and vivacity of the subject and her reminiscences. Incidentally, Mrs. Lingfield must have known enough of Mrs. Lavant's past triumphs to be able to reproduce them in any quantity required. Annabel Dorset, David Wiston and his father appeared on the scene, but were not allowed to approach near enough for the two former to detect any defects in the impersonation. A little while ago I pointed out that it was strange Dr. Wiston had not been recognised. Mrs. Lavant would probably have done so, but Mrs. Lingfield couldn't, for she had not previously met him. Except possibly long ago, at the time of the death of Madame Tallinn.

"So far, so good. But there was the problem of the future to be faced. If Mrs. Lingfield were to become Mrs. Lavant, what explanation could be given of the disappearance of Mrs. Lingfield? This, I feel pretty sure, was how that problem was solved. That evening Lingfield went in the car to a public telephone somewhere, rang up his sister-in-law, and asked her to come down at once. He met her at the station and, avoiding Hopton's eye, smuggled her to The Brake by the northern entrance. There were then, as before, two women at The Brake, who could in turn play the parts assigned to them.

"Look how beautifully it all worked out. Mrs. Neston is not an actress, and is probably incapable of impersonating Mrs. Lavant. But this was quite unnecessary, for her role of Mrs. Lavant was played only off the stage. It was she who stayed in bed in the morning, and was the recipient of the breakfast tray, taken up by Mrs. Lingfield. It was thus perfectly simple to prevent the Edgefields detecting the imposture. Of course, Mrs. Lingfield only assumed the personality of Mrs. Lavant when necessary, that is when visitors were expected. And visitors were only received by appointment.

"Consider again the visitors since zero hour. Annabel recognised Mrs. Lavant as the lady of the photograph. Never having previously seen Mrs. Lingfield, she was quite ready to accept Mrs. Neston as her. The only possible clue was the photograph of Lance and Linette in the drawing-room. And I dare say the sisters resemble one another sufficiently for no suspicions to be aroused by a photograph taken some time ago.

"The same remarks apply to us. Having then no reason to suspect that things might be otherwise, we both accepted Mrs. Lingfield as Mrs. Lavant, and Mrs. Neston as Mrs. Lingfield. I said just now that Mrs. Neston knew very well who you were. Of course she did. She recognised you as one of the visitors in the drawing-room that afternoon.

"But the visit to The Retreat was a far more delicate matter, and it was avoided as long as possible. But when Sir Julius rang up, it was impossible to delay any longer. A reply that Mrs. Lavant was indisposed could only be a postponement. Besides, Sir Julius's concern might have induced him to come to The Brake himself. The risk must be taken, relying for safety upon the failing eyesight of Sir Julius. But every precaution must be taken against Mrs. Moffatt seeing the spurious Mrs. Lavant. It was Lingfield's task to engage her in conversation and keep her out of the way.

"Then we come to the final scene. I don't know what convinced the Lingfields that the curtain must be rung down upon the comedy. Perhaps they may already have decided to end it. The spurious Mrs. Lavant's apprehension may have been assumed to account for her departure. The letter received on Friday morning may have had something to do with it. At all events they cleared out. The Lingfields left in the car, taking Mrs. Lavant's jewellery with them. Mrs. Neston walked to the northern entrance, where the Lingfields picked her up. The rest, my friend, is up to you."

"Thanks very much," Arnold replied. "But I'm not going to rush round chasing the figures of your imagination. I'm going to get all this rigmarole straightened out first. We'll begin with what you call zero hour. Mrs. Lavant was in fact dead when those two young people saw her. How did she die?"

Merrion smiled. "That's just the question. She didn't die as the result of an accident. She may have passed away quietly in her sleep as a result of heart failure, not an impossible event in the case of an old woman of eighty. Or she may have been murdered, by an injection of some kind. Murder involves a murderer, certainly not the Lingfields. For one thing, their prospects depended on keeping Mrs. Lavant alive. And for another, if they had murdered her they wouldn't have left her lying in the hammock while they chatted with Mrs. Moffatt. I'm quite sure they had no idea that anything was wrong until they heard that private telephone call from Annabel."

"I'm not so sure about that," Arnold objected. "Even you will admit that their behaviour was a trifle suspicious. When they found her dead, why didn't they behave as people normally do in such circumstances? Send for a doctor, for instance?"

"It may have been panic," Merrion replied. "After all, since they lived with Mrs. Lavant, they might have expected her murder to be laid at their door. But I think there was more in it than that. I've just said that their prospects depended on keeping Mrs. Lavant alive, and that, apparently, is what they decided to do."

Arnold shrugged his shoulders. "Most reasonable people would say that they concealed the crime because they had committed it themselves. Or put it this way, if not the Lingfields, who, then?"

"Don't forget that Mrs. Lavant may have died a natural death," Merrion replied. "But if you insist on hunting for a murderer, I don't mind joining you. The only other person who was legitimately on the premises at the time was the keeper, Hopton. His motive must remain obscure, for all that could happen to him as the result of Mrs. Lavant's death was the loss of his job. The doorway in the wall would allow Sir Julius to reach The Brake unobserved, but again there is a complete absence of motive. And on the subject of motive, there's this to be borne in mind. Mrs. Lavant had nothing to leave, beyond her personal belongings. Her income reverted automatically to Mrs. Dorset, Annabel's mother."

"Well, that may be," said Arnold. "I have an idea you've

someone else in mind."

"Yes," Merrion replied. "Was it entirely a fluke that brought Annabel and David Wiston to The Brake at zero hour? What was David doing while Annabel was slumbering beneath the trees? Henry Dorset thinks and expects that Annabel will marry David some day. And, as I tell you, Annabel's mother inherits Mrs. Lavant's income."

"I'll have a few words with the young fellow myself," said Arnold. "Now, here's the snag in this precious theory of yours. You say that when Mrs. Lingfield saw what had happened, she set to work to impersonate Mrs. Lavant. Made herself up to look like her, took off her dress and jewellery, and put them on herself. Yes, but what about the body?"

"Her husband joined her before very long," Merrion replied. "Between them—their acrobatic tricks show that they are pretty muscular—they carried the body to the house and hid it in a cupboard. Later on, when the newspaper men had gone, they disposed of it permanently."

"Yes, but where?" Arnold insisted. "Nowhere on the premises, that I'll swear. Between us, we've combed every inch of the grounds. And your idea of looking in the boat-house first didn't come off, if you remember. And it's no good talking about what we found there last week. Most certainly the skeleton wasn't Mrs. Lavant's. And the body was that of a woman of about forty, not about eighty."

Merrion nodded. "You're quite right there. This may be what happened. What was to prevent the Lingfields loading the body into the car that night and taking it away somewhere? There are plenty of places in the Forest where a body might be hidden, and where it might remain hidden indefinitely."

"As usual, you're distressingly vague," Arnold grumbled. "It'll be the deuce of a job to search the whole Forest."

"Why not search for the Lingfields instead?" Merrion asked. "You can arrest them at sight, and charge them with any number of crimes. The murder of Mrs. Lavant, if you like, though that particular charge will be difficult to support till you can produce the right body. The concealment of her body, anyhow. The theft of the jewellery. Confronted with that lot, they'll probably find it in their best interests to tell the truth. And I dare say we can persuade Mrs. Neston to tell us where they are. Shall we go along to her flat now and interview her together?"

Arnold agreed to the suggestion, and they set out. "I hope she hasn't bolted," Arnold remarked as they reached Bamey Gardens.

"She's not likely to have done that," Merrion replied. "I don't suppose she has anything more serious on her conscience than a little innocent play-acting. However, we can only ring the bell and see what happens."

They did so, and after an interval the door opened. Merrion knew at once that his imagination had not played him false. His recognition of the woman who stood in the entrance was instantaneous. "Good afternoon, Mrs. Lingfield," he said pleasantly. "We've met before, you remember. At The Brake, last Tuesday afternoon."

"That's not my name," she replied nervously. "You've made a mistake. Mrs. Lingfield is my sister."

"Yes, and I've met her too," said Merrion slowly, giving weight to every word. "And on the same occasion. You are Mrs. Neston, but I thought you would prefer to be addressed by the name you were using then."

She seemed so appalled by his convinced tone that she could only stare at him aghast. "We must ask you to let us in," he went on quietly. "The only alternative will be for Inspector Arnold to apply for a warrant for your arrest."

"My arrest!" she exclaimed wildly. "I haven't done anything wrong. Only what Lin and Lance asked me to."

"Unfortunately that has placed you in a very compromising situation," said Merrion gravely. "If you have any explanation to offer, we are ready to listen to it. But we can't go on talking on the doorstep here."

"Come in, then," she replied, almost eagerly. "I can explain everything." She led them upstairs to her flat and took them into a small but comfortably furnished lounge. "Now, what is it you want to know?" she asked.

"We want to know what has become of Mrs. Lavant," Merrion replied sternly.

"I don't know," she replied. "They didn't tell me. Only that she'd had to go away very suddenly, and didn't want any one to know about it. That's why Lance rang me up and asked me to come to The Brake at once."

"You'd better tell us all about that," said Merrion quietly.

"I'll tell you everything," she replied. "There wasn't any harm in it really. Lance rang me up, on Wednesday evening, the week before last. He said that something very serious had happened, and asked me to catch the next train to Ridhurst, where he would meet me at the station. I asked him if anything had happened to Lin, and he said he'd tell me when we met.

"I went down at once, and found Lance on the platform. He told me that Lin was all right, but that they were in a difficulty, and wanted me to help them. He had a car, and drove me to The Brake, where I never was before. There I found Lin, and it was then she told me that Mrs. Lavant had gone away. She said that it was a highly confidential matter, connected with her late husband's relations, and that nobody, even Sir Julius, must know anything about it. If any one came to the house, she would make up as Mrs. Lavant and pretend to be her. All she wanted me to do was to pretend to be her."

"Your part was harmless enough, I dare say," said Merrion. "But was it to last indefinitely?"

"They said it would be only for a few days, till Mrs. Lavant came back," she replied. "But time went on and she didn't come back, and they kept asking me to keep it up a little longer. And I began to get frightened, especially after that day you and Mr. Arnold came to The Brake. I felt there must be something very wrong that they hadn't told me, and I was afraid of getting mixed up in it."

"Did you recognise the brooch that Mr. Arnold brought with him that day?" Merrion asked.

"No, I didn't," she replied. "I only said what they expected me to say. I hardly knew Loretta. Lin brought her here once or twice before the war, when my husband was alive, but I haven't seen her since then. Lin told me that she had stayed with them at The Brake for some time, and then gone to Australia."

"Was there any particular reason why our visit should have frightened you?" Merrion asked.

"I was nervous, and thought I might be found out," she replied. "But it wasn't only that. Lin and Lance knew that you were coming, and they were very uneasy about it. When I asked them why, they told me it was because they were afraid you had found out where Mrs. Lavant had gone to. But after you had gone, they seemed very much relieved."

"Your sister played her part very well," Merrion remarked. "Had they told you what had been found in the boat-house?"

Mrs. Neston shook her head. "Not a word. The first I heard of it was from your conversation. And I had seen nobody else. All the time I was at The Brake I spent the morning in bed, in Mrs. Lavant's room, out of the way of Mrs. Edgefield."

"Well then, we come to last Friday," said Merrion. "What induced the three of you to leave so suddenly that day?"

"It wasn't really sudden," she replied. "I had told them that even if Mrs. Lavant didn't come back I wasn't going to keep it up beyond the end of the week. And then, on Thursday, Lin had to go to The Retreat to see Sir Julius. She didn't want to go, for she was terrified of meeting Mrs. Moffatt. And when she came back she was very much upset, and said that she was sure Sir Julius suspected something. Then, next morning, a letter came from Annabel Dorset saying that she was coming again that afternoon. I struck at that, and said I wouldn't play up again. So Lance said that the only thing to be done was to go up to London and wait for Mrs. Lavant there. They would leave the house open so that she could get in, if she came back before they could tell her where they were."

"And where are they?" Merrion asked quietly.

"I don't know," she replied. "They drove me back here, and left two large suitcases, which they said they'd call for when Mrs. Lavant had joined them. They didn't tell me where they were going, and I haven't seen or heard of them since."

Merrion glanced at Arnold, who took the hint at once. "I must see those suitcases, Mrs. Neston," he said.

"Very well," she replied. She led him out of the lounge, and Merrion took the opportunity of making a rapid survey of the flat, sufficient to assure him that the Lingfields were not hiding in it. He then rejoined Mrs. Neston and Arnold in what appeared to be a spare bedroom. On the floor were the two suitcases, locked, and as Arnold found when he lifted them, unusually heavy. He was about to say something when Merrion interrupted him sharply. "That's all right. We must hurry along, we're late already." Then, turning to Mrs. Neston, "Thank you so much for what you've told us, Mrs. Neston. Your explanation is, of course, perfectly satisfactory. I apologise for the misunderstanding. Good afternoon." And almost before Arnold knew where he was, Merrion had bundled him out of the fiat.

"Here, what the dickens are you playing at now?"Arnold demanded when they had reached the street.

Merrion laughed. "Just a little finesse, that's all. You needn't run away with the idea that those suitcases contain Mrs. Lavant's dismembered body. I've a much better guess than that. They're full of her jewellery."

"Stolen property," Arnold replied. "If that's the case, I ought to have taken them to the Yard."

"Nonsense!" Merrion exclaimed. "Don't you see? They're the bait which will catch your fish. I'm quite ready to believe that Mrs. Neston doesn't know where the Lingfields have gone to. But it's quite possible that before they call on her again, they'll take the precaution of ringing her up. That's why I tried to give her the impression that we were perfectly satisfied, and shouldn't be troubling her again. All we've got to do is to arrange for your people to watch the flat. Then, when the Lingfields call to collect the jewellery, you've got them in the bag. Now, you can go along to the Yard to fix that up, and then come and have dinner with me."

Merrion went back to his rooms feeling fairly satisfied. His theory of impersonation had been proved correct, and that was a step in the right direction. But the death of Mrs. Lavant remained unexplained, as did the method of disposal of her body. And, most puzzling of all, was the behaviour of the Lingfields. They surely could not have hoped that the deception could be continued indefinitely.

Arnold kept his appointment, and after dinner they reviewed their conversation with Mrs. Neston. "She was telling the truth all right," Merrion said confidently. "We showed her that we knew so much already that she couldn't do anything else. The Lingfields had told her just enough to achieve their purpose and no more. She has no idea what happened at The Brake on the afternoon before her arrival there, and accepted the story that Mrs. Lavant had gone away. You'll notice that to the very end they kept up the pretence that they would rejoin her before long."

"We can't be sure that Mrs. Lavant is dead till we find her

body," Arnold remarked.

"She's dead right enough," Merrion replied. "But I'm becoming more and more convinced that she wasn't murdered. As for the body, I expect you'll be able to persuade the Lingfields to tell you about that when you've bagged them. By the way, bodies seem to be rather a tender point with them. There was one point in Mrs. Neston's story that seemed rather obscure. Why were the Lingfields uneasy before our visit, and relieved when we were gone?"

"That's easy," said Arnold. "Because they were afraid that we should see that the woman who was supposed to be Mrs. Lavant was actually Mrs. Lingfield."

"How could we, when neither of us had seen either of them before?" Merrion asked. "That the woman was made up was perfectly obvious, but there was nothing suspicious about that. Mrs. Lavant was notoriously a vain old woman, and might be expected to make up to look as young as possible. No, there was more in their uneasiness and subsequent relief than that. They hadn't told Mrs. Neston about the boat-house body, which was what we were inquiring about."

Arnold grunted. "Perhaps you'll condescend to tell me what's in your mind?"

"Not now," Merrion replied. "I haven't got it straight yet. For the present you'll have to try to disentangle the skein for yourself. It's certainly in a bit of a mess. You've got a skeleton and a body, neither of which you can account for. On top of that, you've got a dead woman whose body can't be found. That little lot should give you a bit of a headache."

"The Lingfields will cure that," said Arnold grimly. "What next?"

"A final visit to The Brake, I suggest," Merrion replied. "We'll drive down there to-morrow morning. And I'll arrange to pick up Annabel Dorset on the way. She seems to have taken a fancy to the place lately."

XIX

"I've rung up Annabel," Merrion said when Arnold joined him next morning. "She's quite ready to come with us. I shouldn't say very much to her if I were you, at all events at first. Better leave her to me, as a friend of her father's."

They drove to Surbiton, where they found Annabel waiting for them, and continued their journey, Annabel sitting in front beside Merrion, with Arnold in the back of the car. "I'm glad you were able to come. Miss Dorset," said Merrion gravely. "I wanted the chance of talking to you. I've some bad news for you, I'm afraid."

"Bad news?" Annabel replied quickly. "About Auntie? Have you found out what's happened to her?"

A pretty shrewd guess, Merrion thought. "Mrs. Lavant is dead," he said simply.

"Dead?" she exclaimed. She was silent for so long that Merrion wondered whether the fact was indeed news to her. And when she did speak his suspicions that she was already aware of something were strengthened. "How do you know? Who told you?"

"You were the first to tell me," Merrion replied. "You were not mistaken, after all, that Wednesday afternoon."

"Not mistaken?" she repeated wonderingly. "But I was. I saw Auntie alive and well not an hour later. And two days afterwards I had tea with her. I can't understand what you mean, Mr. Merrion."

"There is such a thing as optical illusion," Merrion replied lightly. "But you suffered from no optical illusion when you first saw Mrs. Lavant. There is no doubt that she died that afternoon. Have you see David Wiston lately?"

Annabel shook her head impatiently. "I've only seen him once since then. On Friday, when he spoke to me in Ridhurst. I think he must be ashamed of the way he behaved that day."

"His apparent mistake?" Merrion suggested. "As it turns out, he wasn't mistaken after all."

"Not only that," she replied. "He was very silly when we

met—met Tom, Tom Hopton, the keeper, I mean."

Her confusion was so obvious that Merrion wondered what could be the cause of it. "You were at The Brake on Sunday, I'm told," he said. "Naturally you wanted to find out if there was any fresh news of Mrs. Lavant. But Hopton obeyed his orders and didn't let you go up to the house. He was quite right, of course. Did you have any further conversation with him?"

"Oh, no," she replied evasively. "Nothing of any importance, that is. He told me that he had come to The Brake from Scotland, and talked about looking for another job. I am enjoying this drive so much, Mr. Merrion. It's ever so much nicer than going by train to Ridhurst and walking all the way out to The Brake from there."

It was quite obvious that for some reason she did not want to discuss Hopton, whom oddly enough she had, after an instant's hesitation, called Tom. Merrion allowed the conversation to drop, and she showed no inclination to revive it. She sat silent, apparently wrapt in deep thought, until they reached Ridhurst. Having there picked up the sergeant with the key, they set out on the last lap of their journey, to pull up outside the gate of The Brake.

Merrion turned to the girl at his side. "I wonder if you would mind if we dropped you off here?" he said. "We have some formal duties to carry out which wouldn't interest you in the least. And perhaps you'd join us at the house in half an hour's time, say."

Annabel accepted the suggestion with curious alacrity. By this time Hopton had appeared and swung open the gate. "No, sir, nobody's been here since you were here last," he replied to Arnold's question. Annabel got out of the car, and Merrion drove on up the drive with his two remaining passengers.

Annabel and Roy Rayner were left by the gate, confronting one another. "Well, and what does this mean?" he demanded sulkily. "What were you doing in the car with those policemen? You haven't been telling tales, have you?"

"No, I haven't," Annabel replied firmly. "Mr. Merrion rang up and asked me to come here with him, I don't know why. And now I'm here there's something I want to ask you."

"Then you'd better come into the lodge," said Roy. She followed him into the little kitchen, which was just as she had seen it a couple of days before. He motioned her to the chair and seated himself on the table. "Now, what is it?" he asked.

"On the way down, Mr. Merrion told me that Mrs. Lavant was dead," Annabel replied accusingly. "You knew that when you were talking to me on Sunday. That's why you were so sure that neither of us would see her again."

Roy swung his legs idly. "Your Mr. Merrion seems a pretty knowing fellow," he said. "Who told him that Mrs. Lavant was dead?"

"I don't know," Annabel replied. "He told me that she died that Wednesday afternoon when David and I were here together."

Roy frowned. "So that's what he told you, is it? Well, if he told you that Mrs. Lavant was dead, I suppose he's in a position to prove it. In future, the trustees will expect to pay her share of the income to your mother, believing the legitimate heir to be dead. And the only way you can avoid disappointing her is to marry me."

"I don't want any more of that impertinence!" she exclaimed. "You know very well I shall do nothing of the kind."

"Why not?" Roy asked banteringly. "I don't have to remind you that we're second cousins. I may have been a bit wild when I was younger, but I'm quite a reformed character now, I assure you."

"How am I to know we are second cousins?" she countered. "You haven't shown me any proof that you are Roy Rayner."

"You'd better take my word for it," he said. "If I have to prove it, your mother won't get the money."

"I don't care!" she exclaimed angrily. "I'm going to get all this cleared up. If Mrs. Lavant was dead when David and I saw her, who was it who pretended to be her afterwards? You must know that."

"I don't, but I could hazard a guess," he replied. "Whoever it was, it wasn't Mrs. Lavant."

"You knew she was dead, then!" Annabel exclaimed. "I see it all now. You killed her because you wanted the money."

Roy flushed angrily at this accusation. "Oh, so that's what you see. Well, I see things rather differently. You've never given any explanation of what you and that young fellow were doing here that afternoon. I've said nothing until now, but I've a pretty shrewd idea that the pair of you killed her between you for the sake of the money."

Annabel stared at him in speechless indignation. "How dare you say such a thing!" she exploded at last.

"You've just dared to say something exactly similar," he replied. "I don't see it's any less likely that you should have killed Mrs. Lavant than that I should have. If you like, we'll compromise by saying that your precious David killed her without telling you. The best thing we can do is to keep it to ourselves and think no more about it."

For a moment a horrible doubt swept through Annabel's mind. That doze under the trees, from which David had awakened her and led her to the lawn at The Brake. The meeting with him, barely a couple of miles away, on the day that she had found The Brake deserted. But this was ridiculous. Roy, if he really was Roy, must be bluffing. And the time had come to call his bluff. "I know now that you killed Mrs. Lavant," she said, rising from the chair. "I'm going up to the house now, and I'm going to tell them who you say you are."

He slipped off the table and stood between her and the doorway. With the light behind him she could not see the dangerous glint in his eyes. "Do you mean to break your promise and give me away?" he asked in a curiously level tone.

"I do," she replied firmly. "You can't hold me to it, for when I made it I didn't know you were a murderer."

His manner changed, and he laughed shortly. "I know when I'm beaten. All right, do as you think best. But, as we're second cousins, and in compensation for your broken promise, I'll ask you a favour. Give me a sporting chance. Don't go up to the house until ten minutes after I've gone. Will you do that?"

"I oughtn't to really," she replied doubtfully. "But I will."

"Then I'll go and collect my few possessions," he said. As he disappeared into an inner room, shutting the door behind him, Annabel sat down again. She could offer to give Roy the sporting chance he asked for, for she was bluffing herself. Even now she was not really sure that he was a murderer. It was a thousand pities that he hadn't kept straight instead of getting mixed up in that smuggling business. There was so much that was likeable about him, and things might have been so different. What if she were to keep her promise, after all? Tom Hopton would get away, and no one but herself would ever know who he really was. And then, some day, perhaps—

Roy reappeared, dressed as she had seen him on Sunday. "Well, good-bye, Annabel," He said lightly. "We're not likely to meet again. I think you've chosen the wrong course, but you must do as you think best."

As he moved to the outer doorway, she might even then have called him back. But he was too quick for her. With a swift movement he took the key from the inner side of the lock. In an instant he was out, slamming the door behind him. She heard the key turned on the outer side, and realised that she was a prisoner.

Merrion did not stop at the house, but drove on past it towards the northern entrance. "I want to have a last look at that boat-house," he explained. "I fancy there's something there that we've overlooked so far. Or rather I should say underlooked. We can leave the car at the top of the drive."

They walked to the boat-house, unlocked the door and entered. Merrion smiled as a leaf fluttered down at his feet and pointed upwards. "You see?" he said. "Where that shingle's missing. It's a pretty wide gap. Any one not too stout could get through it easily."

"If they could reach it," Arnold replied. "It must be ten feet at least above the floor. They'd want a step-ladder."

"Ordinary people would," Merrion agreed. "But not an acrobatic team. Number one could be lifted up to reach it and scramble through, stretch an arm down and the other could climb up this till he got a hold of the woodwork. And that may possibly explain how it came about that the door was locked with the key on the inside."

They spent a few minutes looking round, then returned to the car. "We'd better see that everything is all right in the house," said Arnold. "It would be easy enough for any one to break open a window and pinch something."

Merrion turned the car and they drove back. He pulled up at the front door, but as they were about to get out he pointed ahead of him. "Where's all that smoke coming from?" he asked.

Arnold looked at the cloud billowing towards them. "Someone's lighted a bonfire, by the look of it," he replied.

Merrion put his head out of the window and sniffed. "It

doesn't smell like a bonfire to me. Far more like oil burning. We'd better go and see what it is. Come along!"He let in the clutch, and they raced down the drive. As soon as they came in sight of the lodge, the source of the smoke was apparent. A black reek was pouring from it, and flames were shooting from a window at the back. These had already caught the branches of an overhanging tree, which were crackling merrily.

As Merrion pulled up the car with a jerk they tumbled out and raced to the lodge. As they approached it they heard a pounding on the door, and a female voice screaming desperately. Merrion realised that the voice must be Annabel's. "All right, we're here," he shouted. "We'll get you out in a jiffy. Are you alone?"

"Yes, I'm alone," the voice replied. "Roy locked me in when he went away. Oh, be quick!"

Merrion did not pause to wonder who Roy might be. His problem was to fulfil his promise to get Annabel out in a jiffy. A glance showed him that the windows, narrow and barred, were set high above the ground. The door was of stout oak, and would not yield to his favourite tyre-lever. Then he had an inspiration. "Stand back!" he shouted. "As far away from the door as you can."

He dashed back to the car, started up and swung off the drive. The car lurched and bumped over the uneven ground towards the lodge. At a steady speed Merrion drove it at the door, till the projecting bumper caught it fairly. The door cracked and splintered, but the lock held. Merrion backed the car a few yards, then viciously drove it forward again. This time the door yielded and flew open with a rending crash. With the inrush of air, a sheet of flame roared through the interior. As Merrion backed the car away to give them passage, Arnold and the sergeant dashed in, to drag out Annabel, her face and hands so blackened with smoke that she was almost unrecognisable.

Merrion left the car and joined them. "This is my fault," he said gravely. "We'll take you along to Dr. Wiston's surgery."

But Annabel shook her head. "I'm all right," she replied, gasping and coughing. "It's only the smoke, I'm not burnt. But you were only just in time. Let me sit down out here in the open for a few minutes."

Arnold led her to a patch of grass at a safe distance. With the opening of the door, the lodge had become a mass of flames, threatening the trees clustered round it. "We shall have the whole Forest alight if we aren't careful," said Merrion. "It's a job for the fire brigade. Where's the nearest telephone?"

"At the Verderers' Arms, sir," the sergeant replied. "About a mile along the road from here."

"You can drive?" said Merrion. "Jump in the car and put the call through. Give me the key of the house before you go."

The sergeant went off, not without some grinding of gears in his haste. Merrion shuddered at the sound. "Poor old car!" he muttered. "A badly bent bumper, and a not improved gearbox. It's my own fault, but I never imagined anything like this would happen?" He walked over to where Arnold was keeping an anxious watch over Annabel. "I don't suppose you'll ever be able to forgive me. Miss Dorset," he said contritely. "Are you quite sure you aren't hurt?"

"Quite," she replied, gazing ruefully at her blackened hands. "If only I could have a wash, I should be all right."

"Do you think you could walk as far as the house?" Merrion asked.

"I'm sure I could," she replied. Merrion helped her to her feet, and the three walked slowly up the drive. Merrion unlocked the back door and took Annabel up to Mrs. Lavant's bathroom, which was equipped with every possible toilet requisite. "There's only cold water, I'm afraid," he said. "But I dare say you can manage with that. You'll find me waiting for you downstairs when you're ready." He went down, to rejoin Arnold in the kitchen. "Well?" Arnold asked.

Merrion shook his head. "You'll have to possess your soul in patience for a bit. It's no good expecting a woman to tell a coherent story when she feels she's looking a fright. We'll talk to her when she comes down."

The sergeant reached the Verderers' Arms without misadventure. As he left the inn after calling the fire brigade, he met Joe Edgefield, coming for a morning pint. "Morning, Sergeant," said Joe. "Tom Hopton's gone along to fetch what you sent him for."

"Tom Hopton!" the sergeant exclaimed. "What! Have you seen him, then?"

"Why, to be sure I have," Joe replied. "He came to my place

a little while back all poshed up. Tom said you'd sent him to Ridhurst to fetch a key from the police station. He asked to borrow my bike, and I let him have it."

"I never sent him," said the sergeant. "Which way did he go?"

"Why, Ridhurst way," Joe replied. "And he seemed in a bit of a hurry by the way he rode the old bike along."

The sergeant paused irresolute. Should he give chase in Mr. Merrion's car? On the whole he decided he bad better not. If Hopton was bent on escape he was far too cunning to keep to the direct road. He would certainly thread a devious course through the lanes, and any attempt to pick up his track would be futile. "You'll be lucky if you see the old bike again," he said bitterly as he got into the car. Leaving Joe and the fugitive to their own devices, he drove back to The Brake.

By some feminine miracle, Annabel came downstairs with all traces of her adventure removed. "It wasn't really your fault, Mr. Merrion," she said brightly as she entered the kitchen. "It was entirely mine. I never ought to have gone into the lodge at all. But it never entered my head that he would play me a trick like that."

"It was attempted murder," Merrion replied gravely. "But the motive escapes me."

"Well, you see," said Annabel, hesitatingly and in some confusion. "I'd promised him that I wouldn't tell any one who he really was. But then when you told me that Auntie was dead when I saw her, I knew that he must have killed her. Of course I couldn't keep my promise after that, and I told him so. He asked me to give him ten minutes' start before I came up here and told you. And when he went out he locked me in."

"Having previously upset a can of paraffin and set fire to it," Merrion remarked. "Who did he tell you he really was?"

"My second cousin, Roy Rayner," Annabel replied.

Arnold pricked up his ears. "Roy Rayner!" he exclaimed. "Why, Mr. Merrion and I were talking about him only the other day. Hopton was pulling your leg. Miss Dorset. Roy Rayner lost his life in a smuggling affair three years ago. His body was identified by Mrs. Lavant herself."

Merrion smiled. "I think we may disregard that identification. The man who called himself Hopton was speaking the truth for once in his life."

"I'm sure he was," Annabel agreed. "He wouldn't have told me he was wanted by the police if he hadn't been."

"He's still more badly wanted now," said Arnold grimly. "But you needn't worry about that. It won't be long before we lay hands on him."

"When did he tell you that he was Roy Rayner?" Merrion asked.

"When I saw him on Sunday," Annabel replied. "He told me then that neither of us should see Auntie again."

"He had good reason for knowing that," said Merrion. "You believe that he murdered the lady of the hammock?"

"The lady in the hammock?"Annabel replied. "Auntie you mean? Yes, I'm sure he did. You see, as Roy Rayner, her money would go to him. And when I asked him who it was who pretended to be Auntie the second time I came here, he said he didn't know for certain but he could guess."

"I wonder how much he really knew, all along," Merrion remarked thoughtfully. "However, we can talk about that another time. Meanwhile, there's that conflagration. We'd better see what's been done about that."

As they left the house the sergeant drove up in Merrion's' car. "I've called the Brigade, sir," he reported to Arnold. "And I've heard news of Hopton. He's taken Edgefield's bicycle and gone off on it."

"That's all right," Arnold replied. "I know within a little where he'll go to." They walked down the drive, to find the lodge and one or two trees round it burning furiously. A small crowd had collected in the roadway, among them Mrs. Moffatt and Amos Wanstead. With its bell clanging angrily, the fire-engine swept in, and the crew tumbled off it. With a speed born of long practice, a hose was run through the trees to the southern end of East Moon. The pump started with a roar, and two steady jets were directed upon the burning building. A dense hissing cloud of steam floated up and the flames flickered out as though by magic. The fire was under control.

"Well, that's that," Merrion remarked. "We'd better be getting back. You'll be late for lunch. Miss Dorset, I'mafraid."

They drove first to Ridhurst, to set down the sergeant. As he got out at the police station, a constable came out of the building and spoke to him. The sergeant turned to Arnold.

"There's a message just come through for you from the Yard, sir. If you will ring up Sergeant Wighton, he has some news for you."

Arnold went in and returned in. a few minutes with a triumphant expression. He got into the car, which Merrion drove away towards Surbiton. But Arnold said nothing until Annabel had been deposited at home. Then, as soon as he and Merrion were alone in the car, "It worked!" he exclaimed. "And quite simply too."

"I knew it would," Merrion replied tranquilly. "You mean, I suppose, that your people have got the Lingfields?"

"Him, at all events," Arnold replied. "This is what Wighton told me on the phone just now. He was watching Barney Gardens this morning when a taxi drove up, in broad daylight, about eleven o'clock. A man got out and told the driver to wait. He rang the bell, and a woman let him in. A little later he came out with one of those suitcases, and put it in the taxi. Then he went in again and fetched out the other. He got into the taxi and told the man where to drive to. Then Wighton got in beside him and told the driver to take them to the Yard. When he was charged there with the theft of jewellery, the man gave his name as Lance Lingfield. We'll go straight there and hear what he's got to say for himself."

"Not much!" Merrion replied. "We're going to have some lunch first. It won't hurt Lingfield to cool his heels for a bit."

XX

After lunch, Merrion accompanied Arnold to a room at Scotland Yard. "Before you send for Lingfield I'd like to make a suggestion," Merrion said. "As I've warned you before, the tangle is pretty complicated. I fancy I've unravelled most of the threads, but a few snarls still remain. You'd better let me do most of the talking."

"I don't mind that," Arnold replied. "As long as you get out of Lingfield what's happened to Mrs. Lavant."

Merrion smiled. "I know now what happened to Mrs. Lavant. She wasn't murdered, you can set your mind at rest about that. I even know where her body is. I'm pretty sure that when we've got Lingfield's story out of him, I shall find I am right."

Arnold issued his instructions by telephone, and Lingfield appeared under escort. He looked, not unnaturally, ill at ease, but it seemed to Merrion that his bearing was fairly confident. Rather that of a man who, finding himself in a hole, felt quite able to climb out of it. Arnold dismissed the escort, told Lingfield to sit down, and cautioned him. Then he turned to Merrion, and nodded to him encouragingly.

"Well, Lingfield, so it's come to an end at last," said Merrion quietly. "You must have known that you couldn't keep it up indefinitely. And by this time so many crimes may be charged to you that one hardly knows where to begin. You may be able to clear yourself of some of them, but I think you must see that the only way you can do so is by telling us the exact truth. To start with, why did you and Mrs. Lingfield abandon your music-hall career and go to live with Mrs. Lavant at The Brake? Was the initiative yours or hers?"

"It was Mrs. Lavant's," Lingfield replied. "She had known my wife for many years, and had become very much attached to her. When war broke out and Mrs. Lavant went to The Brake, she begged us to come and live with her, at her expense. I wasn't at all taken with the idea, but the war had made things very difficult for us. We couldn't get an engagement, and at last we consented. I looked at it as a temporary arrangement, for Mrs.

Lavant was a very old woman, and couldn't live much longer. Perhaps, when she died, things in our line would have improved, and we could go back to the halls."

Merrion nodded. "So you went to live at The Brake. You found there Mrs. Lavant and Madame Tallinn. Later, your half-sister. Miss Loretta Sowley, joined you. Who suggested that she should do so?"

At the mention of Loretta's name Lingfield looked profoundly uncomfortable. "Again, Mrs. Lavant," he replied. "Loretta had been ill, and when we told Mrs. Lavant she said she must come to The Brake for a rest."

"Be careful!" Merrion rapped out sharply. "I warned you a moment ago that your only hope was to tell us the exact truth. I put it to you that Loretta's illness had nothing to do with it. A not too scrupulous actress was required for your purposes, and you chose your half-sister to play the part."

Lingfield stared at him in amazement. "Well, that may have had something to do with it," he admitted reluctantly. "But I assure you that, to begin with, it was entirely Mrs. Lavant's idea that the part should be played at all."

"You can hardly expect me to believe that," said Merrion scornfully. "Why should she want someone to impersonate her?"

"Believe it or not, but it is perfectly true," Lingfield replied. "Mrs. Lavant was in many ways an extraordinary woman. Her likes and dislikes were grotesquely exaggerated. Her heart was affected, and she knew she had not much longer to live, though she resolutely refused to see a doctor. She had an unreasoning hatred of her husband's family, and couldn't bear the thought of her income going to them when she died. Her husband's grandson, Roy Rayner, would come into it, and him she detested. If he were killed in the war, as was quite possible, the money would go to her husband's niece, Mrs. Dorset, and Mrs. Lavant seemed to think that was nearly as bad."

Merrion could easily believe this, for it conformed well enough with what Henry Dorset had told him of Mrs. Lavant's character. "It was Mrs. Lavant's idea that you should enjoy her income after her death?" he suggested.

"That my wife should," Lingfield replied. "Mrs. Lavant's devotion to her was remarkable. She might have played the part, but she didn't feel capable of sustaining it, and her disappearance would have been difficult to account for. And there was another reason why Mrs. Lavant wished that her death should remain secret. She had a romantic affection for Sir Julius, and hated the idea of his comfort being disturbed in any way. She was afraid that if The Brake became empty, it would be requisitioned for some purpose he wouldn't like."

"Sir Julius was not in the secret?"Merrion asked.

"Nobody was in the secret but my wife, Loretta and myself," Lingfield replied.

"Not even Madame Tallinn," said Merrion. "Now, tell us the truth, Lingfield. Who pushed her into the lake?"

"Nobody!" Lingfield replied earnestly. "She drowned herself, there is no doubt about that."

"Most considerate of her, from your point of view," Merrion remarked. "What made her take her own life?"

"Her mind was affected," Lingfield replied. "She had been behaving very oddly for some time. The evidence on that point given at the inquest was perfectly true. She knew, or guessed, that Mrs. Lavant was at the point of death, and was profoundly distressed. She probably dreaded being abandoned, without any friends she could call upon."

"And your half-sister?" Merrion asked. "Was it with Mrs. Lavant's consent that Miss Sowley understudied her?"

"Not only with her consent, but at her desire," Lingfield replied. "Mrs. Lavant was an actress herself, you must remember, and she thoroughly enjoyed coaching Loretta. The three of them, the third being my wife, spent hours together in Mrs. Lavant's suite. She taught Loretta the whole of her past, her experiences and the people she had known, and made her rehearse every mannerism and every gesture over and over again. My wife helped Loretta to make up, and I was called in once or twice to criticise the result. The effect was uncanny. I could hardly tell the false from the genuine."

"If you couldn't, nobody else was likely to," Merrion remarked. "Well, now that the preliminaries are cleared up, I can tell the rest of the story myself. When the end was imminent, Miss Sowley took on the impersonation permanently. It was given out that she had left The Brake and, subsequently, that she had gone to Australia. Mrs. Lavant died, and most conveniently for the success of the imposture, Madame Tallinn died almost simultaneously. Do you still maintain it was suicide?"

"I swear it was!" Lingfield exclaimed. "Mrs. Lavant died in the evening, and next morning I found Madame Tallinn's body in the lake."

"Well, it's too late now to disprove your story," said Merrion doubtfully. "But this second body was a godsend to you. You concealed Mrs. Lavant's body in one of the rooms, a perfectly simple matter, since there was no resident domestic staff at The Brake. Madame Tallinn's body was laid out in another, for all the world to see. The inquest was held, and your half-sister gave a most convincing impersonation of Mrs. Lavant. The undertakers came to The Brake, and laid Madame Tallinn in her coffin. During the night before the funeral you exchanged this body for Mrs. Lavant's. Madame Tallinn's you conveyed to the boat-house, where it remained until it was discovered, as a skeleton, last week."

Up till now, Arnold had been listening intently, without interruption. But at this he could no longer restrain himself. "What!" he exclaimed. "You mean to tell me that Mrs. Lavant has been dead three years and more?"

"Dead, and buried in Ridhurst cemetery," Merrion replied.

"And, until what I have called zero hour, Loretta Sowley reigned in her stead. But, before we come to that, there's another point to be cleared up. Had your half-sister ever met Roy Rayner, Lingfield? In the old days, before the war, I mean?"

Lingfield shuddered. "She had never met him, though of course Mrs. Lavant had told her all about him. Nor had my wife or I ever seen him. And then one day, not long after Mrs. Lavant's death, two policemen turned up in a car at The Brake. The sight of them gave us a nasty shock, for we supposed that somehow the deception must have been discovered. We were very much relieved when it turned out that they had come to tell Mrs. Lavant that her husband's grandson had met with a grave accident, and that her presence was required."

Merrion nodded, and glanced at Arnold. "I told you this morning that we could disregard that identification. The police as good as told Loretta Sowley that the body she was asked to identify was that of Roy Rayner. That being so, she had no option but to agree, as, even had the dead man been Roy

Rayner, she would not have recognised him. And I can understand what a relief the event must have been to the party at The Brake. They must have been looking forward to Roy's return from the wars with considerable misgiving. Isn't that so, Lingfield?"

"It is," Lingfield replied. "After that, we felt that our greatest danger had been removed. Of the people who had known Mrs. Lavant intimately, only Sir Julius remained. We were very anxious when Loretta first visited The Retreat as Mrs. Lavant. But her make-up was proof against his failing eyesight, and her voice had been so carefully trained that he detected nothing. Any change in her manner or inflexion he would have ascribed to distress at Madame Tallinn's death."

"And, for a matter of three years, the deception continued," said Merrion. "There was, in fact, very little risk of its discovery. None of the people in the neighbourhood who had seen the true Mrs. Lavant were likely to have any suspicions when confronted with the false. Their acquaintance with the original had been of the most fleeting nature. Dr. Wiston, Mrs. Moffatt, the clerks from the bank, for instance. By the way, the mention of the bank brings us to the signature. In addition to her other accomplishments. Miss Sowley could faithfully imitate Mrs. Lavant's signature, I take it?"

"Perfectly," Lingfield replied. "She had taken great pains with that when Mrs. Lavant was coaching her."

"And, since somebody from the bank saw, once every quarter, the person they believed to be Mrs. Lavant, no suspicions would arise there," said Merrion. "But what about the cheque you cashed on Friday? Who signed that?"

Lingfield hesitated. "Well, as a matter of fact, my wife did. She, too had learnt to imitate the signature."

"You seem to have taken every precaution," Merrion remarked. "And now we come to that fatal Wednesday, a fortnight ago. When you engaged that keeper, Tom Hopton, you had of course no idea that he was in reality Roy Rayner, whom you believed to be safely dead and buried?"

Lingfield stared at him. "You know that too?" he exclaimed.

"You may take it that there's very little about the whole affair we don't know," Merrion replied easily. "That's one reason why I warned you that your only hope was to tell the exact truth.

Why did you engage a keeper?"

"Because we wanted to have someone about the place," Lingfield replied. "Several times inquisitive people had made their way into the grounds in the hope of catching a glimpse of the once famous Claire Gabriel. What finally decided us was the fact that about six months ago we heard someone prowling round the house at night. You'll understand that we had every reason for keeping our secret hidden from prying eyes. So we put an advertisement in the local paper."

"I shouldn't be surprised if it turned out that the nocturnal prowler was Roy Rayner," Merrion remarked. "You put an advertisement in the paper, and he presented himself to apply for the job?"

"He did," Lingfield replied. "He gave his name as Tom Hopton, and produced a reference from a gentleman in Scotland by whom he had been employed. We wrote to this address, and received a reply, confirming the reference and recommending Hopton as a good worker of sober habits. I engaged him, and he seemed perfectly satisfactory. We congratulated ourselves that we had found the very man we were looking for."

"While he congratulated himself on being installed on Mrs. Lavant's doorstep," said Merrion. "Go on."

"We thought all was well until the day before it happened," Lingfield replied. "On warm afternoons Mrs. Lavant had always liked to lie in the hammock on the lawn after lunch, and Loretta, who followed her example to the last detail, kept up the practice. My wife and I were usually about the place, but on Tuesday, a fortnight ago to-day, we had occasion to drive into Ridhurst. We went out by the lodge entrance, Hopton, as we believed him to be, saw us, and must have realised that this was his first opportunity of seeing Mrs. Lavant alone.

"We were away for an hour or more, and when we came back we found Loretta in a state of dithering terror. She told us that everything was discovered, and that we must make a bolt for it while there was still time. It was quite a while before we could get her to tell us clearly what had happened. But at last we calmed her down and she told us the story.

"It seems that she had dozed off in the hammock, and had woken with a start to find Hopton standing over her. She asked him what he was doing, and he replied by asking her who she was. She said that she was Mrs. Lavant, his employer, and told him to go about his business. At that he shook his head. However well she might have made herself up to look like Mrs. Lavant, he knew better. He had lived long enough in Mrs. Lavant's house not to be taken in by any impersonation. However, if she liked to keep it up, that was her affair. Only, of course, he would expect some reward for keeping his mouth shut.

"Loretta tried her best to brazen it out, but she could make no impression upon him. He told her that, clever though she might be, she couldn't alter her ears, which weren't the same shape as Mrs. Lavant's. And then, when she asked him how he could possibly have known Mrs. Lavant so intimately, he told her that he was Roy Rayner, and that he had lived for years with his grandfather and Mrs. Lavant after his mother's death. That being so, he was of course the heir to Mrs. Lavant's income. But he would be content to let things go on as they were, on condition that he shared fifty-fifty. He told Loretta that if she didn't agree to that, he would blow the gaff. And he said he'd give her a day or two to think things over."

Merrion nodded. "That's very much what I imagined had happened. And I think I can guess your reaction. You pointed out to your half-sister that there was really no danger. Rayner could not expose her without revealing his own identity, and that would lead to his immediate arrest. All she need do was to refuse to yield to blackmail."

"That's about it," Lingfield replied. "We wondered whether we should give the so-called Hopton the sack, but we were rather afraid of what he might do. On the whole, it seemed a better policy to let him stay where we could keep our eyes on him. Loretta agreed that if he tackled her again, she would threaten to inform the police."

"A game of bluff on both sides," Merrion remarked. "You left your half-sister alone in the hammock again on Wednesday?"

"Yes, we did," Lingfield replied contritely. "We never for a moment supposed that anything could happen to her. And, in case Rayner should turn out troublesome, we arranged to be not far away. We went to The Retreat to see Mrs. Moffatt. And we took care that Rayner saw us leave The Brake. While we were at The Retreat, we arranged matters so that we should hear the telephone bell if it rang. Mrs. Moffatt was easily persuaded to leave the door of her room open on a hot day."

"Mrs. Moffatt was summoned to the library," said Merrion. "And then the telephone bell did ring, and you answered it. What did you think when you heard a strange and agitated voice demanding to be put through to Dr. Wiston?"

"I didn't know what to think," Lingfield replied. "You know about that? Who was it?"

"It was Annabel Dorset," said Merrion. "Didn't you recognise her when she called at The Brake two days later?"

Lingfield shook his head. "How could I recognise her? I had never seen her before then."

"You had," said Merrion. "She appeared at the edge of the lawn for a moment while the interview was taking place."

"She never told us that," Lingfield replied. "I paid no attention to those people. I supposed that having heard there was to be an interview they had just wandered in out of curiosity. Besides, I was too intent on what my wife was saying, ready to prompt her if she had forgotten the right answer to any of the reporter's questions."

"Well, let's go back to the moment when you heard the voice on the telephone," said Merrion. "You didn't know what to think, but you guessed that something alarming must have happened. One of you at least must get back to The Brake immediately. So you revived the Lance and Linette turn and projected Mrs. Lingfield over the wall. Then you went out by the way you had come, trusting in Amos Wan-stead's brain being dull enough not to wonder how it was that while he had let two people in, he only let one out. Did you see Rayner as you came back?"

"No, I didn't see him again that day," Lingfield replied. "When my wife told me what had happened, I supposed that he had bolted. But he hadn't, for he was at the lodge again next day."

"When Mrs. Lingfield arrived on the scene she found your half-sister dead," said Merrion. "Did you find out how she had been killed?"

Lingfield shook his head. "No, we didn't. There was no sign of violence whatever. But we knew, of course, that Rayner must have done it."

"Being a crook, Rayner would know where to get hold of a hypodermic syringe and a deadly drug," Merrion remarked.

"Mrs. Lingfield took over the impersonation. She was so used to helping Miss Sowley make up that she found this fairly simple. You concealed the body and later took it to the boat-house. It was quite a neat trick to lock the door, leave the key on the inside, and make your way out through the hole in the roof. But what made you add to your list of crimes by becoming accessories to murder? Why didn't you inform the police of what had happened?"

Lingfield spread out his hands in a despairing gesture. "How could we? How were we to account for the body? The medical examination would have revealed that it couldn't be Mrs. Lavant's. The whole deception would have been exposed, and we should probably have been accused of having committed the murder ourselves. We were naturally panic-stricken, and took what seemed to us the only possible course. There was no time to think about it, for the newspaper men were expected within the next half hour."

"Add to that, that you wanted to go on enjoying Mrs. Lavant's income," said Merrion. "Now for the sequel. Madame Tallinn's body had never been found, so you had every reason to hope that Miss Sowley's would not be. You had clothed it in some of her own clothes, and fastened the dress with a pin belonging to her. But the body was found, and Mrs. Edgefield told you the news on the following Tuesday. How much did you know of this when we saw you that morning?"

"Only that a body had been found in the boat-house and had not yet been identified," Lingfield replied. "I didn't know that it was in such a state as to be unidentifiable. I was afraid that it would somehow be discovered to be Loretta's. If it was, I should be called upon to view it, and should have to admit the fact. That's why I hedged when you told me about the pin."

Merrion nodded. "I see. If it were proved that the body was Miss Sowley's, it would have looked suspicious if you had denied all knowledge of a pin she habitually wore. I understand now your relief at the outcome of our afternoon visit. You learnt then that the body was unrecognisable, and that there were therefore no grounds for connecting it with The Brake. It was quite safe for your wife, as Mrs. Lavant, to explain how the pin could not be Miss Sowley's. Now, one thing more. You had enlisted Mrs. Neston to play the part of the third member of the household. But that couldn't have gone on for ever. How did you propose to deal with the situation?"

"I'd got it all worked out," Lingfield replied. "I was going to stage a violent quarrel one morning in Mrs. Lavant's suite, apparently between Mrs. Lavant and Mrs. Lingfield. I should have arranged for Mrs. Edgefield to overhear this, but of course not to see it. That afternoon Sophie Neston would have gone back to London, and I should have given out that my wife had taken mortal offence at something Mrs. Lavant had said to her and left her for good, in spite of all my efforts to dissuade her. My wife, as Mrs. Lavant, would have elaborated the story to Sir Julius. But Sophie wouldn't play up any longer, and my wife got cold feet after her interview with Sir Julius on Thursday. She felt she would never be able to keep up the impersonation, as Loretta had. So we decided that it was time to ring down the curtain."

"Taking Mrs. Lavant's jewellery with you," Arnold remarked grimly. "That's the present charge, but as you probably understand quite clearly, other charges will be preferred against you."

For the first time Lingfield smiled, though rather wanly. "On the present charge at least I am innocent. Before Mrs Lavant died, she made a will, which I can produce. It was signed in the presence of Loretta and a man from the bank, who witnessed it. In it, Mrs. Lavant left everything she had the power to leave to my wife. Her personal jewellery was, of course, included."

"We'll see about that," Arnold replied, pressing the bell-push on his desk. The escort reappeared and Lingfield was removed from the room.

XXI

"You can take what you've just heard as true in the main," said Merrion, as he and Arnold were left alone. "It's the only explanation which could account for what we've found out. The only point I'm doubtful about is the death of Madame Tallinn, but you can't hope to clear that up after all this time. And I expect it's right about the will, which, however, is of no effect until it has been proved. You'll have to find some more substantial charge."

"No difficulty about that," Arnold replied. "The concealment of two bodies will be enough to be going on with. And what about fraud? He and those two women of his have been pocketing Mrs. Lavant's income all this time."

"To the detriment of Roy Rayner, as I suppose you realise," Merrion remarked. "My friend Henry Dorset must be scratching his head over his untimely resurrection. Of course, there's no doubt now that he murdered Loretta. And, from what Annabel Dorset didn't tell us, I can hazard a pretty shrewd guess as to what was in his mind."

Arnold was about to reply, when the telephone on his desk buzzed. He picked up the instrument and listened. "Yes, come along," he said. Then, turning to Merrion, "That was Wighton. You may as well stop and hear what he has to say."

Wighton appeared and made his report. "When I had brought Lingfield here, sir, I went on to the address he had given to the taxi-driver. It was a boarding-house in Bloomsbury, and I made inquiries there. The woman of the house told me that a Mr. and Mrs. Leyton had come to stay yesterday afternoon. They had come on Friday afternoon to see her, but she had told them that she would not have a room vacant till Monday. I showed her the photograph, and she recognised the couple at once. She told me that Mr. Leyton had gone off in a taxi this morning, and hadn't come back yet."

Arnold nodded. "That was no news to you. They had parked the jewellery with Mrs. Neston till they were settled. Go on."

"I inquired for Mrs. Leyton, sir," Wighton replied. "She had gone out too, to do some shopping, the woman told me. So I waited, and half an hour ago she came back. I told her that her name was Linette Lingfield, and that I held a warrant for her arrest. She didn't deny it, and I brought her along here. She's down below now, sir."

Arnold glanced at Merrion, who sighed wearily. "Yes, I suppose so," he said. "But it's up to you, this time."

Arnold told Wighton to fetch Mrs. Lingfield, and in a few minutes she appeared. Merrion looked at her with interest, and the first impression he received was that she was a very frightened woman. She was trembling all over, and almost collapsed into the chair Arnold pointed out to her. She was in the forties, with a sisterly likeness to Mrs. Neston, but her face was weak and lined. It was clear to Merrion that her husband was the dominant partner.

"Well, Mrs. Lingfield, we've met before," said Arnold mockingly. "I'm bound to say that you look a lot younger now than you did then. Will you allow me to congratulate you on your skill as an actress?"

She made no reply, but her terrified eyes wandered from Arnold to Merrion and back again. "Now, listen to me," Arnold went on in a sterner tone. "There are several very serious charges pending against you and your husband. We have just had the pleasure of his company in this room, and he has made a statement. We are going to give you the opportunity of doing the same."

"My husband!" she exclaimed faintly. "You—you've arrested him?"

"We have," Arnold replied. "So, you see, you can gain nothing by attempting to hide the truth." Having cautioned her, he took her through the whole course of events at The Brake, since she and her husband had joined Mrs. Lavant there. Under his interrogation, she told substantially the same story as her husband. She, too, swore that Madame Tallinn had taken her own life. But she confessed that the letter apparently written by her had been a forgery. Mrs. Lingfield had written it herself, at her husband's instigation. Between them they had destroyed all Madame Tallinn's belongings, so that nothing should remain to afford a comparison of handwriting

Arnold questioned her closely regarding her discovery of

Loretta's death. She declared that the shock of it had completely
paralysed her for the moment. But, as her faculties returned,
she realised that something must be done, if only to gain time.
She had felt equal to impersonating Mrs. Lavant for the benefit
of the newspaper men, who were complete strangers. It was her
husband who had insisted that she should adopt the role
permanently, and that her sister should be called in. But she
had felt unequal to the strain, and her interview with Sir Julius
had completely unnerved her.

"I can't help feeling sorry for that woman," said Merrion,
when Arnold had dismissed her. "She is, or was, entirely under
the influence of her husband. Loretta, I fancy, must have been
of much sterner stuff. And of course, before she died Mrs.
Lavant dominated the lot of them. She must indeed have been
a remarkable old woman, who stuck at nothing to further her
likes and dislikes. Well, the mystery is solved, so far as I am
concerned. All that remains is the apprehension of a particularly
dangerous killer. And that I can safely leave to you."

Arnold had his ideas about that. When Merrion had left him,
he sent for the records of the information which had led to the
interception of the smugglers. He guessed that Rayner's instinct
would lead him to seek refuge among his old associates of the
underworld. The most promising contact would be the deserter
who had originally named Rayner as the leader of the smuggling
gang.

The records revealed this man's subsequent history. He had
escaped from the prison to which he had been sentenced for
desertion, but had been rearrested in an act of attempted
housebreaking. For this he had received a further sentence,
which had expired a month ago. The man, whose name was
Albert Shipley, was now under the watchful observation of the
police. He was reported to be working as a casual labourer in
Poplar.

Arnold sent for Wighton and gave him his instructions. He
was to find out from the police of the Division concerned where
Bert Shipley was to be found. He was to shadow him that
evening until he found an opportunity when he was alone. Then,
without any one else becoming aware of it, he was to spirit him
to the Yard. "I'll be here to meet him," Arnold concluded. "And
mind what you're about. You've got to bag this chicken without

disturbing any of the other fowls in the roost"

"I know how to manage that, sir," Wighton replied confidently. He went out, leaving Arnold to consider the situation. There was no doubt that Rayner would return, at least temporarily, to his particular haunts in the London underworld. Only there could he find the help necessary for his immediate maintenance. But, even when he had been located, his capture would have to be organised with the greatest care. Once before he had slipped through the meshes of the police net, and Arnold had no intention of allowing such a thing to happen again. The list of crimes with which he would be charged was formidable enough. The policeman whom he had wounded during the smuggling affray had never fully recovered from his injuries. No one, having a knowledge of the circumstances, could doubt that he had murdered Loretta Sowley. And his brutal attempt to murder Annabel Dorset was proved up to the hilt. He was, as Merrion had said, a particularly dangerous killer.

Late that afternoon Arnold received a telephone call from the sergeant at Ridhurst. "I've got some information for you, sir," the sergeant reported. "We've seen nothing of that chap Hopton. But Edgefield's bicycle has been recovered. It was found in a ditch a few hundred yards from the next station to Ridhurst on the line to London."

"Good enough. Sergeant," Arnold replied. "I've got some news for you in return. We've arrested both the Lingfields and got statements out of them. You'll be glad to hear that your local problems are solved. The skeleton was all that remained of Madame Tallinn, whose inquest you will remember. And the body was that of Loretta Sowley."

"So that's cleared up, sir," said the sergeant. "Excuse me asking, sir. What about Mrs. Lavant?"

"Mrs. Lavant was buried in Ridhurst cemetery rather more than three years ago," Arnold replied. "That makes you think a bit, doesn't it? I'll be down to see you to-morrow and explain the mystery."

As Arnold rang off he uttered a grunt of satisfaction. The finding of the bicycle went a long way towards confirming his theory. Rayner, avoiding Ridhurst, where he might have been recognised, had taken a train to London. No doubt he was in the Metropolis now, hidden in the secret ramifications of the underworld.

Arnold broke off for a meal, and returned to his room at ten o'clock. As the minutes passed, he occupied himself with the papers which had accumulated on his desk during the day. He found it difficult to concentrate upon them, for his eyes strayed continually to the hands of the clock. At last, a few minutes before eleven, the telephone buzzed, and he snatched up the receiver. "Well?" he asked eagerly.

Wighton's voice replied. "I've got Bert Shipley here, sir. I traced him to a pub near the East India Dock and waited till he came out. None of his pals saw us together, and I brought him along in a taxi. Will you see him now, sir?"

"Bring him along right away," said Arnold. Wighton appeared, escorting an under-sized man with furtive eyes and rat-like features. "Good evening, Shipley," Arnold said briskly. "We're old friends, aren't we, and I don't have to warn you to tell the truth. Sit down there. Now then, you remember, some years ago, telling me about a friend of yours. Roy Rayner. Have you seen him again lately?"

"Whatever makes you ask me that, Mr. Arnold?" Shipley replied glibly. "You know very well that Roy was killed by the cops not very long after I spoke to you about him."

"Don't you try any of your games with me," said Arnold sternly. "It was not Rayner who was killed, but one of the others, as I expect you knew all along. I saw Rayner myself, no longer ago than this morning, so it's no use telling me that he's dead. Answer my question. Have you seen him lately? Come on, out with it."

"Well, I never!" Shipley exclaimed, no whit abashed. "Fancy you seeing him, Mr. Arnold. I've seen him, too. One evening it was, I saw him first. About a fortnight ago, I dare say."

"You saw him a fortnight ago?" Arnold asked. "How was that? Tell me where you met him."

"It was in the pub where I was this evening," Shipley replied. "There wasn't any harm about it. I was standing there at the bar having a drink when someone tapped me on the shoulder. I turned round sharp, and I couldn't hardly believe my own eyes. There was Roy, who I hadn't seen all that time, looking just the same as he always did. He said he wanted a word with me and we went out together. I asked him where he'd been, and he said he'd been keeping out of the way. He told me that he'd just got a job in the country, and that he'd have to get back that same evening."

"Yes, I dare say," said Arnold impatiently. "But it wasn't only to tell you that that he wanted a word with you. What was it?"

"Why, nothing much, Mr. Arnold," Shipley replied. "He only wanted to know if I could tell him where to get hold of a syringe and some dope. He must have taken to doping himself since I'd last known him."

Arnold let this pass. It was most unlikely that Rayner had divulged the use to which he meant to put the drug. "Were you able to help your friend?" he asked easily.

"Why, yes, it so happened that I could," Shipley replied. "One of the chaps had found a case of stuff that must have belonged to a doctor, and I knew he wouldn't mind parting with it for a decent price offered."

"By found, you mean pinched," said Arnold. "The chap had stolen the case from a doctor's car, I don't doubt. But never mind about that now. You told Rayner where he was to be found. This was a fortnight ago. What day of the week was it?"

Shipley scratched his head. "What day? Let me see now. It was the day after I'd started on the job I'm on now, and that was on a Monday. Tuesday evening it must have been when Roy spoke to me."

This was probably the truth, Arnold reflected. It had been on a Tuesday afternoon that Rayner had revealed his identity to Loretta Sowley. In the interests of his own safety, he had resolved to kill her if she refused to comply with his demands. The scene on the lawn at The Brake on the following day could easily be reconstructed. Rayner had approached Loretta again, and asked her what she meant to do about it. She, as arranged with the Lingfields, had called his bluff, and told him that she was going to tell the police who he was. Rayner had plunged the syringe, already charged with some deadly drug, into her arm. She had probably shrieked, but the sound would not have penetrated to The Retreat. And so rapid had been the action of the drug that within a minute or two she had become unconscious.

Arnold turned once more to Shipley. "Have you seen Rayner again since that evening?" he asked.

Shipley blinked uneasily. "See here, Mr. Arnold. Roy won't never know that you've been talking to me about him?"

"He won't unless you tell him," Arnold replied. "And you're not likely to have the chance of doing that. So out with it."

Shipley leant forward in his chair. "I haven't seen him again myself," he replied, hardly above a whisper. "But he's in town, and I know where. It was this way. I was talking to one of the chaps this evening, and he asked me if I knew that Roy was about again. I said that I'd heard he had a job in the country somewhere, and the chap said that he'd given that up. He said he'd seen Roy only a few hours back. Roy said that he was looking for somewhere to doss down, and the chap, who used to be a pal of his at one time, told him that he could muck in with him and his brother for a bit."

"Who was the chap who told you that?" Arnold asked.

"No names, no pack-drill," Shipley replied with a cunning leer. "But I'll tell you where he stops. Number 6, Ellam Street."

Arnold nodded. Ellam Street was a notoriously disreputable cul-de-sac in the dockland area. Just the sort of neighbourhood in which Rayner might have been expected to seek refuge. "I'll pay him a call," he said. "You won't want to be mixed up in this, Shipley. We'll put you up here for the night. We can provide you with a thoroughly nice cell, fitted with all modern comforts. And if it turns out that you've given us false information we shall know where to find you."

When Shipley had been disposed of, Arnold and Wighton set off in a police car, and drove to the police station nearest to Ellam Street. There they left the car and picked up a reinforcement of a sergeant and a squad of constables. It was well after midnight when the party set off in pairs, each pair taking a different route. A few shadows were flitting about the dingy, narrow streets, but on the appearance of the blue uniforms these vanished as though by magic.

Arnold advanced alone to investigate. Number 6 was one of a row, and had three storeys. Its main door opened on Ellam Street, and there was a second door opening into a narrow alley behind. Windows looked out upon both street and alley, and there might be a trap-door giving access to the roof.

Arnold posted his men to guard all possible ways of escape. Then, holding their torches ready, he and Wighton tried the door. As he had expected, it was not fastened. The inmates of such a house would need to be able to get in at any hour of the night without causing a disturbance. They entered, and found themselves in a narrow passage, with no light showing, and reeking of the stuffy smell of overcrowded humanity.

Switching on their torches, they thrust open the doors on either side of the passage. The rooms seemed full of people, men, women and children in all states of dress and undress. At the sudden flash of light a babel of curses arose. One or two slinking figures picked themselves up and sidled out. Arnold let them go, knowing that they would fall into the clutches of the men outside. Having satisfied himself that Rayner was nowhere on the ground floor, Arnold and Wighton climbed the creaking stairs at the end of the passage.

By the time they reached the first floor pandemonium was raging. The lodgers above, aroused by the disturbance beneath them, were swarming like angry bees, expostulating in every known tongue except English. Arnold and Wighton rounded them up, flashed their torches upon the faces of each in turn, and drove them downstairs, until the landings and rooms were cleared of surging humanity.

But, amid all this turmoil, one door had remained closed. It was that of a room at the back of the house, on the first floor. Arnold tried the door and found it fastened. He flung his weight against it, the flimsy lock yielded, and the door burst open. By the light of his torch Arnold saw three men within. Two of them were sitting up half-clothed on iron bedsteads, and one of these flung up his arms in a gesture of surrender. Arnold beckoned to Wighton, who hustled them from the room.

The third man lay wrapped in a heap of sacks beneath the window. He did not stir until Arnold approached him. Then a hand shot out from under the sacks and Arnold, seeing the glint of metal, leapt aside. As he did so there was a flash and a deafening report. Arnold felt the bullet graze the side of his head, and recoiled with the shock. In the instant, the man sprang up and flung open the window. As he vaulted through the opening, Arnold, recovering himself, leapt towards him. The man, holding to the sill with one hand, hung suspended. The other hand still held the automatic. A second shot rang out, but this went wide.

It all happened in a split second. Simultaneously with Arnold's leap, Wighton, with uplifted truncheon, dashed across the room. He struck, not at the man's head, just visible above the window-ledge, but at the hand holding the automatic. The weapon flew from the man's grasp, discharging itself with a third report. There was a sharp cry, as it seemed of astonishment. The hand grasping the sill relaxed, and with a dull thud the man fell into the alley below.

Arnold and Wighton raced downstairs and out of the house by the back door. Two policemen were already bending over the dying man. The last bullet from the automatic had penetrated his neck, and blood was gushing in spurts from the artery. In a last flicker of consciousness he bared his teeth in a mocking grin as Arnold dropped on one knee beside him. Roy Rayner had paid the penalty of his crimes.

XXII

A few evenings later, Merrion dined at Surbiton with the Dorsets. When he arrived at the house, he was secretly amused to find that he was not the only guest. David Wiston and his father were already there, and David seemed in some subtle way to have become a member of the family.

During dinner the conversation suffered some restraint, for the subject uppermost in everybody's mind was carefully avoided. But afterwards, when Annabel and her mother had retired to the lounge. Henry Dorset could contain himself no longer. "Now then, Merrion!" he exclaimed. "You're the only person who can tell us the inside story. I've heard Annabel's version, and Matthew here has told me what's being said in Ridhurst. But what's the truth behind if all?"

As simply as he could, Merrion ran through the facts as he knew them. "That is the whole story of the last few years," he concluded. "To sum up the points that interest you most. It is established beyond any doubt that Mrs. Lavant died a natural death rather more than three years ago. Roy Rayner, after his brief reappearance from the grave, has finally returned to it."

"I suppose there's no doubt that he really is dead this time?" Dorset asked, a trifle anxiously.

"Not the slightest," Merrion reassured him. "Arnold has taken no chances. He has exhibited the body, not only to Bert Shipley, a crook pal of Rayner's, but to two people he dug up who had known Rayner when he was living with his grandfather. All three have identified the body beyond question. You can rest assured that there's no mistake this time."

"I'm glad to know that," Dorset replied. "Nobody can be expected to waste any sympathy upon him. Or the other scoundrels either. It strikes me that the Loretta woman only got what she deserved. As for the Lingfields, I hope they both get whacking sentences for their share in the dastardly fraud. They've received the income that ought to have been coming to Irene all these years. Is there any chance of recovering it from them?"

Merrion shook his head. "I doubt it. I fancy their only asset is the jewellery. Lingfield has produced a will, which appears to be perfectly genuine and is dated five years ago. In it, Mrs. Lavant appoints Mrs. Lingfield her sole legatee and executor. The will, of course, has not been proved. Whether it can now be proved so long after the testator's death, whether that death can be assumed in the absence of any certificate, or whether a prisoner in custody can act as an executor, I am not sufficiently versed in the law to say."

"I shall see the solicitors to the trustees to-morrow!" Dorset exclaimed. "They're answerable for paying the money to this gang of swindlers. If we can't get it out of the Lingfields, they ought to fork it out themselves."

Merrion glanced at Matthew Wiston. "When did you first make the acquaintance of Mrs. Lavant, Doctor?" he asked.

"Soon after she went to live at The Brake," Wiston replied. "Certainly during the lifetime of the genuine Mrs. Lavant. I must repeat that from that time the occasions on which I saw her were infrequent. I had no suspicion whatever that the woman I saw during the past three years was not Mrs. Lavant herself, though I did think it wonderful that she never seemed to grow a day older."

Merrion smiled. "That seems to me the solicitors' line of defence. Loretta succeeded in imposing upon all those to whom she chose to show herself. Even had one of the partners made a practice of handing the quarterly instalments to his client in person, it would have been impossible for him to detect the imposture. After Loretta's death it was a different matter, for Mrs. Lingfield didn't feel equal to the impersonation. She wouldn't meet you, for instance. Doctor."

"Well, I mean to get what's due to us out of somebody," said Dorset firmly. "To think that this has been going on for three years and more. And the exposure is entirely due to you, Merrion. It was the best idea I ever had to tell you that queer story of Annabel's, What did you really think when you had heard it?"

Merrion glanced significantly towards David Wiston, who was toying impatiently with his wine-glass. "You must be getting bored with the conversation of us old fogies, David, my boy," said Dorset, taking the hint. "Go into the lounge and join the ladies. You'll find them more entertaining, I don't doubt."

As David rose his father followed his example. "I think I'll go into the lounge too, if you don't mind. Henry," he said. "I shall have to be getting along soon, if I'm to catch the last train to Ridhurst. And I'd like the chance of talking to Irene and Annabel before I go."

So Merrion and Dorset were left alone in the dining-room. "I'll answer your question quite frankly," Merrion said as the door closed. "I thought it not impossible that David had been playing tricks. On the following Sunday night I went exploring in pursuit of that idea. And it was then that I discovered Loretta's body."

"Eh?" Dorset replied. "So it was you who found the body? I didn't know that. Well, I'll be equally frank with you. Annabel, too, had her suspicions that David might have been mixed up in it. When you brought her back here the other day she was pretty badly shaken up by what she'd gone through, and she told her mother and me everything. A good deal more, I gather, than she had seen fit to tell you and Mr. Arnold. And she was full of remorse for what she'd thought about David."

Merrion smiled. "I wonder what she told you about Roy Rayner," he remarked.

Dorset struck the table with his fist. "The bloodthirsty young villain! My word, Merrion, she had a lucky escape, and I don't mean from being burnt alive. You won't believe it, but that young thug had the insolence to ask her to marry him. And, if she hadn't found out his true character, she might have consented. He'd somehow turned her head, and in her eyes he appeared a thoroughly romantic character. But there, as I say, you won't believe it."

"I do believe it," Merrion replied truthfully. "And David?"

"She's going to marry him," said Dorset. "I always thought she would. Reaction from Rayner's nearly fatal charm brought matters to a head, I suppose. Safety first. Better marry a steady young chap like David before another firebrand shows up. She must please herself, and she's old enough to know her own mind. Anyhow, now that that crook of a second cousin of hers is safely dead, she'll be a rich woman one day."

Merrion left Dorset to wrestle with the legal problems involved. The Lingfields were brought to trial, and received sentences of imprisonment on the charges brought against them. Sir Julius was naturally indignant when the deception was explained to him. His chief concern, however, was for the future of The Brake. Fortunately for his peace of mind, he found a suitable tenant. But he had the door in the wall removed, and the opening securely bricked up.

After the suspicions he had harboured, Merrion thought he could do no less than send a particularly handsome wedding present.

CPSIA information can be obtained
at www.ICGtesting.com
Printed in the USA
BVHW072059210122
626680BV00002B/62

9 781515 425434